THE WHISPER GIRL

A JAKE CASHEN NOVEL

DECLAN JAMES

ONE

Eighteen hours ago ...

She looked at him, those piercing, ice-blue eyes filled with fear. Those eyes. That dark hair. He reached down and curled a strand between his fingers. She flinched, tried to scramble backwards, but she couldn't find a good grip in the dirt with her hands taped in front of her at the wrists.

"This was always gonna be the dead giveaway," he said, smiling. She squeezed her eyes shut, trying to hold back tears. If he'd taken the tape off her mouth, he knew she would have begged him. Or played dumb. Like he didn't already know what she was. Like her words would make any difference.

"Where did you think you were going to go?" he asked. "Did you really think it was going to work out for you? That things would be better out there than here? There's as much pain for you out there, maybe more. I'm doing you a favor."

She shook her head. He reached forward, pulling the tape from one side of her mouth. It turned out he wanted to hear what she'd say, after all.

"No," she whispered. "No. Please. I won't do anything. I just went for a walk."

No. Not interesting at all. He pressed the tape back over her mouth.

"Get up, Adah," he said. "You want to go for a walk? We'll go for a walk."

He wrenched her arm, pulling her to her feet. She nearly lost her balance. He caught her, put an arm around her waist and pushed her forward so she could see where they were.

"See," he said. "It's a long way down." She pressed back against him, realizing he was the only thing keeping her from falling down the edge of the ravine. It was probably a thirty-foot drop over jagged rocks and thorny branches. If she lost her footing ... if he did ... she'd die right here.

"What was so bad about it?" he asked. "You had everything you needed. People who cared about you. A roof over your head. Whatever they told you about the other side of the hill? You have no idea how bad it can be. How quickly you would have lost your soul. But don't worry, I'll make sure you never have to find out."

She let out a muffled cry. He pulled her away from the edge and shoved her forward. She staggered, fell down on one knee. Tried hard to get back to her feet but her bound wrists made it difficult. He pulled her up, gripping her shirt.

"Adah Lee. You think you're some special prize. You have no idea how much trouble everyone has gone through for you. You don't care. You don't appreciate it. You think just because of who you are, you're entitled to something you've never deserved."

He pushed her forward. He would take her through the woods on the other side of Red Sky Hill. No one would ever think to look for her there. It was a harder path around the hill. They would assume she went the other way, past the old lady's house. It would have been the smart thing to do. But he doubted she'd ever been smart.

"Keep walking," he commanded. "You don't stop until I tell you."

It would be a long walk back out for him, too. But it would be pitch dark soon. No one would think to look for her here. They'd never think she was brave enough to try to leave. And if they figured it out, they'd all think she deserved whatever came to her, just like he did.

She was slow, taking halting steps, trying not to lose her footing as the brush grew thicker. At this rate, they'd be here all night. He couldn't afford that. Maybe he needed to end this now. Maybe he'd had all the fun he was going to. He felt again for the hunting knife strapped in a sheath on his belt. He hadn't realized how thrilling it would be when he showed it to her. She must have seen her own eyes filled with fear, reflected in the blade. It was almost poetic.

Slowly, he drew the blade out of its sheath, never taking his eyes off of Adah. He knew she must have felt his hot breath on her neck as she kept trudging forward. She didn't cry. That part was over. He wondered if she'd even try to scream again if he took the tape off. Maybe he wanted her to. Surely they were far enough away from anybody's hearing.

"Stop," he said. "Turn around. Slowly."

She took another step forward. Her whole body trembled as she stopped. She started to turn around. He was wrong. It seemed she still had tears left, after all.

His heartbeat kicked up a notch. The thrill of what he could finally do coursed through him. He took a step toward her.

The ground shifted beneath him. He stepped on a rock or something. It broke loose. He lost his balance, rolled his ankle, and fell to one knee. But he never lost his grip on the knife.

Adah turned back toward the woods. Her dark hair flew behind her like a banner as she started to run.

"Dammit," he muttered. "Stop!"

But she didn't stop. She was quicker, more agile than he would have given her credit for. He stopped to watch her flee, just for a moment. It gave him a different kind of thrill he hadn't expected.

"Do it," he whispered to himself. "Run."

He sheathed his knife and took off after her.

Two

"Serving the people of Worthington County has been one of the great honors of my life. I'm grateful and humbled to be entrusted to continue as sheriff for another four years. We're going to finally, fully take this department into the twenty-first century ..."

Detective Jake Cashen heard muted whispers behind him. A cackle. Sheriff Meg Landry had just been sworn in as sheriff after a heated election a few months ago. An archaic rule in the county charter set inaugurations in April rather than January.

If Jake didn't know better, he'd say Meg seemed choked up. She wasn't a particularly emotional person. She could come off as downright cold until you got to know her.

The cackling behind him got louder. Jake turned. When he zoned in on who the hecklers were, it didn't surprise him. Jeff Hammer had been demoted from sergeant to the graveyard of the property room after he'd withheld information that could have helped a murder investigation. Deputy Sullivan McCloud covered his mouth and whispered something to Hammer. Sully still spoke loud enough for Jake to hear.

"She's a token. It's gonna be a long four years."

Jake clenched his fists. He leaned forward, stepping out of line so he could see Landry's family standing just one row ahead of him. Phil Landry beamed at his wife. Mercifully, Sully and Hammer's voices hadn't carried up to the front row.

Paige Landry, Meg's daughter, stood behind her father looking more grown up than Jake had ever seen her. Paige favored her mother with her tight curls and short stature. Phil put his arm around Paige and kissed her cheek. Paige let him. She had always been closer to her father than to Meg.

"These are just some of the goals I have for the next four years," Meg continued.

Sully and Hammer would not shut up. Jake turned. "You two wanna shut your yaps for at least five minutes. Or take it outside. There's a row of reporters standing about ten feet from you. Or hadn't you noticed?"

Hammer glared at Jake. He blamed him for his demotion. In Jake's opinion, the property room had been a gift. If it had been up to him, he'd have asked for Hammer's badge.

"Sorry," Hammer said. "Forgot you're the teacher's pet."

"Thank you," Meg said at the podium.

"Enough!" Lieutenant John Beverly stood directly behind Sully and Hammer. He'd heard the whole thing, just like Jake. Beverly shot Jake a look that read "stand down."

"Hammer, you want to be on night duty in the property room for the rest of the year? I'm sure Landry will sign off on it."

Scowling, Hammer stared straight ahead. The room filled with modest applause as Landry finished her speech. Meg stepped off the podium and headed for her husband and daughter.

Jake was proud of her. She'd come under heavy fire during the election. A lot of people still didn't think she deserved to be sheriff at all. She was never supposed to have that job. The previous sheriff, Greg O'Neal, hired her to serve as his undersheriff and her role was supposed to be strictly administrative. But when O'Neal died of a sudden heart attack, it thrust Meg into the role. In Jake's opinion, she excelled in it. Though Hammer and Sully's "teacher's pet" comment riled him.

"Jake," Meg called out. "We're going to take some pictures. I'd like you to stick around."

Jake heard Hammer and Sully snicker as they moved with the dispersing crowd.

"You know this isn't really my thing," he told Landry. "You, Phil, and Paige are the stars today."

"You did great," Phil said as he hugged Meg. Even Paige was in a good mood today. It wasn't easy being an almost seventeen-year-old girl in the 2020s. Never mind being the child of a public figure like she was.

"How about over here in front of the flag?" the photographer said.

"I'll leave you to it," Jake said.

Meg got into position with Phil on one side and Paige on the other. "Don't go too far," Meg said. "I'll let you off the hook on the pictures, but go wait for me in my office. We need to talk."

Her tone didn't seem ominous, but Jake wondered what she could want to talk to him about right after her ceremony. There was a reception at the union hall. Jake was hoping to skip it, but Meg certainly couldn't.

"Okay, boss," he told her. Meg smiled for the camera. Phil positively beamed. Paige made an attempt at a smile, but she was outside of her comfort zone, too.

Jake left them and headed up the elevator and down the hall to Meg's office. He hadn't been in it since Meg finished her redecorating. Gone were the dark paneled walls from Greg O'Neal's time. She'd painted them a light beige and had new, tan carpet installed. Meg had gotten rid of the monstrosity of a desk that probably dated back to the seventies. In its place, she'd chosen a smaller, sleeker, solid white oak piece.

It was nice, Jake thought. It made the whole room feel bigger and brighter ... more Meg.

He sat on one of the caramel-colored leather couches she'd picked. It was comfortable enough. There was a matching couch next to it, perpendicular on the opposite wall.

A few minutes later, Meg walked in. Phil was right behind her. Meg turned and kissed him. "I'll see you over there," she said. "Just give me about fifteen minutes."

"Hey, Jake!" Phil waved. "Don't keep her too long."

Jake smiled. "I'll try not to."

Phil left and Meg shut the door. Her face was flushed, her wide smile still fixed in place.

"Was it okay?" she asked. "I hope I didn't bore anybody to death."

"It was fine," he said. "You did good."

"Thanks for hanging back. I knew you were probably planning to duck out. I'll let you. But not before I pick your brain about something."

"Is it that important?" Jake asked. "You're gonna miss your party."

She waved a dismissive hand. "We'll be fine. The county commissioners are going to make the whole thing about them anyway."

"What's up?"

"I wasn't kidding with what I said about dragging this department into the modern era. I'll cut to it. I've been in communication with the Columbus Field Office. They're forming a Violent Crimes task force. FBI, Secret Service, detectives from the surrounding counties. It took some wrangling, but I got us a seat at the table. They've asked me to submit a name from this department. There's no question I want it to be you."

Jake let out a breath. "I hate task forces. The FBI hates me."

"This one will be different. You'll have access to state-of-the-art equipment. I've seen the proposal. The feds are actually going to put real money and muscle behind this one. I need you to think about it. Then I need you to do it."

"In my spare time?"

"The feds are paying for it. It could be a significant bump to your take home. Your overtime will be billed at double your current hourly rate. It'll be a raise, Jake. It's part time. You can negotiate your hours. I'm handpicking you for this one. It's a fantastic opportunity for both you and this department."

Hammer and Sully's teacher's pet comment replayed in his mind. He could only imagine the scuttlebutt that would go on behind his back when word got out about the money.

"I don't know," Jake said. "I told you. I can barely handle the caseload I have. Half the time I'm doing Majewski's job in property crimes too. He's on medical leave again for what, twelve weeks this time?"

"I know. But ..."

Jake knew the bottom line. "Meg," he said. "If I'm even going to consider taking on something like this, getting me a partner ... an official one ... needs to take priority."

"I know," she said. "It's going to happen. Now that the election's behind me, I'll have the power I need to make some real changes around here. This is one of them."

"It has to be Erica Wayne," Jake said. "She's practically already been my partner on the last few cases. We work well together. She deserves it."

"I know that too," Meg said. "Of course, Erica's at the top of any list to make detective. But there has to be a formal promotional process. My hands are tied on that. It's in the collective bargaining agreement. I'm posting the position tomorrow morning. Just make sure Erica puts in for it. We have to jump through the hoops but of course she'd be the frontrunner."

Jake also knew a lot of the rank and file would hate it. Erica had only been with the department for a couple of years. She'd also served in the Army Intelligence for close to a decade before that. Jake knew of no one more qualified to work with him.

"She'll put in for it," he said. "She wants it. She deserves it. Will I be part of the interviewing process?"

"Probably not," Meg said. "You can't be objective and you've made no secret of that."

There was a knock on the door. Andrea, Meg's newly hired and much-needed office assistant, poked her head in.

"Sorry to interrupt," Andrea said. "I was actually looking for you, Detective Cashen."

"It's Jake," he said.

"Jake." Andrea blushed. She was a sweet girl, Jake thought. Just a few years out of college. "Anyway, there's someone here to see you."

"It's Friday," Jake said. "After four. I'm off duty."

"I know. That's what I told her. But she wouldn't take no for an answer. And she said you'd want to see her."

Puzzled, Jake looked at Meg.

"You better skedaddle then," Meg said. "We'll talk more on Monday morning. I'll expect your answer. It better be yes." Meg winked.

"I put her in the interview room just outside your office," Andrea said, opening the door wide enough so Jake could pass.

"Thanks," he told her. He made the quick jaunt down to his office. He'd locked his door when he left. The interview room two doors down was the only light on. Jake gripped the knob and hoped whatever was behind this door wasn't going to ruin his day.

He stopped short when he saw her. She somehow looked smaller here than what he remembered when he'd met her on her turf on the other side of Red Sky Hill.

"Jake," she said. She was Melva Bardo, matriarch of one of the biggest organized crime families in the region. She lived in a remote area in the northern part of the county and belonged to an isolated hilltop community rarely seen in town. In Jake's experience, they didn't trust outsiders and were armed to the teeth.

"Mrs. Bardo," he said. He extended his hand to shake hers but she waved it away.

"This won't take long," she said. "But it's time I collected what you owe me."

THREE

"What is it that you think I owe you?" Jake asked. Melva Bardo had taken a chair against the wall in the corner of the room. She sat with her arms crossed, a scowl on her face. She looked so much like her son Rex, the leader of the Hilltop Boys. His gang had run guns, moonshine, and any number of other criminal enterprises. Despite Rex's RICO conviction a few years ago, he was by all accounts still hands-on with the business, even from prison.

"I didn't come to play games," Melva said.

"Glad to hear it. But as I recall, it's you who owes me a favor." Not long ago, Jake had investigated a murder that happened on the edge of Melva's property. His investigation took him to the other side of Red Sky Hill and he almost hadn't survived it.

"We can agree to disagree on that. It doesn't matter. What matters is this."

Melva reached into the pocket of her long sweater and pulled out two dog-eared photographs. She laid them on the table. Jake picked one up.

"Who is she?" Jake asked, staring at the image of a young, pretty girl with dark hair. She had a Mona Lisa smile, her lips slightly pursed, brilliant blue eyes. She was sitting outside on one of the picnic tables Jake recognized from Melva's backyard.

"Adah," Melva answered. "Adah Lee."

"Lee is her last name?" Jake asked. He didn't recall any family with the surname of Lee among the people he met on the other side of that hill.

"No," Melva said. "She doesn't have a last name. Not formally. She's just Adah. She's a whisper girl."

Jake put the photograph down and picked up the second one. This was a full body shot of Adah standing in profile. In this one, she was laughing, her head thrown back. She held a red ball in her hands.

"Whisper girl?"

"I call them the whisper kids. There are a few families that live deeper in the woods. They don't come out a lot when we have gatherings. They used to. But they mostly keep to themselves. I don't know how many there are."

"Why do you call them whisper kids?"

"The kids have never been on the other side of the hill, Jake. They're born and raised back there. Like ghosts. Whispers."

"So, what's with this one?" Jake asked.

"She's gone," Melva answered. "Disappeared. I'm worried."

"How do you know she's gone if she doesn't come to your part of the woods? Or any gatherings."

"I just know."

Jake put the photograph down. He had the strong sense he wasn't going to make it home anytime soon.

"Mrs. Bardo," he said. "I think you better start from the beginning."

"It was Adah's birthday yesterday. She turned seventeen. We threw a party for her. She never showed."

"But you said these whisper families, whisper kids don't generally come to your gatherings."

"I said they don't come often. This one was different. We'd been planning it for a while. Adah helped me plan it. Then she didn't come. And nobody knows where she is. She's not at home. She's not with any of the other families. She's just ... gone. And I know something bad happened."

Jake rubbed his forehead. "I'm going to need a lot more to go on."

"There isn't more. Those pictures I gave you are the only ones of her the way she looks now. I might have one or two from when she was little. But that's it. When I said those kids don't go to the other side of the hill, I mean they *never* go. Those kids don't exist as far as you're concerned. No birth certificates. No social security cards. No school records. Nothing."

"She's completely undocumented? Good lord, have any of them ever seen a doctor? Been vaccinated?"

Melva shook her head. "They don't trust the government. They don't trust people in town. I'm talking about the parents. A lot of the kids ... well ... maybe they think differently."

"Does Adah think differently?" Jake felt his anger rising. It was one thing that these people lived off the grid. But if they weren't providing basic medical care for their children, that was something else entirely. "How many are there?"

"Not sure," Melva said. "But Adah has five older brothers and one younger sister. She lives with her daddy, Warren Sommers. Her mama is Scarlett."

"What does Adah mean to you?"

For the first time, Melva's face softened. She blinked rapidly, as if she were forcing back tears.

"She's one of the good ones," Melva answered. "Smart. A hard worker. But she's got a rebel heart. It sometimes gets her into trouble."

"With her parents?"

Melva nodded. "And some of the others. I took Adah under my wing a couple of years ago. She helps me around the house and the garden. I taught her how to read. How to do her figures."

"You're telling me the other kids can't do any of that? They've had no schooling?"

"Not sure. Certainly not formally. But Adah's always been a quick study. I've got a kind of soft spot for her in my heart."

"I can see that. So tell me more about yesterday and what you think happened?"

Melva took a deep breath. "It's like I told you. There was a party. A big one. Everybody came out for it because I told them to. Adah helped me earlier in the day. She frosted her own cake. She went home and was supposed to come back to my kitchen about an hour before the party started. She didn't. I thought maybe she'd just decided to come with the rest of her family. She didn't. Warren insisted we have the party without her. I think he figured she'd just wandered off to sulk. She did that sometimes when she got into a fight with one of the boys or Warren and Scarlett."

"You're saying Adah's own parents weren't worried about where she was?"

"Didn't seem overly concerned, no. But I'm telling you, it's not like Adah. She wouldn't have not told me where she was going. She wouldn't do that to me. And now it's been almost twenty-four hours and nobody's seen her."

"Did you check back with her parents?"

"Of course I did. She's just gone. Vanished. I think something bad happened to her."

"Mrs. Bardo, I understand your concerns. But you're telling me Adah is a seventeen-year-old girl who doesn't always get along with her parents or siblings and she's got a rebellious streak? What makes you think she didn't just run away? I'll be honest, that's always the most likely scenario in cases like this."

"Not. Adah," Melva said firmly.

"Why not?"

"Because if she was gonna do something like that, she'd have to come to me. I don't think you understand. Adah didn't have money. None of them do. No credit card. No bank account. Nothing. She's just ... gone. Poof. And I'm worried."

"Okay," Jake said. His wheels started spinning. This girl was completely undocumented. As far as the rest of the world was concerned, she didn't exist. How in the hell was he supposed to figure out what happened to a girl who didn't exist on paper in the first place?

"Whatever happened to her, it was bad, Jake. I need you to do your job."

"Why aren't Adah's parents the ones who are asking?"

"You'd have to ask them that. And I wish you would."

"Do you think someone in Adah's own family might have hurt her? Punished her for this rebel heart you're talking about?"

Melva dropped her chin. She got quiet. Then, slowly, she lifted her eyes to meet Jake's. "They have before."

"They've hurt this girl?"

"I've seen bruises on her, yes. Adah wouldn't ever come out and say it. Not even to me. But yes. She was afraid of her daddy. Most people are."

"Are you?"

"I most certainly am not. But it's like I said, I need you to do your job. Every second that goes by, things could get worse."

Jake checked the clock. It was nearly five now.

"When was the last time anyone saw Adah, to your knowledge?"

"Her party was supposed to start at six. She left my house around three o'clock, but like I said, she was supposed to come back. I don't know who saw her after I did."

"Have you asked any of them?"

"I asked one of her brothers. He told me Adah never showed up. He said he saw her about a half an hour before the party was supposed to start. Then never again."

"Mrs. Bardo, can you appreciate how tough this is for me? You're telling me a girl's missing but that her own family doesn't seem concerned about it. You're telling me the girl herself wasn't really getting along with them? She doesn't go to school. I'm assuming she doesn't have any formal work history. The only thing you've got are two grainy pictures of her. Do you know what she was wearing?"

"She was wearing some jean overalls and a red sweatshirt. Both of those were hand-me-downs from one of her brothers. But that's what she had on the last time I saw her. I couldn't say if she changed her clothes after that."

"And you're telling me you have reason to believe her father might have done her harm?"

"I'm saying it's a possibility."

Jake found the whole thing strange. He knew most of the people on the other side of that hill revered and feared Melva Bardo. She had dozens of strong, young, heavily armed men loyal to her. If she wanted to make Warren Sommers's life difficult, she easily could.

"Why me?" Jake asked. "Why aren't you handling this in-house, so to speak?"

"Something happened," Melva said. "Something bad. Isn't this what you do? Investigate when someone gets hurt?"

"Yes."

"So do that. You have my permission to come back over the hill."

"It has to be different this time, Melva. Do you understand what I'm saying?"

She remained stoic, unreadable. "Yes."

"It has to be my rules, not yours. If I come up there to investigate this girl's disappearance, I'll do so my way. With backup. With my own vehicle. I'm not dealing with your bandana-wearing muscle on ATVs. They'll stay out of my way. They'll cooperate and answer questions I'm gonna have. If you or your kin in any way try to deny me access or make things tougher, I'll arrest them on obstruction charges and bring even more backup in. Do you understand?"

"I understand," Melva said. "Just find this girl, Jake. No matter what it takes."

He hoped she meant it. He didn't think for a minute the people on the other side of that hill would cooperate. There were a million places to hide bodies and make evidence disappear. He knew in his soul if Adah Lee's family wanted to make her disappear, they could, and not even Jake or a hundred other cops would be able to find her. In a dreadful way, he knew Adah had a better chance if she had simply run away and faced some bad guy on Jake's side of the hill.

But as Melva sat there, holding his gaze with her cold, hard eyes, he knew she'd become something he never thought he'd see.

Melva Bardo was terrified.

FOUR

I t was just past six before Jake finished with Melva Bardo. She left, promising again that she would cooperate and tell her people to stand down if he came up the hill. She also left him a hand-drawn map showing a hidden two-track road where he could drive straight in.

He sent a quick text to Birdie. Though everyone else called her Erica, he'd been calling her by that nickname since she was three years old.

> Are you still in the building? And if you're not, how fast can you get here? Bring your badge and your gun.

He stared at his phone screen, then sent a follow-up text.

> And your vest.

He didn't wait for a response, but shoved his phone in his pocket. There was light coming from Sheriff Landry's office. That surprised him. She should be at her own party.

He knocked on the door. "Come on in, Jake," she called out.

"You okay?" Jake asked. "What are you still doing here?"

"Waiting for you. I figure if Melva Bardo saw fit to come down the hill to talk to you specifically, it'll be something I need to know about. Am I right?"

Jake frowned. "You are."

"Have a seat."

Jake took a chair in front of her desk and filled her in on Adah Lee as best he could.

"I don't like it," Landry said. "Have you ever known any Bardo to come to the cops for help?"

"First time for everything."

"Don't blow me off. You know exactly what I mean. From what you said during the Albright investigation, she's got an army of hot-tempered, testosterone-fueled good ol' boys up there to do her bidding. If she really thinks this girl's family did her harm, why wouldn't she handle it her way?"

"I think she's scared enough to realize she needs more specialized help. And she doesn't know for sure whether Adah is still in her territory or if she's out here somewhere."

"So you want to take this on?" Landry asked.

"I don't think we have a choice. I believe Melva's genuinely worried. It wasn't easy for her to come down here and ask me for help. I think she knew she had no other choice."

"What if the truth is the opposite, Jake? What if it was too easy because she knew you wouldn't be able to say no? What if she's setting you up for an ambush?"

"I made myself clear," Jake answered. "I go up on my terms, not hers."

Outside Meg's window, the sun had nearly set. In a half hour, it would be pitch dark.

"What's your plan?" Meg asked, knowing full well she wouldn't be able to talk Jake out of this.

"Birdie's ... um ... Deputy Wayne's coming back in. I want her on this with me. And I'll take a marked unit. Melva's given me directions to their private access road."

Jake handed Meg the map Melva drew. Frowning, Meg took it.

"I don't get it," she said. "We sent drones out there the last time. There was no road."

"It's hidden by a canopy of trees. The Hill People are smart enough to know someone might want to take an aerial look someday."

"I suppose I don't have to tell you how much I hate this. And I suppose you don't have to tell me you're going up there anyway. But two crews, not just one. I want at least four deputies up there as backup, *plus* Deputy Wayne."

"Not just for today," Jake said. "I want her pulled to work with me on this case from start to finish. I need her. She's the best investigator we've got ..."

"Next to you," Landry finished for him.

Jake wasn't cocky enough to agree with her. "I just need her," he said. "I need somebody I don't have to babysit and who anticipates my moves. Erica does."

"Fine," Landry said. "Set it up for first thing in the morning as soon as it's light out again."

"No," Jake said. "This can't wait that long. This girl's been missing for twenty-four hours. I'm already behind the eight ball. I need to work it right now."

Meg grumbled. "Why did I know you were going to say that?"

"And I want Denning, Stuckey, Bundy, and Holtz. They're all working afternoons today. Bundy and Stuckey are still in the building."

Still frowning, Meg picked up her desk phone. She punched line one. "Andrea," she said. "I need you to have dispatch pull Denning and Holtz. Unless they're in the middle of something serious, I need them back here as soon as possible. Thanks."

"That'll do," Jake said. "I appreciate it."

"Vest," Meg said. "It's non-negotiable. Though a fat lot of good that's gonna do if they've got snipers up in those trees you're talking about."

"They won't," Jake said. "They'll listen to Melva."

"Really? If she's right, this girl's family did her harm. They're clearly not listening to Melva. This is going to end badly. I hate every part of this."

"I know. But you know we might be the only shot this poor kid has."

"You wait for everybody," Meg said. "No unnecessary risk-taking. You going up there right now is bad enough. I agree you need Wayne. Does she know what you've volunteered her for?"

No sooner had she said it than there was a knock on the door. Birdie poked her head in. She was out of breath, her hair barely together in a ponytail. But she was armed, wearing a badge around her neck and holding her vest.

"Where are we headed, Jake?" she asked.

Jake smiled. "You'll ride with me. I'll fill you in on the way."

———

W ithin fifteen minutes, Jake, Birdie, and his two backup crews were on the road. He'd given Birdie the highlights as he turned off Ridgeville Road, heading to the northernmost part of the county.

"What's your gut feeling?" Birdie asked. So far, it was the only question she'd asked. The moment Jake told her he needed her, Birdie dropped everything and got to him. It was one of the many reasons Jake had come to rely on her.

"It's not good," he answered. "Melva isn't somebody I'd expect to cry wolf. If she thinks something bad happened to this kid, I think we're probably already too late."

"So why did she wait so long? Why didn't she have her people all over this girl's family right away? Why let almost a whole day go by before coming to you?"

"I don't know. I think she felt like she didn't have a choice."

"You can't trust her," Birdie said.

"I know. But I'm not worried about an ambush like Landry is. Melva didn't make it a secret that she was coming to the Sheriff's Department. She's not dumb enough to put a target on her own back like that."

"You're getting close," Birdie said, looking at Melva's map. Jake made copies of it for both of the crews behind him. Jake had just driven over a dip in the dirt road. Just ahead, he saw a break in the tree line.

"There!" Birdie said, pointing to his left. Jake hit the brakes, kicking up road dust. But sure enough, he spotted the two-track road. There was no way he'd have noticed it if he didn't know to look. As he made the turn, Melva was waiting, leaning against her ancient pickup truck. She held a hand up to halt him.

"Wait here," Jake told Birdie.

"Nice try," she said. She got out of the car with him. The two cruisers pulled up behind him. Jake gave them a signal to stay in their vehicles.

"Just follow me in," Melva said. "The road's going to branch off in about a half a mile. One of the boys is waiting on an ATV. He'll lead you out to the Sommers's place. It's about six miles north of here. The road's dry. You shouldn't have any trouble getting in or out."

"You're not coming?" Jake asked.

"Better not," Melva answered. "I don't think my presence would help. Let's just say Warren and I tend not to see eye to eye."

"Terrific," Jake muttered. He stood by what he'd told Birdie. Melva had to know if something happened to him or any of his people, Landry would have this whole place crawling with cops within the hour. Still, he didn't like going in blind.

Melva didn't wait for him to say anything else. She pointed again in the direction she wanted Jake to follow, then got back in her truck and drove right around them.

"Just stay close," he told Birdie.

They climbed back into the car and headed north. Just as Melva said, one of her boys waited on a four-wheeler about a half mile up where the road forked. He was just a kid himself, maybe fourteen. In a way, it eased Jake's mind a bit. He didn't figure Melva would knowingly send the boy into danger. But the trees got even thicker as they made their way uphill and down the other side. Long branches scratched the sides of his car.

"Maybe we can bill the Bardos for the new paint job we're gonna need," Birdie muttered.

Jake turned on his high beams. The road narrowed even more. It was barely a road at all. Just a well-worn path that hadn't been cleared. He wondered if anything other than a four-wheeler or a horse-drawn wagon had ever gone this way.

It took almost twenty minutes to reach a clearing. They were deep in the valley now. The kid on the ATV stopped. He pointed to a piece of flat ground about fifty yards to the left. Jake parked and waited for his backup crews to do the same.

Resting his right hand on the heel of his gun, he stepped carefully down a steep incline, with Birdie right behind him. The four deputies fanned out a bit, keeping their eyes on the tree line and the top of the next hill.

"Those are berm houses, earth-sheltered," Birdie said.

She was right. Four long structures built right into the side of the hill. None of the homes would have had any source of heating or cooling beyond the natural protection of the earth itself. An ingenious design, if you weren't claustrophobic.

"Warren lives in that one," the boy said. "I'll try to get him. But I can't promise he'll come out. Just wait here."

Jake found himself scanning the hilltop as well. Meg had been right about one thing. This would be the perfect place for an ambush.

FIVE

"I need you to be the eyes in the back of my head," Jake whispered to Birdie. She was already doing it. Turning her back to Jake, she kept a casual stance, her hand on her hip, just above her gun. The other deputies spread out, two of them with eyes on the tree line behind them, two scanning the hilltop above them. But on a moonless night, it was nearly impossible to see anything in the dark.

"Mr. Sommers?" Jake called out. "I'm with the Worthing County Sheriff's Department. Would you come out and talk to me for a minute?"

He heard shuffling behind the door. Several footsteps. A flickering light came on in the house next to this one. Candlelight. A minute went by. Jake knocked on the door.

"We really need to talk to you, Mr. Sommers. I promise this won't take long."

He heard a deep, male voice shout, "Go back!" Jake didn't know if the man was talking to him or someone inside the house.

Another full minute went by, then finally the front door creaked open and Warren Sommers poked his head out. Jake held a flashlight in his hand, but pointed the beam to the side, away from Sommers's eyes.

"What do you want?" Sommers barked. Jake estimated the man was close to fifty years old. Salt and pepper hair with a goatee. He was missing a canine tooth. He wore flannel and well-worn jeans, work boots with the laces untied as if he'd just thrown them on.

"Do you want to step outside?" Jake asked.

Sommers turned his head, giving a fearsome look to someone inside. Jake heard footsteps running away from the door. Sommers squeezed himself out the door and slammed it behind him.

"What. Do. You. Want?" he barked.

"Do you know where your daughter Adah is?" Jake asked.

Sommers scanned the yard, spotting the four deputies and Birdie. With no immediate threat, she turned to face him, standing a few steps behind Jake and to his left, guarding his weaker side.

"What business is that of yours?"

"I have reason to believe Adah has been missing for a day. We're concerned she might be in some kind of danger. Do you know when you last saw her?"

"No."

"Is her mother here? Do you think she might have some insight into what's going on?"

"Adah is none of your business. You're trespassing on my property."

"And you haven't answered any of my questions. Look, I just want to make sure your daughter is okay. Surely you want that too."

"Adah makes her own choices. She lives with the consequences. Not your business. Not my problem."

"Mr. Sommers, Adah is seventeen years old. She's a minor. She's vulnerable. I'm trying to make sure she hasn't gotten herself into the kind of trouble that could get her hurt."

"I didn't ask for your help, Cashen," Sommers said. Jake had yet to tell Sommers his name, but he knew it anyway.

"It's Adah I'm trying to help. Right now, all I'm asking you is when was the last time you saw her. Do you know of any place she might have gone? A friend? Relative? Anyone else who might have seen her in the last twenty-four hours?"

"And I'm asking you to leave. Get off my property. I know my rights."

"May we come inside?" Jake asked, knowing it was futile. "Maybe have a look around Adah's room?"

"We're done here. You don't take another step onto my property without a warrant and a hell of a lot more backup."

"Are you threatening me?" Jake said, taking a step forward so he was nose-to-nose with Warren Sommers.

"I'm stating a fact. I'm not worried about Adah. She thinks she can take care of herself? Let her."

Sommers turned abruptly and slammed the door in Jake's face.

"That went well," Birdie said. "We're wasting our time."

"Time Adah may not have," Jake muttered. But Birdie was right. In one way, Warren Sommers was right. Without a warrant, he'd get no further. But the man had acted as suspicious as they came.

"Better get going." The boy who'd led them out here reappeared.

"Warren's got a temper. He meant what he said. You can go back out the way you came."

"What's your name?" Jake asked him.

"Tucker."

"Tucker, how well did you know Adah? When did you see her last?"

"Don't know. A couple of days ago. We aren't friends."

Tucker turned and climbed back onto his four-wheeler. He revved the engine, then sped past Jake and Birdie, disappearing into the woods going the opposite direction.

"Should we follow him?" Birdie asked.

"None of the cars will make it through there," Jake said. "And I'm sure as hell not following him on foot in the dark. We'll come back tomorrow. I'll get a warrant to search Adah's house."

Birdie didn't look happy, but she followed Jake back to the car. He signaled to the other deputies. This time, Stuckey and Bundy took the lead, driving back up the rugged trail that brought them here.

"I think Melva's instincts are right," Jake said. "Something bad happened to this girl."

"Or maybe something good," Birdie said. "Maybe she got the hell out."

"She's got no money. No credit cards. No identification. How far do you think she could get without diving headlong into real trouble?"

Birdie turned to answer him, then something caught her eye at the exact instant Jake saw it too.

"Jake!" Birdie shouted.

Jake slammed on the brakes, kicking up dirt. A young, skinny kid stood directly in Jake's path in the middle of the trail. He held up a lantern. It gave his face a ghostly glow.

The other deputies kept driving ahead, not seeing what Jake did.

"Dammit," Jake said. "You got a death wish, kid?"

The kid's expression never changed. He stood frozen in the road as Jake approached him. As he got closer, he realized the kid was older than he first thought. Maybe eighteen or nineteen. He had sandy blond hair and an Adam's apple about as big as a golf ball.

"You the detective?" he asked.

"I'm Jake Cashen. Who are you? Do you know why I'm here?"

"I know why you're here. I'm Isaac. Adah's my little sister."

Jake glanced at Birdie. She holstered her weapon but kept a hand on it.

"Isaac," Jake said. "Do you know something about what might have happened to your sister?"

"She's gone," he said. "Just ... gone. It's not good."

"Tell me what you know, son," Jake said. "Why don't you come with us? We can talk in my office."

Isaac shook his head. "Not leaving. Warren won't like it if he knows I'm talking to you."

"Warren's your father?" Birdie asked.

Isaac nodded. "He's glad she's gone."

"Why is that?" Jake asked.

"I told her. Adah never listened. She has all these ideas in her head. She never can just keep quiet. She's always talking back. Arguing. She does it just to make him mad."

"Make who mad?" Jake asked. "Your father? Isaac, do you think your father had something to do with what happened to Adah?"

"I never said that!" Isaac shouted, clearly angered by the question.

"Okay, okay," Jake said, putting his hands up in surrender. "Just calm down. Why don't you just tell me what you do know?"

"She's just gone. She's not here. I think she's on the other side of Red Sky Hill. She'd been threatening to go for months. She left when she did on purpose. Just to rub it in Warren's face. Ran off before her own birthday party. Broke Miss Melva's heart. Broke my ma's heart. She tells me everything. But she didn't tell me this."

"Isaac, when did you last see your sister?" Jake asked. "It would help if I could understand how long she's been gone."

"Yesterday," Isaac answered. "Four thirty. She came home from Melva's. She was just supposed to clean up and change clothes. She was taking forever and Warren got fed up. The rest of us left for the party without her. She promised she'd be right behind us. I wanted to wait for her but Warren said no."

"You were with him?" Jake asked. "Warren and the rest of your family left with you?"

Isaac nodded.

"And you all stayed at the party together?"

"Yeah."

"You're saying your father was there at the party the whole time? You saw him?"

"I wasn't keeping track of him. There were a lot of people."

"Then what happened? How long did you all stay at the party before realizing Adah wasn't coming?"

"An hour," he said. "I wanted to go back for her but Warren would have been mad. Melva went to all that trouble."

"Didn't anyone question why Adah wasn't at her own party?" Birdie asked.

Isaac shook his head. "It just seemed like her. Adah could be selfish sometimes. I told you. She liked to make Warren angry for the fun of it. We just figured it was that. But then we went home and Adah wasn't there either."

"Did you go out and look for her?"

"We did. Me and my brothers."

"How many brothers do you have?" Jake asked. "Older, younger?"

"All older. There's seven of us including me. Elias, Joseph, Jeremiah, Paul, then me, then Adah, then Zennia ... Zenni. She's the baby."

Birdie took out her pad and wrote it all down.

"And all your brothers and your younger sister, they were at the party too? The whole time? Nobody stayed back?"

"No, sir. We went together."

"Who lives in those other houses?" Birdie asked. "Next to Warren."

"Elias and his wife live in one with their kids. Joseph and Jeremiah live in the other. My grandmother lives in the last one further down the hill."

"Warren's mother?" Jake asked.

"Yeah."

"So it's just you, Adah, Zenni, and your parents in the main house?" Jake asked.

"And Paul," he answered. "But he's moving out this summer. He's building a house closer to the big hill. He's gonna get married."

"How old are you, Isaac?" Jake asked.

"I'm nineteen."

"Is there anyone you know that might want to hurt Adah? Or anyone she might have been talking to on the other side of Red Sky Hill?"

"I don't know. I don't think anybody was mad at Adah, if that's what you mean."

"She never told you she was having trouble with anyone?" Jake asked.

"No."

"You said she was selfish," Birdie asked. "Did that irritate your father or your brothers, or anyone else on this side of the hill?"

"Warren and Adah were always butting heads. She wasn't scared of him."

"Should she have been?" Jake asked. "Have you ever seen Warren hurt Adah or any of your brothers and sisters?"

Isaac didn't answer. "You better go now. Warren's gonna be expecting me. He won't like it if he knows I talked to you."

"But you're worried," Jake said. "You think something bad happened to Adah?"

"Can't be anything good. She wouldn't have just disappeared without telling me."

"You were close with her," Jake said.

"She talked to me," Isaac answered.

"Did she tell you she was going to run away?"

"She just said she was curious about what things were like in town. She was always asking to ride in with one of Miss Melva's people. She never got to go. But she didn't tell me she had plans to go herself." Isaac took a step back and lowered his lantern. "Are you gonna find her?"

"I'm going to try," Jake said.

"Good. That's good. I want her to be all right."

"I want that too, Isaac. But I really wish you'd come with me. Let me take a formal statement from you down at the station. It would help. I'd like to know who Adah's friends were."

"Most of the girls around here got in trouble if they hung out with Adah. They thought she was a bad influence. But sometimes she hung around Grace and Sarah. They live in the houses south of here. By Miss Melva's."

"Did she have a boyfriend?" Jake asked.

"No," Isaac said. "She would have told me. Plus, she was already ..." His voice dropped off.

"She was already what, Isaac?" Jake asked.

"I can't talk anymore. I gotta get back."

"Isaac, wait. What were you about to say? Adah was already what? Was she promised to somebody?"

"I hope you find her," he said. "There's nothing else I can tell you."

Jake took a step forward. Isaac was quicker. He bolted sideways and disappeared into the woods. Birdie ran after him.

"Dammit," Jake muttered. "Birdie, wait!"

He followed her. But neither of them made it more than a few yards. The underbrush was thick, tangling around their ankles.

"Stop," Jake said. "Birdie, it's no use. We can't chase that kid through here in the dark. We don't know what's out there and we'll end up lost and cut off from our backup."

She let out a growl. "I hate this place."

Jake understood her feelings. "I'll get the warrant. We'll come back when it's daylight. We need to talk to everybody we can out here. And I need to get inside Adah's house."

They trudged back to the car. Jake saw burrs sticking to Birdie's back. He picked them off. He turned and she did the same for him. He knew they'd be all over his pant legs, too.

"He has an alibi," Birdie said as soon as Jake started driving. "That kid said his whole family was at Melva's during the time frame Adah vanished."

"If he's telling the truth," Jake said. "And I have no idea if Warren could have sent someone back for her. And Isaac pretty much admitted he didn't have eyes on Warren the whole time. He could have slipped away for a bit while everyone else was distracted at the party."

"Jake," she said. "I keep feeling worse and worse about this. Something happened to that girl. Something bad. You have to sense it too."

Jake didn't want to give voice to it. But as each hour ticked by, he knew Birdie was right. The only explanations he could think of for Adah Lee's disappearance were awful ones.

He breathed a sigh of relief as he saw the road out of the hill country up ahead. "Let's just work the case," he said. "And not think too far ahead."

Six

The next morning, Sheriff Landry wanted a status report. She came down to Jake's office. He had his warrants written and Birdie's promise to babysit them through the court until Judge Finneas Cardwell signed them. He expected her back any minute.

"We got almost nowhere," Jake told Landry. He filled her in on everything that happened over the hill last night. Before Meg could even respond, Birdie appeared in the doorway.

"How good do you think your warrants will be now that Warren Sommers knows you're coming back?" Meg asked.

"It is what it is," Jake answered. "I have a lot more people to interview. Adah's brother at least gave me a starting point. As soon as Erica gets those warrants signed, we'll head back out this afternoon."

"What do you need in the meantime?" Landry asked.

Jake picked up the copy he'd made of the two photographs Melva Bardo gave him. "These need to go out to all local law enforcement and nationwide. We need to get this girl's face out there as much as we can."

Landry kept her frown. "This is going to get press, at least locally. There are still a lot of folks in town who have some strong prejudices about the people over that hill."

"That's gonna have to be their problem. I'd also like to get a drone up within the hour."

"How good do you think that will be?" Birdie asked. "We couldn't even see the access road through those trees."

"I don't expect a miracle. But we have to try."

"If the hill people don't shoot the damn thing out of the sky," Landry muttered.

"It's a possibility. I'll get word to Melva to expect it. Tell her people to stand down. She promised me she would."

"I don't know, Jake," Birdie said. "The Sommers's encampment didn't seem to get Melva's memo that they should cooperate."

Jake felt his own frustration building. This could turn out to be an impossible case.

"How do you find a girl who doesn't exist as far as anybody else is concerned?" Landry said, giving voice to Jake's main fear.

"The same way you look for any other undocumented victim. This one's going to take more boots on the ground. I'm going to have to figure out a way to talk to every household on the other side of that hill."

"Cardwell should be in chambers by now. I'll head over there," Birdie said.

"I'll get you your drone," Landry said. She picked up the

photocopies of Adah's picture. "And I'll get Darcy to distribute these within the hour."

"Thanks," Jake said. "I'm headed over to Tessa and Spiros's. It's Tuesday. The Wise Men should be there. I checked the archives. Virgil Adamski worked on a drug case that involved a few witnesses up there. He might have an approach I haven't thought of. When I get back, we'll head back up the hill."

Birdie and Meg had their marching orders. Jake grabbed his jacket and decided to walk the two blocks over to Papa's Diner. The Wise Men included three retired cops Jake had grown to trust. Virgil Adamski, Chuck Thompson, and Bill Nutter.

It was just after nine when he walked through the front door of the diner. Spiros's bell clanged as the door shut behind him. The lights were off in the main dining area. Jake walked around the counter. The three Wise Men always took up the large round table at the very back of the diner. It was empty.

"Spiros?" Jake called out. This was odd. The diner should be bustling with the breakfast crowd. Adamski, Thompson, and Nutter usually got here by eight and hung out all the way through lunch.

Jake heard voices coming from deeper in the kitchen. He walked behind the counter and pushed his way through the stainless steel double doors.

He stopped short when he saw Tessa Papatonis. She slumped forward in a chair against the wall, her face buried in a kitchen towel, her body wracked with sobs. Spiros stood over her with his hand on her back, comforting her.

"What's wrong?" Jake asked. Tessa didn't look up. Hesitant to leave his wife's side, Spiros hugged her, then motioned for Jake to step back out into the diner with him.

"Where is everybody?" Jake asked.

"Oh Jake," Spiros answered. "The ambulance just left. Virgil fell over in his chair right after Tessa brought him his eggs."

Jake's heart dropped. Virgil was only sixty-five years old and as far as Jake knew, in relatively good health. Though he smoked off and on.

"Heart attack," Spiros continued. "The paramedics got here so fast, thank God. Chuck and Bill rode with him. We didn't know what to do. Tessa got an aspirin down him, but that's all we could think of."

"That's good. That was quick thinking," Jake said, praying they'd gotten him to the hospital in time.

"Jake," Spiros said. "We were going to follow. I had to close up the diner. We can't even think about having service right now."

"Of course not."

"But ... we ... Tessa. She can't go to the hospital. It's too much for her. Maybe for me too."

Long ago, Tessa and Spiros had lost their only child, a daughter, to violence. They'd learned of her death while standing in the emergency room. Jake could completely understand their aversion to ever being in a hospital again.

"Will you go, Jake? Will you call me and tell me if Virgil's going to be okay?"

"Of course," Jake said, his eyes darting to the wall clock. It was nine fifteen. He'd have at least an hour before Birdie got back to him with signed warrants.

"I have time," he told Spiros. "I'll call you just as soon as I can. Tell Tessa not to worry. Virgil's too stubborn to die."

Ten minutes later, Jake walked through the lobby of County Hospital. The emergency room was to his left, down a winding hallway. He didn't stop at the front desk. The receptionist there recognized him and buzzed him through the doors.

With each step, dread coiled through him. He hoped what he'd told Spiros was true. Virgil Adamski couldn't die.

He spotted Chuck and Bill almost immediately. They were huddled together in the waiting room, too agitated to sit.

"Chuck," Jake called out. Chuck looked up. Relief flooded his face when he saw Jake.

"What happened?" Jake asked.

"He just keeled over," Bill answered. "We were just sitting there shooting the breeze like always. Virg turned grey, started coughing, then fell off his chair to the ground. It was chaos."

"What are they saying?" Jake asked. "Has anyone called his daughter?" Virgil's daughter Crystal lived in Florida.

"I just got off the phone with her," Chuck answered. "She'll be on a two o'clock flight out of Tampa. She'll be here this evening."

"Good. What are the doctors telling you?"

No sooner had Jake asked than a male doctor in green scrubs walked up to them.

"Are you here for Mr. Adamski?" he asked. "Do you know who his patient advocate is?"

"I am," Chuck answered, surprising Jake. "Virg thought it would be good if he put me on it too. Cuz Crystal knew it might take her a few hours to get here. Virg's brother lives in Phoenix."

"Smart," Jake said.

"I'm Dr. Dormer," the doctor said. "Let me fill you in on what's happening with Mr. Adamski. He has indeed suffered a heart attack. We've given him some thrombolytic medication but he's not responding to it as well as we'd like. We'll be taking him up to the fourth floor very shortly where Dr. Hinzel, one of our cardiologists, will perform an angioplasty. He'll thread a catheter through Mr. Adamski's coronary arteries to try to remove the blockage and place a stent. He may need bypass surgery, but we won't know that until the cardiologist is able to take a closer look. If it's just the angioplasty, that should take a couple of hours. After that, he'll be admitted for a few days."

"How bad is it?" Bill asked.

Dr. Dormer looked at Jake. "You're his son?"

"No, just a close friend. His daughter is on her way. Should be here in a couple of hours." Jake turned to Chuck. "I can arrange to pick her up from the airport and bring her straight here."

"It's taken care of," Chuck said. "Gemma's doing it."

Jake's sister Gemma had been good friends with Crystal Adamski, now Holstein, growing up. He had two unread texts from his sister. He knew he'd catch hell for not answering them.

"That's good," Dr. Dormer said. "We really won't know how much damage there was to the heart muscle until Dr. Hinzel sees what's what. There's a family waiting area in the cardiology wing. You'll be more comfortable there."

"Can we see him before you take him up?" Jake asked.

"Of course," the doctor said. "Though I should warn you he's pretty out of it. But he's stable. His vitals are good. He's on oxygen. I don't know how responsive he'll be. But don't let that alarm you. And try not to agitate him. He was pretty volatile when they brought him back. Altered."

"We'll be careful," Chuck said.

"All right. But just for a few minutes. We really do need to get him upstairs. Transport should be here any minute."

"We just want him to know we're here," Bill said. "Let him know his daughter's on the way."

"That would be good," Dr. Dormer said. "Follow me."

Jake, Chuck, and Bill followed the doctor to a curtained area down the hall. When Dormer pulled back the curtain, Chuck and Bill gasped.

Virgil looked terrible. His skin was waxen and gray. Jake didn't need to see the results of any test to know the heart attack had to have been major and Virgil was lucky to have survived long enough to get here.

Chuck stepped forward and put a gentle hand on Virgil's right foot. Virgil stirred a bit and opened his eyes. He couldn't talk through the oxygen mask. He tried to pull it off but Jake stopped him.

"You need to leave that on, buddy. It's helping you get better," Jake said. "But you're okay. You hear me? You're getting good care and you're going to be just fine. You have to have an operation, but these doctors know what they're doing."

Virgil locked eyes with Jake. He looked terrified. Jake tried to keep his face neutral, but he felt just as terrified. In the span of an hour, Virgil Adamski looked like he'd aged forty years. Maybe he had.

"Crystal's flying in," Bill said. "She'll be here by dinnertime. She wanted me to make sure you know she loves you, Virg. That's a great kid you raised."

Virgil nodded. He squeezed his eyes shut. When he opened them, they were filled with tears.

"We need to let you rest," Chuck said. "But me and Bill aren't going anywhere. We'll be here when you get out of surgery. We got you. You hear me? We got you."

Chuck leaned forward and kissed Virgil's forehead. Seeing it cut a hole in Jake's heart.

"I'll have someone show you to the waiting room," Dr. Dormer said.

"You're gonna be okay, Virgil," Bill said as the three of them walked back to the elevators.

"I'm glad you came," Chuck said to Jake. "Virg needs all the support and good thoughts he can get."

"I see that," Jake said as they waited for the elevator doors to open. "I wish I could stay. But you both have my cell. You let me know the second you hear what the doctors say."

"What's up?" Bill asked.

"We can talk about it later," Jake said.

"We got time, Jake," Bill said. The two men stepped away from the elevator doors, eager to hear what Jake had to say.

"I'm working a missing person case," he said. "Girl from the hilltop vanished a day and a half ago. She's undocumented. Never been to school. Never seen a doctor. Seventeen years old. Melva Bardo came down and recruited me to find her. I came to the diner hoping Virgil could give me some pointers. I know he worked a drug case and interviewed a few witnesses up there."

"That was ages ago," Chuck said. "I remember that one. Damn. Virgil will be jazzed to talk to you about it. You have any leads?"

"Not yet. Though her father's at least a person of interest. I'll know after I go back up there. I'm waiting on a few warrants. But I'll be honest. I've got a gut feeling this girl's already dead."

"That's gonna be a rough one," Bill said. "You let us know if you need anything."

The elevator doors opened. "You better catch that one," Jake said.

"We'll be in touch later," Chuck said. "Thanks for coming down."

"Thanks for staying with him," Jake said. "Thanks for getting him here so quickly."

A moment later, a text came through from Birdie. She'd secured the warrants in record time.

"I gotta go," he said.

"You headed back to Red Sky Hill?" Bill asked.

"Yep."

"Watch your back," Chuck said. "I know Virgil hated every second he had to be there."

"So do I," Jake agreed. The two men got on the elevator. Jake waited until the doors shut, then texted Birdie back.

"I'm on my way. Get two crews to follow us."

"Already waiting," she answered. "We'll get going as soon as you get here."

SEVEN

Warren Sommers stood sentry like a gargoyle in the hallway outside Adah's room. She shared it with her younger sister, Zenni. Zenni was fifteen. She looked nothing like Adah. Where Adah was dark-haired with blue eyes, Zenni had the same sandy blonde hair as her father, deep-set brown eyes she kept downcast as she waited at her father's side.

There wasn't much to look through. Adah didn't have a cell phone. No computer. Only a few dresses hanging in the closet, all shapeless brown or blue cotton that would have probably hung past her knees. Certainly nothing a normal seventeen-year-old would want to wear.

But Jake tried not to judge. Just because they lived differently didn't mean it was wrong. But the house itself seemed oppressive. Only the rooms at the front had any natural light. Zenni and Adah's room was cut into the hillside. No windows. Not even a door. Just a doorway. It felt like a tomb.

"Did she keep a diary?" Jake asked. Though Warren Sommers hadn't uttered a single word since Jake served the warrant on him.

Adah's mother had opened the front door and let Jake and Birdie in. He put two deputies on Sommers, the other two posted at each end of the longhouse to prevent any of the other occupants from getting in the way.

"I'll talk to the mother," Birdie said. Jake half expected Warren to impede Birdie's way. But he kept still, glowering at Jake.

There was simply nothing here. No notes. Adah seemed to have left with only the clothes on her back. She had no other shoes so Jake assumed she'd been wearing the only pair she owned.

"Mr. Sommers," Jake said. "I need to know what your daughter was wearing the day of her party. Can you tell me that? It will help if I can get an accurate description out. In case someone might have spotted her."

Sommers said nothing but pushed Zenni forward. The girl looked terrified. She'd been crying when Jake first entered her bedroom.

"She had denim overalls," Zenni said, her voice barely above a whisper. "She liked those."

"Long ones?" Birdie asked, having just come back down the hall. "With pants or a skirt?"

"Pants," Zenni answered. "They were too long on her so she cut them. They were frayed at the bottom."

"A raw hem," Birdie said.

"She had a red shirt under it," Zenni said.

Jake wrote it down in his notepad. It wasn't much, but it was something.

"When was the last time you talked to Adah?" Jake asked.

"The morning of her party. I woke up before she did. I was out in the garden. When she didn't come out, I came back in to wake her up. She's supposed to help me. We needed to weed before breakfast."

"How did she seem to you?" Jake asked. "Was she upset about anything?"

"No. She was just Adah. Normal. We didn't talk much."

Warren Sommers scowled at Jake, then abruptly left the hallway and went out the front door.

"Zenni," Jake said. "Do you know if Adah was seeing someone? Like a boyfriend?"

Zenni shook her head.

"Do you think she could have kept something like that a secret from you?" Birdie asked.

"No. She's just gone. Adah didn't want to be here. She wanted to go to college. But she wasn't mad or anything that day. She was just … Adah. There's nothing else I remember. I wish I did."

There wasn't much more they could do here at the house. He'd gotten nowhere with Warren, Adah's mother, or the rest of her brothers. Their stories stuck closely with what Isaac had said last night. Adah was at Melva's in the later morning. She came home to change and wash up. Her family started off for Melva's for Adah's party. Adah stayed back. Her family went ahead without her and none of them saw her after that.

Only one member of the family was conspicuously absent today. Isaac was nowhere to be found.

"Do you know where Isaac is?" Jake asked Zenni.

"Probably fishing. Or out checking his snares. That's where he is most of the time."

Jake didn't like the look of Zenni. Her hair was dull. Her skin, flaky and sallow.

"Zenni," Jake said, lowering his voice. "Do you feel safe here?"

Zenni's eyes went wide. "I don't have anything else I can tell you. I'd like to go back to my room now. Are you finished?"

Birdie glanced at Jake. She was worried about the same thing he was. But there were no outward signs of abuse or neglect with Zenni. He hated leaving her behind, but had no legal basis for removing her.

"We're finished for now," Jake said. "But I do have a question. I understand Adah was friends with a girl named Grace and a girl named Sarah. Do you know where they live?"

"Sarah's about a mile east of us. She lives with just her mom. Her dad died when she was little. Grace lives more south, closer to Miss Melva. Mom and Dad didn't really like it when Adah hung around with her."

"Why is that?"

"She goes to town a lot. Adah always wanted to go with her."

"She wasn't allowed?" Jake asked.

"You'd have to ask Grace. I need to go now."

With that, Zenni darted down the hall and went outside to join her father.

"Come on," Jake said. "We're not gonna get anything else out of these people right now. Let's see if we can find this Grace. If she's not one of these so-called whisper kids, she might be more willing to talk."

Jake, Birdie, and the deputies left the Sommers's compound. Scarlett stood glued to her husband's side. As much as Jake didn't like the look of Zenni, Scarlett looked downright terrified. She never met Jake's eyes. She kept them focused on the ground. Her whole posture was off. She was trying to make herself smaller, unnoticeable. He'd seen that kind of thing too many times to count. But like Zenni, Jake saw no obvious signs of abuse. It might not be physical, but he had no doubt Warren Sommers ruled his family with an iron fist.

Sommers curled his lip and spat on the ground as Jake walked past him.

"We'll be in touch if we find anything," Jake said. "If you hear from Adah, please get word to me."

"Do you think you'll find her?" Scarlett said, shocking Jake.

"I hope so," Jake said.

Scarlett hiccupped. There were tears in her eyes. Warren put an arm around her and held her up. It tore at Jake to leave her and Zenni there. But he had no other choice.

Adah's friend Grace was easy to find. There was a group of houses near the base of Red Sky Hill. Melva lived in the biggest. It was built near one of the roads leading out. The others were nestled in the woods. They likely wouldn't be viewable from the air. Grace Bowen ended up living in the first door they knocked on.

She was pretty, with a full figure and round, rosy cheeks. She had a light in her eyes missing from Warren Sommers's children. Grace's mother, Barbara, even offered Jake and Birdie some tea and cakes. They declined. The Bowen house was cheery, with tons of natural light coming in from a large bay window in the front. Though it was log-built, the interior was painted a soothing white.

"When was the last time you saw Adah?" Jake asked all the standard questions. Grace's answers were consistent with what he'd already heard from Melva and the Sommers family.

"Did you find it strange that Adah didn't show up to her own party? Or that the party went on without her?"

"Kind of. Not that Adah didn't show up. That was typical Adah. She was always in open warfare with her dad. She knew it would embarrass him if she didn't show up after all the trouble everyone went to. Whatever Adah could do to tick him off, she'd do it."

"Everyone says Adah wanted out. She had ambitions to live in town. Or somewhere else. Is that true from what you knew of her?"

"Oh yeah. Adah had these big dreams. Wanted to go to New York or Hollywood. But she was so dumb. Like she didn't even know how far away those places were. Or how she'd afford to live there."

"She didn't learn basic geography?" Birdie asked.

"No." Grace laughed. "I tried to teach her some. I got a lot of flack for hanging out with her."

"Why's that?" Jake asked.

"Because those kids out there, they're weird. Backwards. There's rumors some of them are inbred. It's been like that since before I was born."

"She's telling the truth," Barbara said. "I'd say it's been about thirty years since a few of the families started cutting themselves off from the rest of us. I know what people think. That we're hicks. Hillbillies."

"I don't think that at all," Jake said.

"Well, they are. The Sommerses, Pruitts, Nagels, the Garrs. It's not right what they're doing to those kids. They should be in school with the rest of our kids. Going to the doctor. We like our lifestyle out here. It's remote. Quiet. But we're not freaks. Those parents are turning their kids into freaks, though. I felt so bad for Adah. She wanted so badly to see more of the world. I once offered to let her live with us. Her parents wouldn't hear of it. They stopped her from coming out of the valley for months after that. I felt guilty."

"Do you think Adah tried to run off that day?" Jake asked.

"Probably," Grace answered. "She turned seventeen. She knew what was gonna happen in a year if she didn't find a way out."

"What was going to happen?" Jake asked. Barbara Bowen's face fell.

"Grace, that's a rumor."

"No, it's not. Adah told me. It was in confidence, but now that she's gone, I don't suppose it matters. If it could help you."

"What is it?" Birdie asked.

"Adah's dad was going to make her get married when she turned eighteen. To Rance Pruitt."

"Grace! That's got to be a lie," Barbara said.

"It's not a lie."

"Who's Rance Pruitt?" Jake asked.

"He's a grown man," Barbara said. "He's got to be at least fifty years old."

"Did Melva Bardo know that?" Jake asked. "I know she was close with Adah. That she was trying to help her."

"Nobody in this part of the valley knew," Grace said. "I think Adah was too scared to tell her. Melva sure wouldn't have liked it. She probably would have had a thing or two to say about it. Adah swore me to secrecy. She was afraid her father would try to keep her from working for Miss Melva if they got into it."

"I take it Adah had no desire to marry this man?" Jake asked.

"God no," Grace said.

"Grace! Language," her mother said.

"Sorry. But no. Adah said there was no way she'd go through with it. One time she told me she'd slit her wrists before she let that old man touch her. She knew it was only because Old Rance wanted a son. His first wife couldn't have kids. She had some kind of female problem. Then she died trying to have one anyway."

"I think it was an ectopic," Barbara said. "Maybe ten years ago. She just collapsed out at the greenhouse one day. It was just awful. We wanted to get her to a hospital but Rance wouldn't allow it."

"Good grief," Birdie said. "That's barbaric."

"It certainly was. Melva was beside herself."

"Where can I find this Rance Pruitt?" Jake asked. He hated to think about it. But if he'd caught wind of the fact Adah might not go through with what her father arranged, it might provide a motive to kidnap her ... or worse.

"Do you think Pruitt would have tried to hurt Adah if he found out she had other plans for herself?" Birdie asked, going down the same road as Jake was.

"I'd hate to think it was something like that," Barbara said. "But I haven't seen Rance up this way in years. And when I did, he was just a sour, angry man. He does have a temper."

"Worse than Warren Sommers?" Birdie asked.

"You don't think Adah's dad did something to her, do you?" Grace said.

"Do you think he's capable of it?" Jake asked.

"I don't ... I don't know. But he was here. He was at the party. The whole time."

"Are you sure?" Birdie asked. "You never saw him leave?"

Barbara took a moment to answer the question. "I don't know. I suppose he could have. I saw him arrive with the rest of his family. I saw him leave with them. The middle part? I can't say I was focused on him at all."

"What about Rance Pruitt?" Birdie asked. "Was he here?"

"No," Barbara said. "I told you. We haven't seen him down here in years."

"Where can I find him?" Jake asked.

"I'll draw you a map," Barbara Bowen said, concern filling her eyes.

If Warren Sommers and his family lived in the middle of nowhere, Rance Pruitt's homestead was even more remote. Two miles deeper into the woods, Jake and Birdie had to take the last half-mile on foot. Jake didn't like it. Too many places for someone to lie in wait in the woods.

It was late in the day. There was only maybe another hour of sunlight. Jake wanted to be as far away from the valley as he could before dusk.

Pruitt's cabin was in a state of disrepair. The chimney leaned to one side. Half his roof shingles had peeled away. Two shaggy dogs growled and barked as they approached, but they were luckily fenced off. Though with the noise they made, there was no hope of catching Pruitt by surprise.

As they approached, Jake heard something crash. The sound of shattering glass. Instinctively, Jake drew his weapon. Birdie did the same.

"Hello!" Jake called out. "This is the Sheriff's Department. I need you to come outside!"

Jake heard a door open and shut. Birdie leaned sideways, peering around the house. "He's making a run for it," she said.

"Pruitt!" Jake yelled. "We just want to talk!"

Birdie was already on the move. She bolted around the side of the house, giving chase. She grabbed Pruitt's shirt. He whipped around and landed a sucker punch across her jaw.

"Birdie!" Jake shouted. But Birdie barely flinched. She lost her grip on Pruitt and he sprinted further down the hill with Birdie right behind him.

"Christ," Jake muttered, taking off after her. Pruitt's house was on a slope. From their uphill vantage point, Jake had a clear view of Pruitt as he dodged bushes and branches, heading deeper into the woods. Birdie was nimble, avoiding getting tangled in the brush. Jake ran down, praying he wouldn't twist his knee and aggravate an old wrestling injury.

Birdie was almost on him. Then Pruitt dodged left and turned the other way. He hadn't seen Jake. He was heading straight for him. Jake reacted, diving at Pruitt's legs, pulling him down to the ground and knocking the wind out of him.

Barbara Bowen was right. Pruitt looked to be about fifty years old, gone full gray with a potbelly and ripped shirt.

He was unarmed, but kicked at Jake as he lay on the ground. But Jake had him in a hold he'd never get out of. Birdie caught up, holstered her weapon, and took out her cuffs. Pruitt made a last attempt to break Jake's hold.

"Stay down!" Birdie commanded. Pruitt finally put his hands up in surrender.

Jake got Pruitt on the ground face down, his knee in his back.

"Enough!" Jake said.

Pruitt spit dirt. "I know why you're here. I know she sent you. I won't let Melva make some fool out of me. That girl is poison. She's got Bardo blood through and through."

"Melva?" Jake said. "What the hell are you talking about?"

Birdie slapped her cuffs on Pruitt and helped Jake haul him to his feet.

"What's he talking about?" Birdie said.

"You know why we're here, Pruitt. I think you need to tell me what you know about Adah Lee."

He spit on the ground. "They want to saddle me with their trash," Pruitt said. "You tell Warren Sommers this is his mess, not mine. I don't want a damn thing to do with some Bardo whore."

"Bardo ..." Jake said, then stopped short. Saddle him. Bardo whore. Warren's mess.

Bardo. Adah? His mind flashed with the image of Zenni and Isaac with their sandy blond hair and brown eyes. Even Scarlett was fair-haired with a light complexion. What he'd seen of the rest of

Warren Sommers's children matched. All except for Adah. Dark hair. Ice-blue eyes that seemed to pierce right through you.

"Jake?" Birdie said, clearly piecing it together at the same time he did.

"She's a Bardo, isn't she?" Jake said. "That's why Melva's so interested in getting her back. Adah's her ..." Jake's mind spun. Melva Bardo had three sons. Floyd, the family screw-up, was father to three children, all of whom he'd met and none of them had children of their own. Her youngest son, Alton, had died in combat in the Middle East decades ago, well before Adah was born. Nyla was Melva's daughter. But Jake had never heard of her having any other children but her worthless son, Zeke, who died childless in a shootout a few years ago.

And Rex. Head of the family. Rex ... with the dark hair and smoldering blue eyes. God. Why hadn't he seen it before? In the pictures Melva had given him, Adah Lee was the spitting image of King Rex Bardo.

EIGHT

"You have no cause to arrest me," Pruitt shouted as Birdie hauled him out of the backseat of the cruiser. They'd driven him back to the base of Red Sky hill. Deputy Denning stood ready to wrestle him back to the ground if necessary. Jake ignored Pruitt's protests.

"You assaulted an officer!" Jake shouted. "Get him into an interview room," he told Birdie. "I'll get there as soon as I can."

Birdie nodded to Denning. Denning jerked Pruitt forward and led him to the back of one of the patrol cars. He put his hand on Pruitt's head and put him in the car.

"Are you okay?" Jake asked Birdie. He reached for her chin and tilted her head to the side so he could get a look at her jaw. There was a small bruise forming, but she moved her mouth from side to side. Nothing was broken. She pulled away from him.

"I'm fine. He hits like a toddler. I'll ride with Denning," Birdie said. "What are you thinking?"

"I'm thinking I need to have another conversation with Melva Bardo." Though he knew Birdie came to the same conclusion as Jake about Adah's possible paternity, she said nothing.

Birdie, Deputy Denning, and Pruitt drove off. Jake climbed behind the wheel of his own cruiser and tore off for Melva Bardo's.

Someone may have gotten word to her that he was coming. That Rance Pruitt just got taken out in handcuffs. Jake felt the trees up here had eyes, and maybe they did. He had a creepy sensation running up his spine as if he were being watched. Melva stood on her back porch looking cross. Jake did not care.

"Inside," he barked at her. He was done giving her any sort of reverence. She raised a brow, but took his direction.

One of the men he'd seen around her the last time he came to her door was up there, standing guard in her living room.

"Luc," she said. "You can wait outside. I'll be fine. Detective Cashen knows his manners."

Luc looked dubious, but did as he was told. Melva shut the door behind him. "I made some sweet tea. Would you like a glass?"

"I didn't come here for tea time, Melva," he said.

"All right." She walked to her kitchen table and sat down. Jake didn't wait for an invitation. He jerked a chair out and sat on the edge of it.

"I talked to Rance Pruitt," Jake said. "You wanna guess what he told me?"

Melva looked genuinely puzzled. "I wouldn't have the first idea. Rance keeps to himself, mostly. His wife was more social. But Arlene passed away a long time ago."

"Are you going to sit there and pretend you didn't know Warren Sommers was going to force her to marry Rance next year?"

Melva's eyes gave away nothing. She stood up, walked over to the counter and calmly poured herself a glass of tea. She added sugar and stirred it with a long spoon. Then she sat back down across from Jake.

"I had hoped to avoid anything like that," she said.

"What do you mean?"

"I had a hunch Warren might do something like that. Adah certainly had concerns. But no, I had no idea Warren had actually arranged anything formal."

"Grace Bowen told me," he said. "She said Adah told her. You want me to believe you and Adah were close, and yet she never mentioned it to you?"

"No. She didn't. But I understand why. She'd know I wouldn't stand for something like that. I would have had it out with Warren myself. She probably didn't want to start a fight."

"Melva, it's time you stopped lying to me."

Melva narrowed her eyes. "You better be careful, Jake. I'm a lot of things. A liar isn't one of them."

"Who is she?" Jake shouted. "The truth. Now. Rance Pruitt seems to think he knows Adah's secret."

Melva took another sip of her tea.

"Dammit Melva. You came to me. You asked me ... practically begged me to find this girl. I'm in it now. I've risked my people to come up here against the sheriff's wishes. Meg Landry wanted to send an army up here. She still might. You could have law enforcement from three counties crawling all over this land. And they'll all be forced to act if they see something illegal. You have crops up here that might interest the DEA. Child Protective Services will want to clean out that whole compound. Your whisper kids. Right now, I can't think of a good reason not to let them."

"If you have something you want to ask me, you'd better just come out with it."

"Is Adah your granddaughter? Is Rex her father?"

For the first time, Melva flinched. He knew she had to have expected the question.

"What gives you that idea?"

Jake slammed his fist on the table top. "Stop playing games with me. You think you're in control here. Not anymore. I told you from the beginning I was going to handle this investigation my way. But you haven't been fully honest."

"I told you, I've never lied to you."

"If Adah Lee is Rex's daughter, that is a critical fact, Melva. You know that. If Rance Pruitt knows it, it's not a secret."

"I. Never. Lied. To. You."

Jake bolted out of his chair. He wanted to punch a hole in the wall. He wanted to shake sense into Melva Bardo.

"You withheld vital information. Who else knows she's Rex's?"

Melva closed her eyes and let out a deep breath. "I don't know."

"I don't believe you."

She opened her eyes again. "I mean, I don't know for sure whether Adah is Rex's."

"Does he think she is?"

"He suspects," she said. "There was … an opportunity for it."

"Scarlett Sommers had five sons before she had Adah. She's been married to Warren for what, almost thirty years?"

"She was only seventeen," Melva said. "It wasn't a love match."

"I can see that. Does he beat her?"

"Probably," Melva said. "Eighteen years ago, Rex got himself into a bit of trouble. There was an attempt on his life. He stayed here for a while."

"Trouble? Let me guess, the cops were looking for him. Or the feds. He was hiding out."

"What difference does it make why? I'm telling you he spent maybe six months here. He met Scarlett. She was still in her twenties then. With five kids under eight years old. She was drowning. Rex grew fond of her. Warren was … let's just say Scarlett and Warren were having some domestic difficulties and Scarlett needed a place to rest. To sort things out. Rex spent time with her."

"He slept with her," Jake said.

"Yes. I didn't condone it. No matter their difficulties, Scarlett was a married woman. I threw Rex out when I caught them together."

"And nine months later, Scarlett delivered a bouncing baby girl with dark hair and blue eyes. Is that right?"

"Yes. But we don't know for sure if Rex is the father. Scarlett and Warren were together in that time frame, too."

"Does Warren know she might not be his?"

"I don't think so, no."

"How can you be certain of that? I told you. Rance Pruitt suspects it. Said he wasn't going to go through with the match because she was a Bardo whore."

"He said that?" Melva asked, anger deepening her voice.

"Which is it? You're angry that he called Adah a whore? Or angry that he rejected Adah for it?"

"Stop it," she said. "I loved Adah. Everything I've ever done was to protect that girl."

"How was lying to me protecting her? If Adah is Rex's … and it doesn't even matter whether she is or not. It matters that certain people think she is. Your son has dangerous enemies. I know you know that. Enemies who would use that girl to get to him."

"That's why she's here!" Melva said. "That's why I didn't tell you or anyone who she might be. And I don't know for sure. I told you. There's just as good a chance she's Warren's daughter as anything."

"Look at her," Jake yelled. "Warren has six other children who nobody could mistake as being anything other than his, or siblings. Except Adah. She has Rex's coloring. Yours. I don't think you need a DNA test to know whose genes are flowing through her veins. I should have realized it the second you showed me those pictures. Except I trusted you to tell me the truth."

"I've never lied to you. Call me a liar one more time and …"

"And what?" Jake rose from his seat. He towered over Melva. She stared him down.

"Nobody knows she could be Rex's. Nobody. Anybody who says otherwise is spreading false rumors."

"Do you know someone in particular who would want to hurt Rex? Someone from this community?"

"No," she said, turning her back on him. "No one here would ever be that stupid. People may have their opinions about my family, even Rance Pruitt. But they respect us. And they know I'm not someone they'd want to cross."

"Except somebody did. And Adah is the one paying for it."

Melva took a stagger step forward. She clutched her chest and slowly sank back into her chair. She pressed her fist to her forehead.

"They can't," she said. "They don't know about Rex and Scarlett. Rex has never claimed Adah. He's never even set eyes on her but from a distance."

"You should have told me immediately, Melva. She's been missing for forty-eight hours. With each second that goes by, the odds of finding her alive dwindle. I know you know that."

"They wouldn't kill her. If it's someone who wants to hurt my family, they wouldn't kill her. They'd know she's more valuable alive."

"Maybe that's true. But I need names."

"I don't know," she said. "You can believe me or not. But I have nothing to do with my son's business. If he asks me for help, I give it. I would fight to the death for him or any other member of my family. But I'm not involved with what he or any of the rest of them do."

"But you matter to him. That's why you still live out here. Because Rex knows you're safer. So that you can hide his messes. That makes you involved. And everyone up here knows Adah's special to you. She's been a target from the second she was born."

Melva buried her face in her hands. "It's not about Rex. It can't be."

"You can't be sure of that."

"Now you're the one withholding things. I told you. If someone wanted to use Adah to get to us, they would have gotten word to Rex that they took her."

Jake pursed his lips. She was right. He'd known it from the second he realized who Adah might be. Forty-eight hours with no word from any of Rex's enemies. It didn't mean one of them hadn't taken her. But as each minute went by with no word, it meant they weren't using her for leverage. She wasn't a hostage. She was more likely a murder victim. A message.

"What do you want me to do?" Melva said, her voice trembling. "I won't apologize for trying to protect Adah. That's all I've tried to do. You can't go public with who she might be."

"No," he said. "If she's still out there somewhere, it would put her in even more danger."

Melva's shoulders sagged with relief.

"Were you trying to get her out?" Jake asked. "Did you make a plan to get her away from Red Sky Hill? Away from Warren?"

"She didn't ask me for that," Melva said. "I didn't want her out there. I knew I wouldn't be able to keep her safe on the other side of that hill."

"Would she have gone to someone else for that kind of help?"

Melva flipped her palms upward. "I don't know who. I was the only one she trusted as far as I know. The only one who was strong enough to stand up to Warren."

"You asked me what you could do now. You tell me everything. Every detail. I could charge you with obstruction right now, Melva. I may still."

"There's nothing else," she said. "I never even spoke to any of my family up here about my suspicions. I've never uttered a word to a single soul until today. Only with Rex. And even then, we talked around it."

"But they know," Jake said. "Or they suspect. Your nephews. Luc. All the men who protect you up here and do your bidding. They have eyes too."

"I've never asked them. They've never brought it up to me. I told you. I've protected Adah. I've protected my son."

Jake bit back the thing he wanted to say. The thing even Melva herself must have come to realize. She hadn't protected Adah well enough. She might be paying for that failure with Adah's life.

NINE

"I know I don't have to talk to you," Rance Pruitt said. He still had cuffs on. He banged them loudly against the table. Birdie set him up in the interview room across from Jake's office. He knew she sat behind a one-way mirror, watching.

"That's right, you don't."

"What if I want to leave?"

"That's gonna be a problem, Rance. You hit my partner in the face. You fled when I just wanted to talk to you. That makes me feel like you've got something to hide."

"You were trespassing on private property. My property. I know my rights."

"You keep saying that. And yet, here we are."

Rance frowned and stared at the wall. Jake let him sit in silence for a few minutes. It made him antsy. He kept tapping his foot, looking like he was about to vault out of his seat. Good, Jake thought. He knew the type. He would sit there thinking he had control. But the longer Jake said nothing, the stronger Pruitt's urge to talk would get.

Just before ten full minutes of silence, Pruitt snapped his head and stared at Jake. "Are we going to just sit here? Aren't you going to ask me any questions?"

"You know exactly what I want to talk to you about, Rance."

"And I know exactly what you think of me."

"What's that?"

"Only God can judge me. Not you."

"I suppose that's true," Jake said. "So explain it to me. Make me understand why you hated Adah Lee so much."

Pruitt curled his upper lip. "I didn't hate her. She was nothing to me."

"Was?"

"Is," he said. "Whatever happened to that girl, I had nothing to do with it."

"So you say. But humor me. Tell me again where you were the night of Adah's birthday."

"Where everyone else was. Where she was supposed to be. At *her* party. There were probably fifty people there. Ask around."

"I have," Jake said. "Barbara Bowen said you weren't there. But it's interesting. Except for you, everyone is eager to provide alibis for everyone else. And yet, Adah didn't just vanish into thin air. It was her party. No one seemed to care that she wasn't there. You all just carried on like nothing was wrong. Why didn't you go look for her?"

"Adah does what she wants. Warren has never been able to control that girl. Despite all his promises."

"Talk to me about those promises, Rance. He promised her to you, isn't that right?"

"We had an arrangement. There's nothing illegal about that. Adah would have been eighteen before we got married."

"But you wanted out of it. You told me she was damaged goods in your eyes. How did Warren feel about that? Did he expect you to honor your end of the deal?"

"You'd have to ask him."

"I'm asking you."

"Warren and I weren't talking over the last few weeks. You'll have to ask him."

"You had a falling-out. Was it over Adah?"

Pruitt's eyes were dead cold. He clasped his hands together, making the cuffs clang against the table. "I told Warren exactly what I thought."

"Which was?"

"He lied to me. Adah wasn't who he said she was. She wasn't pure."

"What do you mean by that? That she wasn't a virgin?"

Pruitt's face contorted with horror. "I don't know. But like mother, like daughter. Warren's own wife was a whore. It's in her blood."

"And Adah had Bardo blood. That's what you think?"

"Scarlett made a fool out of Warren. A cuckold. If he chooses to let that slide, that's his prerogative. I don't have to. So I didn't. I was done with her. I don't want to so much as look at Adah, much less marry her."

"Lucky for Adah," Jake muttered.

"There. You show me contempt over things you don't understand."

"So make me. Tell me how a fifty-year-old man forcing himself on a teenage girl isn't worthy of contempt? Or judgment in the eyes of God."

Pruitt banged his closed fists against the table. "Nobody forced anyone. Adah would have been blessed to be my wife. I was offering her the world."

"The world. Your world. Only she didn't like that, did she? She had other ambitions. She wanted to see what more the world could offer her beyond Red Sky Hill."

"Yes! That's Warren's fault for not keeping control of her. Or Scarlett's. With me, Adah would have been protected. She never would have wanted for anything, the rest of her life. I would have kept a roof over her head. A warm bed. She'd never be hungry. She would have had a good, moral purpose to her life."

"A moral purpose," Jake said. "You mean bearing your children?"

"I told you. I won't be judged by you."

"You're certainly judging Warren Sommers though. And Adah. You're blaming her for sins her mother committed. Her father. She's just a kid, Rance."

He shook his head. "I don't blame her. I blame her parents. Both of her parents. Her mother and the man who spawned her."

"When did you last talk to Adah? Last see her?"

"I don't know. Weeks ago, maybe. She was working in her father's barn the day I told Warren I wanted nothing to do with her or her family."

"Was Warren angered by that?" Jake asked.

"He called me vile names. Took a swing at me. He missed. I went home. That was the end of it."

It was a nice story, Jake thought. It would certainly have given Warren Sommers a solid motive for wanting to do Adah harm. If he viewed her as soiled as Rance did.

"Did you tell Warren you suspected Adah wasn't his daughter?"

"He's a fool if he can't see it for himself," Rance answered. "But I'm not responsible for that. It's Warren's cross to bear. Not mine. I'm out of it."

"Did you talk to Adah directly about any of this?"

"Of course not. It was none of her business what went on between Warren and me."

Jake laughed. "None of her business. The two of you were just bargaining away the rest of her life. She had no say in it."

"She would have been blessed," Rance repeated. "I would have protected her. Taken care of her."

"To me, that sounds like a prison sentence. And I'm getting sick and tired of hearing all of you tell me how you were protecting Adah. None of you actually did. She's out there somewhere. Maybe dead. You don't care. Warren doesn't care. So give me a reason to believe you didn't have anything to do with what happened to her."

"I don't care what you believe. You have no evidence against me. Just your closed mind. And Adah? Whatever happened to her was what she deserved. She brought it on herself. She'd been warned her whole life about what could happen if she defied her father. If she insisted on living in sin on the other side of the hill. So if she chose to go out there anyway? You can't expect me to feel sorry for her."

Jake had the urge to knock Rance Pruitt's teeth out.

"How do you know she brought something on herself? How do you know she tried to run away? For that matter, how do you know she isn't Warren's daughter? You have no proof of that."

"I have eyes and ears."

"But if she's a Bardo, wouldn't that be good for you? To marry her? You know how powerful that family is. Wouldn't it have been an even more fortuitous match for you?"

Rance spit on the ground. "That family is darkness. Pure evil. They walk with the devil. And I'm not afraid of them. I don't want children with evil blood running through their veins."

"Melva Bardo is revered on the other side of the hill."

"Not by me."

"She's lived among you her whole life. She's been loyal. Worked to make sure all of you were safe. Protected, as you say."

"You know what they are. You would have helped put Rex Bardo in prison if you'd been here when his sins finally caught up with him. He's a criminal. Soulless. He deserves to be in hell. And he will be."

Jake couldn't argue with the first part of that statement. He would have done whatever he had to to bring Rex down back in the day.

"What about Adah? Does she deserve to be in hell? Did you try to put her there, Rance?"

"No."

"She made a fool of you. Or she would have. Pretending to be something she wasn't. Bearing your children as if she were pure."

"Which is why I ended it. Warren is the fool. Not me."

"What did she ever do to you, Rance?"

He went silent.

"She was a good kid. She helped others. She worked for Melva. A lot of the kids in your community did. You're not calling any of them evil. From what I can tell, other than being spirited, Adah lived a pretty wholesome life."

"She did no such thing. I saw her. I know what she was planning."

"What was she planning?"

"She was under bad influences."

"From whom? Melva? Adah never set foot beyond Red Sky Hill."

"She didn't have to. Evil had a way of finding her. She was a magnet for it."

"What evil? What influences?"

"I saw her!" Rance shouted.

"Saw her what? When? Did you see her trying to run away? Did you see her the night of her birthday party, Rance?"

"No!"

"Then what did you see?"

"She wasn't always at Melva's."

Jake sat back. "You followed her? Spied on her?"

"I had a right to. I had a right to know who she associated with."

"Who, Rance? Who did you see Adah with? If someone hurt her, then that's a sin as well."

"She lied to her father all the time. Told him she was going to Melva's to help her cook. Garden. Do chores around the big house. Sometimes she did. But sometimes, she didn't. Sometimes, she met with the she-devil herself."

Herself?

"What she-devil?"

"Melva's granddaughter. She comes here wearing tight dresses so her breasts can almost be seen. Paints herself up. Wears vulgar jewelry. Defiles her own body with ink."

"Melva's granddaughter," Jake said. "Do you mean Kyra Bardo?" It was the only other Bardo granddaughter Jake knew of.

"Yes."

"You saw Adah talking to Kyra Bardo?"

"Talking to her. Hugging her."

"Was Melva with them?" Jake said, his blood boiling. Melva hadn't said a word about it. Even now, she was still lying to him. Damn that woman.

"Not when I saw her," Rance said. "They thought they were meeting in secret behind the big barn. Hidden by the trees. But I followed Adah. I knew what she was. I wanted to see the proof with my own eyes."

"When?" Jake said. "When did you see Adah with Kyra Bardo? How often?"

"At least five times. As recently as last week. Kyra gave her something. A small box. I don't know what it was."

Jake's whole body shook with rage.

"Are we done now?" Rance asked. "I've told you everything I know."

"For now," Jake said.

"Then I'm leaving," Rance said, starting to rise.

"I don't think so," Jake said. "You assaulted a cop. You're going to answer for it."

Jake got up. He poked his head out of the door and motioned to Deputy Denning down the hall. "Take Mr. Pruitt down to booking."

"You're just as vile as everyone says you are," Rance said.

"Guess so," Jake said. He turned his back on Pruitt and slammed the interview room door.

Birdie was waiting for him in his office.

"Jesus, Jake," she said. "How many more lies is Melva Bardo keeping? What could her purpose possibly be?"

"I don't know. Or she's deliberately trying to mess with me."

"Why call you at all?" Birdie said. "We never would have known Adah Lee existed, much less went missing."

"I don't know," Jake said. He let his anger get the better of him and swept his hand across his desk, sending papers and a cup full of pens flying against the opposite wall.

Unfazed, Birdie sat on the edge of Gary Majewski's desk. "So, how do you want to play this? Bring Melva in? Charge her with obstruction?"

"Not yet," Jake said. "First, I need to have it out with Kyra Bardo."

"Do you want me to come with you?" she asked.

"No," he said. "I need to do this one alone."

TEN

Bardo Excavating was the family's legitimate enterprise, owned by Floyd Bardo, Rex's younger brother. Floyd had turned out to have a bad head for business and struggled to gain any sort of respect from Rex's crew. Though everyone believed him to be the head of the Hilltop Boys, it was a fallacy. In truth, Rex still ran the show from behind prison. And Floyd's daughter Kyra was the only one of Floyd's children with the brains, business acumen, and ruthlessness to act in her Uncle Rex's stead. She wasn't even thirty years old.

At nine a.m. the next morning, Jake spotted Kyra's red Mercedes parked outside the trailer she used as an office. Trying to keep his temper in check, Jake didn't bother to knock. He simply barged in.

Two crew members stood in front of her in work boots and jeans. Kyra looked up from her desk, but registered no shock at Jake's sudden appearance. Instead, she smiled and crossed her arms in front of her.

"Leave," Jake ordered the two men. "Now."

They looked bewildered and turned to Kyra.

"Don't look at her," Jake said. He put his hands on his hips, displaying his side arm and badge. "I said leave."

Her smile widening, Kyra waved them off. She leaned casually backward in her chair, crossing her legs in front of her.

She was beautiful with her Uncle Rex's dark coloring. Sleek black hair and those penetrating ice-blue eyes. She certainly didn't look the part of a gravel pit boss. Slowly, she rose from her chair, revealing a tight, cream-colored skirt. She wore a pink silk blouse with one too many buttons opened. Jake tried not to look.

As she walked out from behind her desk, her four-inch heels put her almost nose-to-nose with Jake. She perched herself on the edge of her desk with feline grace.

"To what do I owe the pleasure this time, Detective?" she purred.

Jake pulled a copy of one of Adah's pictures out of his pocket and slammed it down on Kyra's desk right beside her. She kept the slight grin on her face as she looked at it. Jake tried to detect some change in her face, her eyes, but Kyra Bardo knew how to keep her mask in place. Everything about her felt calculated. From the way she held her head, the curve of her posture as she leaned a bit to get a better look at the photo. The way she tossed her hair back as she turned her focus back to Jake.

"No games, Kyra. Don't sit there and pretend you don't know who you're looking at."

Kyra picked up the photo. "She's one of the hilltop people."

"You know she's more than that. She's your cousin. And you've been meeting with her in secret. I need to know why. I need to know the last time you saw her and what else you know about what might have happened to her."

Kyra's smile finally faltered. "Jake, I ..."

"You were seen," he said. "Whatever you were doing, you were sloppy about it. Every instinct I have tells me you know something about where she is."

"I don't," Kyra said, her confident tone suddenly vanishing. "Who told you this?" In an instant, she dropped her mask. That more than anything surprised Jake. Or was this part of her game as well?

"Are you denying any of it?"

"I don't know where she is," Kyra said. Her eyes darted across Jake's face.

"But you know her. You know who her father is. Your grandmother has told me one too many lies already. If you tell me one more, I'm taking you in, throwing you in jail for obstruction. I suspect Uncle Rex won't be interested in coming to your rescue this time."

Kyra's hands shook as she put the flyer back down on the desk.

"Jake, I swear. I don't know where she is."

"Why were you meeting with her?"

"Not here. Can we go somewhere?"

Jake had the urge to tell her to shove it. The quick dissolution of her cool demeanor was unexpected. She seemed genuinely nervous for the first time since he met her.

"Sure," he said. "We can go down to my office."

"No! No. I can't have anyone see me walk into the police station of my own free will."

"Fine, I'll put you in cuffs. It'll save me some time."

She sank slowly into one of the chairs in front of her desk. "Here then," she said. "Have a seat."

He did. Kyra rubbed a hand over her face. She'd gone pale.

"I didn't do anything to her, if that's what you think," she started. "The only thing I've ever done is try to …"

"Protect her," Jake said, finishing her sentence. "I'm getting damn sick of hearing that. From your grandmother. From Rance Pruitt. From Warren Sommers."

Kyra frowned. "Rance Pruitt certainly had no plans to protect her. Warren Sommers is a vile human being. Adah was trying to get away from him."

"You're gonna tell me you were just trying to help?"

"Yes."

"Did Adah know who she was? Who her father is?"

"Keep your voice down," she said. "These are thin walls and you've already drawn enough attention. You should have called me. I would have met you somewhere."

"You should have called me! Christ, Kyra. This girl has been missing for days. Do you know what that means? The chances of me finding her alive are pretty much zero at this point."

Kyra's eyes filled with tears. Was it an act? Was she trying to play on his sympathy? Something in his core stirred. Some preternatural instinct to protect her. If she'd done something without Rex or Melva's blessing, her life could get very complicated, very quickly. Jake brushed his feelings aside. She was banking on them. He could feel it.

"I didn't know what to do," Kyra said. "I couldn't think of a way out of this that wouldn't make it obvious who she is, or might be.

Because nobody knows for sure. There's as much chance she's Warren's daughter as anything."

"Bullshit. Look at her. She could be your twin sister. There's Melva's blood running through both of you. She knew it. Is that why she asked you to get involved?"

Kyra's eyes widened. "God. No. Jake. No. Melva doesn't know anything. She didn't know Adah came to me. Adah knew that was a condition of my helping her."

"With what?"

"You know what," she said. "Adah wanted out. She wanted to make a life for herself out in the world. She didn't want to be like her mother. And she knew she couldn't get out without someone like me helping her."

"What was the plan?"

"Jake, it's complicated."

"I think it's pretty simple. Did you give her money? Arrange a place for her to stay?"

"That was part of it," she said. "But I couldn't very well just drive up to her house and put her in my car. I told her if she could figure out how to get away, I'd figure out a way to get her somewhere safe. There wasn't a calculated plan. I just knew how she felt and felt sorry for her. That's the extent of it."

"So she was trying to get to you? That's why she didn't show up at her own birthday party?"

"I didn't know anything about any birthday party."

"When did you see her last?"

"I don't know. A few weeks ago. I gave her ..." Kyra shielded her eyes with her hand.

"You gave her what?"

She looked up. "You're going to jump to the wrong conclusions. You have to understand. I couldn't be seen as openly involved. It's a precarious ecosystem on the other side of that hill. If Adah's father knew she was talking to me, he would have made it so she never left the house. Things would have been so much worse. He'd put her so far away none of us would probably ever see her again."

"He found out," Jake said.

"I don't know. Maybe."

"You think Warren killed his own daughter or hid her away somewhere?"

"I think he's capable of that, yes. That's the truth."

"What were you going to say? You said you gave her something. What?"

She slapped her hands on her knees. "I gave her a burner phone, okay? I told her to call me when she figured out how to get away without being seen."

Jake felt ice in his veins. "She called you the night she disappeared. Is that it?"

Tears kept rolling down Kyra's cheeks.

Jake picked up the photo and flipped it over. He grabbed a pen off Kyra's desk and thrust it at her. "Write down the number she called you from. Was it your own cell number you gave her?"

"Of course not."

"Where's your burner phone? Get it."

Her nostrils flared. Jake was ready to flip the damn desk if she went silent again. But she slowly got out of her chair and walked over to a file cabinet against the wall. She opened the top drawer and pulled out a small black flip phone. She tossed it to Jake. He caught it one-handed.

"Yes," Kyra said. "She called me the afternoon she went missing. At least, she tried to. The reception was spotty. I couldn't understand her. The call kept dropping."

"Dammit, Kyra. What the hell have you been thinking? If I'd had this information four days ago ..."

"You would have what?"

"I could have tried to track the signal. You and your grandmother have made this whole thing worse. If you didn't kill her yourself, you might as well have. She withheld Adah's paternity from me. Your uncle has enemies. If someone ..."

"That's why we never spoke of it!"

"Do you even realize what you've done? Do you get that it was criminal? You're trying to cover up this girl's disappearance. You were complicit in it."

"No. I wasn't. I don't know what happened. She never called me again. I don't know if her father found her. Or Rance Pruitt. You already suspect them. So nothing I've done has impeded your investigation. You've ended up in the exact same place you would have anyway."

"You cut off my ability to track down viable leads. You've just tried to cover your own ass at the expense of Adah's safety, maybe her life. So has Melva."

"I told you. My grandmother isn't part of this. She had no idea I was communicating with Adah. Adah didn't want her to know either."

"Melva would have put a stop to it if she knew," he said. "Melva thought she could handle all of this on her own."

"Yes. But she *wasn't* handling it. Adah knew that. Things were getting worse with her father. She was scared. So she came to me instead. Jake, do you understand the position I'm in?"

Her fear was real. Jake realized it wasn't him she was afraid of at all. Kyra had crossed Melva. Maybe even Rex.

"I thought you were smarter than this. Kyra, what you did was stupid and reckless. You encouraged her to walk out on her own? On foot? Alone?"

"There was no other way. You have to trust me on that. I could not just drive up and get her. I could not put my own ass on the line like that. I gave her a way to get in touch with me if she got out."

"Unbelievable," Jake said. "You get this makes you a suspect. At the very least, a material witness. You should have come to me immediately."

"I'll do whatever you want," she said. "Just please, find Adah. I'm sorry. I'm so sorry. It just …"

"You got in over your head," Jake said through gritted teeth. "You thought you could handle this. How? Where were you going to put her if you got Adah out? Tell me the plan."

"I never thought Adah would go through with any of it. I wasn't going to stick my neck out unless she was committed. I gave her the phone. It was up to her to find her own way out. Then I would have helped her find a place to land."

"You left that girl exposed," he said. "You threw her to the wolves, Kyra."

"No. It wasn't like that."

"She tried to reach out to you. Did you even go looking for her yourself?"

She dropped her head. "She was supposed to call me when she made it to the truck stop on County Road Fourteen."

"A truck stop?" Jake couldn't believe what he was hearing. "You sent a seventeen-year-old girl with no money. With nothing but the clothes on her back to a truck stop? If someone picked her up there, do you realize what could have happened to her? She might have been trafficked. Or worse."

"If you arrest me, you might as well just put a bullet in my head. I'll be as good as dead."

Jake felt sick to his stomach. He believed her. But Kyra had essentially signed Adah Lee's death warrant.

"What are you going to do?" she asked.

"Honestly? I don't know."

Before he could say anything else, his phone rang. He pulled it out. Birdie's caller ID flashed on the screen.

"Don't move," Jake ordered Kyra. He stepped outside the trailer.

"What've you got?" he answered.

He could hear traffic sounds in the background. "It's bad, Jake."

His heart dropped. "Go ahead."

"Two tourists on one of the trails at the state park in Blackhand Hills. They found a body. A girl. She fit Adah's description. I'm about five minutes out. I'll send you a pin."

Rage filled him. He turned around and slammed a fist against the side of the trailer.

"Dammit," he said. "I'll be there as soon as I can."

He clicked off and walked back into the trailer. "Grab your coat," he said.

"What is it?" Kyra said, though her face said she already knew.

"They may have found her," he said.

"Jake, I can't ..."

"Yes, you can. If it's her, the least you can do is identify the body."

ELEVEN

The deep gorges in Blackhand Hills had long provided a hiding place for many a dead body. Some believed their ghosts haunted the one called Devil's Eye the most. The last body dumped there was just a few years ago. No one ever knew.

But that isn't where they found this body. No. This body was out in the open, just a few yards off one of the lesser-traveled trails, but still accessible to tourists. That's where the Levy family had chosen to hike the morning of April 16th. Parents Gil and Abby ran a vet clinic together. Their daughters Gracie, twelve, and Mabel, just seven years old, had come down during their spring break from Arbor Hill Montessori School just outside of Ann Arbor.

As Jake pulled up behind Birdie's cruiser, he saw Abby holding Mabel to her chest. The young girl sobbed against her. Gil and the older girl, Gracie, stood off to the side, talking to Deputy Denning.

"I can't do this," Kyra said. She sat in the passenger seat. Those were the first words she'd uttered on the twenty-minute drive here.

"You can and you will," Jake said. "But for now, don't move until I tell you."

Jake slammed the door and walked over to Birdie. She stood in front of crime scene tape. One deputy snapped pictures of the body, partially buried under rotting leaves.

"The little girl spotted her first," Birdie said. "Her mother said she was chasing a butterfly. She tripped over one of the victim's legs."

She lay face up, her ice-blue eyes, now pearled and opaque, staring at the sky. Deep purple-banded bruising around her neck provided an obvious clue to how she'd been killed. Her dark hair splayed out above her head in all directions. Her right leg was bent at an impossible angle.

She wore a red sweatshirt, hiked up exposing her bare midriff. She was naked from the waist down but the leaves had covered the lower half of her torso.

"The rest of her clothes were found in a ball just over there," Birdie said. "Like someone just threw them there, like garbage."

Sure enough, Jake could see a wad of denim and a pair of light brown work boots caked with mud.

"Zenni, her sister, said Adah was wearing denim overalls," Jake said.

One of the other deputies turned away from the body, doubled over, and retched. The wind shifted. The smell of decay was strong.

"She looks like she's been dead for days," Jake said.

"That'd be my guess," Birdie agreed.

"Dammit," Jake said. "I'm not surprised but ..."

"Yeah," Birdie said. "I kind of still had a little hope, too."

"You brought *her* here?" Birdie asked, turning in the direction of Jake's car.

"Yep. We need a positive ID. I'll go get her."

"You could show her a picture," Birdie said.

"No." Jake's tone was harsh. "Let her see it. She needs to know what this was."

"Jake ..." Birdie started to protest. Jake strode to the passenger side of his car and swung the door open.

"Only step where I step," he told Kyra. "Keep your hands in your pockets."

She'd gone pale, but she did as Jake told her. Jake took her around the Levy family and walked up to the scene so they were upwind of the body. From this vantage point, the girl's head was turned slightly toward them.

Jake stopped. He nudged Kyra in front of him. "Take a good look," he said.

Kyra clamped a hand over her mouth. "Oh God. It's Adah. I don't ... I can't ..." Kyra whirled herself away from the body. "I have to get out of here!" Jake grabbed her by the shoulders.

"You're absolutely certain?" he asked. "You need to be sure. I don't want to tell her mother and father unless you are."

Her hand still over her mouth, Kyra nodded. She took her hand away. "Yes. It's Adah."

"Go back and wait for me in the car," he said. "Don't talk to anyone. Don't call anyone. Do you understand?"

"Yes."

"Denning?" Jake called out. "Escort Ms. Bardo back to my car. Put her in it and make sure she doesn't try to use her cell phone."

"You got it," Chris Denning said.

Jake walked over to the Levy family. Gil Levy had his arm around his wife. The two girls sat in the back of Deputy Bundy's cruiser.

"I'm sorry this happened to you," Jake told Abby and Gil Levy. "I'm Detective Jake Cashen. I need to ask you just a few questions. They might be repetitive. I know you've talked to Deputies Wayne and Denning already."

"It's okay," Gil said. "She's just a kid. She doesn't look much older than our Gracie. My God."

"I just want to make sure. Did you see anyone else around here when you came upon the victim?"

"No," Abby answered. "It was only us. Mabel had run ahead. She tripped over that poor girl. At first, I thought maybe someone had just passed out. It's an intermediate trail. We were going to take one of the beginners, but our girls run cross country, both of them. They were up to the challenge."

"Of course. Other than your daughter tripping over her. Do you remember if any of the rest of you touched the victim?"

"No," Gil said. "God no. Mabel just screamed. I picked her up right away. Got her away from it. Told Gracie not to take another step. Abby too. We backed off, sat down on that log over there, and I called 9-1-1. They were here in maybe fifteen minutes. Maybe less. But no, none of us touched anything. We knew not to disturb anything."

"Good. That's really good. You did the right things. Again, I'm so sorry this happened to you. I'm going to give you my card. If you remember anything else, please call me. You've given your contact information to Deputy Wayne?"

"Yes," Gil said. "She's been very kind."

"I'm glad. We just have to wrap up a few more things and then you can be on your way. I'll have one of the deputies drive you back to your vehicle."

"Thank you," Gil said.

Jake went back to Birdie. "Have you called BCI?" he asked.

"First thing," she said. "And another call to Dr. Stone. He told me to call after BCI gets here."

The moment she said it, a blue van pulled up, the words Ohio Bureau of Criminal Investigation emblazoned on the side in yellow block letters. Agent Mark Ramirez climbed down from the front seat. Jake was glad to see him. They'd worked numerous cases together and he was the best crime scene investigator in the business as far as Jake was concerned.

"We have to stop meeting like this," Ramirez said.

Jake shook Ramirez's hand. He took ten minutes to bring Ramirez up to speed. Then he and Birdie got out of his way as Ramirez called the rest of his team over.

Birdie had just clicked off her call to Ethan Stone, Worthington County's Medical Examiner.

"Are you going to tell the family or do you want me to?" Birdie asked.

Jake let out a breath. "I think I might lose it if Warren Sommers acts relieved she's dead."

"Fair point. I can head over there now. Do you want me to bring him in for questioning?"

"Not yet," Jake said. "Just inform them. Do you have a picture you can show him? Kyra's made a positive ID, but she's not next of kin."

"What's she saying?"

Jake shook his head. "It's a long story. But she admitted to having secret meetings with Adah. She had a half-baked plan to get her out and find her a place to live out in the real world. It looks like Adah was trying to kick off the first part of that plan. She ran away the night of her party. She was supposed to meet up with Kyra."

Birdie's eyes widened. "You mean she had that girl hiking over Red Sky Hill all by herself?"

"It gets worse. The rendezvous point was the truck stop off County Road Fourteen."

"By herself!" Birdie cried.

"Jake!" Ramirez called out. "I've got something here you might want to look at."

One of the techs was taking pictures of and collecting Adah's clothing.

Jake and Birdie exchanged a look and walked over to Ramirez.

"Hey, Erica," Ramirez said.

"Good to see you, Mark," she responded.

With gloved hands and a pair of tongs, Ramirez held out a small card. Jake peered closer. It was a driver's license. Ramirez flipped it so Jake could see the front of it.

"Thought you said this girl's name was Adah something," Ramirez said.

"It is," Jake answered. The ID had Adah's picture on it. She was smiling, her eyes bright. But the name on the card was Justine Patterson.

"It's fake," Jake said, feeling his anger rising.

"It's a damn good one," Ramirez said.

"Where'd she get a fake ID?" Birdie asked. Then she turned her head at the same time Jake did. They both stared at Kyra Bardo as she sat in Jake's front seat.

"It seems I've got a few more questions for Ms. Bardo," Jake said.

"I've got this," Ramirez said. "This one's going to take the better part of the evening. I'll call you if I find anything else interesting."

"Thanks," Jake said. "I'll leave you to it. Deputies Bundy and Stuckey will stay here to help control the scene. We'll coordinate with the rangers to make sure this area is closed off to any other hikers."

He and Birdie walked away from the body. "You sure you can handle things over Red Sky Hill?" he asked.

"Of course. I'll call you when I leave."

"Take Denning and another crew with you."

Jake left her and walked back to his car. Kyra still looked pale and a little sick. He climbed behind the wheel and put the car in reverse.

"Are you taking me home?" she asked.

"Not quite," Jake said. He didn't want to look at her, let alone talk to her. She kept asking questions but he ignored her as he drove back to the Sheriff's Department.

S he was still protesting as Jake walked her into an interview room.

"Sit," he commanded. He didn't offer anything to drink.

He pulled out his phone and showed Kyra the picture he snapped of Adah's fake ID.

"You wanna explain this?"

Kyra closed her eyes. It reminded Jake of some little kid trying to hide by covering their eyes.

When she opened her eyes, color had flooded back into her cheeks. Her eyes went cold. She sat straighter in her chair.

A knock on the door interrupted them. Maureen, one of the civilian clerks, poked her head in. A male voice shouted behind her.

"I'm sorry, Jake," Maureen said. "But there's a lawyer out here who says he belongs to Ms. Bardo. He ..." Before Maureen could so much as finish her sentence, a tall, broad-shouldered man in a three-piece suit barged past her. He had slicked-back hair and a gold watch. He was handsome. Everything about him looked expensive.

"You are to cease questioning my client right away, Detective," he said. He pulled out a card and shoved it in Jake's hand.

"Alex Corvell," Jake read. The name seemed vaguely familiar.

"I represent the Bardo family," Corvell said. "Ms. Bardo specifically."

"I have nothing else to say," Kyra said. This time, her tone had taken on her normal confidence. She had to have called Corvell from Jake's car as she waited for him at the crime scene.

"Your client is a material witness in a murder investigation," Jake said. "She's been cooperating with me up until now. She's not under arrest."

"You have been questioning this woman without the presence of her lawyer all day. Anything she's told you up until now won't be admissible in court. You're lucky I don't slap a civil rights suit on you and this whole department."

"Take it easy," Jake said. "You're not doing her any favors."

"We're leaving," Corvell said.

"Your client has already admitted to having clandestine communications with my murder victim. She identified her body. She was found with a fake ID that she sure as hell wouldn't have been able to procure without help. I want to know how she got it. From whom?"

Kyra slid Jake's phone back to him. "I have nothing else to say."

"You sure about that? Because from where I sit, you were the last person to speak to Adah alive. You admitted to directing her to walk over the hill by herself. She was there, alone, because of you. I asked you what your plan was. You told me you gave her a phone. You told her where to go. When to call you. You didn't say anything about fake documents. What else is there? A birth certificate? Social Security card registered to Justine Patterson? Who's probably some dead eighty-year-old from a nursing home."

Kyra stayed silent. She stared at a point on the wall.

"We are done here, Detective!" Corvell's voice boomed. "Kyra, grab your things. Don't breathe another word."

Jake ignored him. "The girl is dead, Kyra. Murdered. She looks like she was strangled. She wasn't at that damn truck stop. She's lying in the leaves ten miles away from where you told her to be. I doubt she got there on foot. You need to tell me the truth. All of it. You're not helping yourself by staying silent. You're sure as hell not helping Adah."

"I know my rights," Kyra said, meeting Jake's gaze with equal intensity. "On the advice of counsel, I have nothing more to say to you."

She rose, grabbed her purse, and walked to Corvell's side. He put her behind him as if she needed a human shield.

"At a minimum, you're looking at an obstruction charge. Or you aided and abetted."

"Then put up or shut up," Corvell said.

"Did you help cover it up?" Jake asked. Corvell and Kyra turned and walked out into the hall.

Jake slammed a fist against the table. Kyra flinched, but kept on walking. Jake followed.

"I'll have a warrant by morning," he said. "I'm going to turn your house upside down. Search your car. Your phone."

"Do what you have to do," Corvell said. "But if you continue to harass my client, I'll have my own court order in place."

"I think it's time for me to pay a visit to your Uncle Rex, Kyra."

Kyra turned. Her expression changed. She looked absolutely terrified.

TWELVE

J ake had no idea what Rex Bardo knew about what was going on with Adah. While Birdie went to talk to the Sommers family and tell them she was dead, the next morning, Jake entered Glenmoor Federal Penitentiary. He asked for a private meeting room. He wanted no risk of being overheard. He got a little pushback from the warden's office, but Jake knew it was all for show. King Rex wielded influence even here.

Rex walked in shackled. Jake sat at a table against the back wall. "Is all that really necessary?" Jake said to the corrections officer. "He's not a violent offender."

Rex stood rod straight, towering over the guard. If he knew why Jake was here, he kept his face neutral. Well, as neutral as he was capable of. Rex had an intense, weather-beaten face. Those cold, ice-blue eyes seemed powerful enough to shoot lasers from them if he wanted.

"He stays in shackles," the guard said. But he removed the belly chains. Rex said nothing. He walked to the table and sat down.

"I'm keeping an eye on him," the guard said.

"And I really need you to wait outside," Jake said. "Talk to your boss, Amstutz. This was prearranged. You've got surveillance cameras in all four corners."

The cameras would not record audio. But Jake knew they would be watched the entire time. Grumbling, the guard left the room. He would stand just outside the door. Jake would have twenty minutes at most to possibly ruin Rex Bardo's life.

Rex sat across from him, still as a rock, though his eyes smoldered.

"Do you know why I'm here?" Jake asked.

"I have an idea," Rex answered.

"Have you been in contact with your mother?"

"Last month she visited," Rex said.

"Rex, I don't know a good way to tell you this. But Adah Lee is dead."

Still, he kept his face neutral, but a tiny twitching of his right eye told Jake the news cut through him. Jake let him absorb it. He would answer the questions he could, but they might be minimal. Legally, Rex had no relationship with Adah. He had no right to be informed about her case.

"Do you want to know what happened?" Jake asked.

"Where did it happen?"

"I'm not fully sure yet. She was found off a trail in Blackhand Hills State Park. She'd been there a few days. I don't think she was killed there. I think she was dumped there."

Rex tightened his fists. Every muscle in his upper body went rigid. A vein popped out in his neck.

"Melva told me who she was. Or who you think she was. I thought you'd want to hear all this in person."

Rex let his chin drop. The man was fighting a war within himself. He seemed to struggle to keep his composure. When he lifted his head, his breathing had changed. He forced air through his nose, flaring his nostrils like a thoroughbred horse after a race.

"What was she doing in Blackhand Hills?"

"I don't know. Trying to run away. I'm still trying to piece everything together."

He said nothing about the fake ID found on her. Nothing about Kyra's involvement. He couldn't.

"Look," Jake said. "I'm trying to find out who did this. I'm *going* to find out who did this. But you're going to have to help me. I need you to be straight with me. There are things I won't be able to tell you. This is an active murder investigation."

"What is it you think you know?" Rex said, his tone thick with contempt.

"I know there's a good chance that girl was your daughter. I know Melva was keeping an eye on her."

"Not a close enough one," Rex snapped.

"Maybe not. But she was trying. I know Adah wanted out. She wanted to be far away from her family. I have no idea if she suspected she was yours."

"Where is Scarlett?"

"She's at home. Her home. With her husband. My partner is out there right now, letting her know what happened. That we've found her."

Rex pounded his fist against the table.

"When was the last time you spoke to Scarlett?"

Rex shook his head. "I haven't. We don't communicate. There's no way."

"Do you love her?"

Rex looked away. His face turned bright red. "That's none of your business!"

"This whole thing is my business now. You haven't written her any letters? Sent her messages through Melva?"

"No! I haven't had anything to do with Scarlett since two months after Adah was born."

"Your mother told me she wanted out once, too. That the two of you grew close when you were hiding out up there."

"It was a long time ago. Scarlett was … She had five other kids at the time. She didn't feel like she could leave them. I need to know. Is she safe?"

Jake considered the question. He'd asked Rex not to lie to him. Though he might have to withhold information from him, he decided he couldn't lie to Rex, either.

"I don't know. When I saw her, she seemed submissive. Maybe afraid of Warren. He did all the talking. He was open about his anger toward Adah. Blamed her for getting ideas into her head that got her hurt. He didn't act like a concerned father. And Scarlett? She just kind of let him say what he wanted to say."

Rex squeezed his eyes shut for a moment. "She's beaten down," he whispered. "I warned her. I asked her to come with me. She wouldn't. I should have made her. I should have made it so Warren couldn't hurt her."

"And I don't want to hear you finish that thought, Rex."

"Did Warren do this? Did that son of a bitch punish Scarlett by hurting Adah?"

"I won't lie to you. The truth is I don't know. Maybe. He's got an alibi. But the way Adah was found, there's gonna be DNA. Physical evidence. Whoever did this was sloppy about it. If it was Warren, I'm going to find out."

"Melva was supposed to keep her safe!"

"From you? From anyone who might want to hurt you? Rex, I know the implications to Adah if it got out that she might be yours. That's why you walked away, isn't it? Hidden away over Red Sky Hill, she was anonymous. A whisper girl. That's what your mother calls those kids up there."

"We have nothing to do with those people," Rex said. "They're ... fringe. Outlanders. They have their own way of life."

"They sure do. Warren was planning to marry Adah off to a man named Rance Pruitt. Do you know him?"

Rex's face darkened. "I know Rance. If he laid a hand on her ..."

"That," Jake said. "That right there. That can't happen. Do you understand me? I need you to work with me. You cannot start planning revenge. You can't start a war over this, Rex."

King Rex began to almost vibrate. His whole body hardened. He was all coiled rage. An eruption waiting to happen. In all the years Jake had known him, Rex Bardo had never once lost his cool. He turned stoicism into an art form. But today, over Adah, he was losing control by the minute.

"I can't let this stand," he said. "That's what *you* have to understand."

"You have to let me do my job. No retaliation. I don't want bodies to start showing up, Rex. Not Warren Sommers. Not Rance

Pruitt. Not anyone, no matter who Adah's killer turns out to be. Do you understand?"

Rex leaned forward, putting himself nose-to-nose with Jake across the table. "Or ... what?"

"Or I'll come after you too. That's a promise. You keep yourself under control. You let me find out who did this. You tell me everything I need to know."

Rex didn't answer. But he didn't move. For now, Jake would take that as acquiescence.

"Nobody knows about Scarlett and me," he finally said. "Nobody knows Adah is anything other than who her family has said she is."

"Adah's possible paternity has to be the worst-kept secret on the hill, Rex. Rance Pruitt knew it. Warren had to have suspected. Pruitt pretty much admitted to throwing it in Warren's face. And by telling you that much, I'm putting my trust in you. You don't touch Sommers or Pruitt. If they're guilty, I'll prove it. They will be held accountable. Right now, there's no evidence that either one of them had anything to do with this."

"What else do you know?"

Jake stayed silent. As much as he wanted to question Rex about her, if he tipped him off that Kyra might be involved, she'd be in danger, too. Rex would probably move to handle things in house with her. There would be nothing Jake could do to protect her or stop it.

"I'll know more after BCI gets done processing the crime scene. After the ME finishes the autopsy." Rex flinched at the last word.

"Look," Jake said. "I didn't have to come here. I didn't have to tell you a single word about this. But like I said, I'm trusting you. I need your help. If this thing was motivated by Adah's possible connection to you ... if someone was trying to hurt you through her, you're the only one who can point me in the right direction."

Rex bolted off the bench. He stormed over to the wall and smacked his wrists against the concrete, making the handcuffs clang and echo.

"I have to get out of here!" he shouted.

"And you know that's not possible. So let it be me. Let me do what you can't. But you have to help me, Rex. Tell me who you think could have done this."

"You've got nothing. You're feeling around in the dark."

"So give me some light. You have dangerous enemies. You know who might be capable of moving this particular chess piece."

Rex whirled around. "Nah. No, man. Not this. We don't do this. This is bad business. We don't go after families."

"Maybe someone out there didn't get their copy of the rule book. And I think you know who. I'll find out anyway, Rex. I'm good at my job. But it'll take days, weeks. Maybe months. The trail could go cold. Adah's case might end up stuffed in the back of some file in the basement along with the other cold cases. But you could help keep that from happening. Tell me the truth. Help me."

"Why should I trust you?"

Jake got up. He walked over to Rex and stared into his face. "Who the hell else have you got? You've been in here a long time, Rex. You're powerful, but not even you can control everything that's happening out there. You know people get antsy. You know somebody might be thinking now's a good time to try to overthrow the king for good."

Rex bared his teeth. He looked like a damn Rottweiler.

"Trust me. Tell me who it could be. I know you know who'd want to hurt you like this. You say it's not your style. So whose is it?"

Rex pounded the back of his head against the wall. "I'm gonna hold you to your promise."

"Good."

"Sit down," he said. Jake followed him back to the table.

Rex cocked his head to the side, as if still considering his options. Finally, he squared his shoulders and locked his gaze with Jake's.

"All right. You remember that old bar out on County Road Three? Up in Navan Township? Murphy's?"

"Sure," Jake said. "I think it burned down."

"Didn't burn down. It exploded."

"Right. A gas leak or something."

"Or something," Rex said. "Let's just say it changed ownership a few months before that. The Iron Voyagers MC bought it. How much do you know about them?"

"I know they're one percenters. Back when I was still with the Bureau, there was a RICO case against their chapter in Chicago. I don't remember all the details. It wasn't my case."

"It was the kind of thing nobody wants here in Worthington County. They were into human trafficking."

A chill went through Jake. God. If that's what this was. If that's what Adah was targeted for, it meant there were worse things that could have happened to her than winding up dead on that trail. Jake sat back. "Your crew? Are you telling me you moved on them? Burned their place down before they could set up headquarters there?"

A flicker in Rex's eyes gave Jake his answer. "Arson," Jake said. "You had the Hilltop Boys, your crew, blow it up?"

Rex didn't answer. He wasn't stupid enough to verbally admit anything.

"Somebody could have gotten hurt," Jake said.

"Can't say anybody would grieve the Voyagers. They're scum, Jake."

"I don't give a damn about the club. But it took almost a day for the firefighters to put that blaze out. They put their lives at risk."

"Nobody got hurt! And the club moved on. You don't see 'em around Blackhand Hills, do you? But you asked me who'd be stupid enough to break some rules to get at me."

"Who's at the top?"

"Their current president is this shitheel named Rascal Buchanan. He's a junkie. The only thing he's got going for him is his old man, the former president. I think if Rascal showed up as some hanger-on with no connections, he wouldn't even have made it to probie status. He's stupid. He's mean. And he thinks he's untouchable."

"Okay," Jake said. "Okay. I'll run it down. I still have some contacts with the Bureau who keep tabs on the brotherhood. It's a place to start."

"You let me know what you find out," Rex said.

"I'll do my best. But I meant what I said. Even if it turns out to be connected to the MC. You sit tight. No vigilante crap."

Rex didn't answer, but he didn't tell Jake to screw off. He would take that as a positive sign.

"There's something else," Jake said. "I told you there will probably be strong physical evidence at the crime scene. On Adah."

That red rage came over Rex again. He knew the implication of Jake's words. Adah had been hurt badly. There were signs of sexual assault.

"Rex," Jake said. "If you want to know for sure. About Adah. They're going to get a DNA profile on her. There are ways you can find out. You'd have to make a formal request. But I can pull some strings there. Again ... if you want to know for sure."

Rex trembled again. "I don't know," he said softly. "I really don't know."

"I get that. I just thought ... well ... it's an option. That's all I'm saying. Think about it. Then let me know."

Jake rose to his feet. Rex stayed seated. It didn't look like he was capable of moving. Jake would ask the officer outside the door to give him a minute before taking him back to his cell.

"I'm going to hold you to your promise, Jake," Rex said, his voice raspy and barely audible.

"I know," Jake answered. "And I'm going to hold you to yours."

Thirteen

"Jake?"

He was underwater. He could see a light above him. A shadow.

"Jake!"

Sheriff Landry shook his shoulder. He was sleeping. Dreaming. It took him a second to remember where he was. As he lifted his head, a line of drool spooled out beneath his cheek and onto his desk.

He wiped his mouth and sat up.

"Did you sleep here all night?" Landry asked. He looked at his watch. It was just past seven a.m.

"I guess so," he said.

"It's Saturday," she said. "You're off. You need it."

"No. It's okay. I was just going to organize a few things."

He'd set up a whiteboard in the corner of the office on an easel. He fell asleep on a stack of photos he'd printed off last night, apparently right before he crashed. The picture of Warren Sommers was on top. Jake had found an old driver's license photo of him taken about fifteen years ago. Surprisingly, Sommers looked almost exactly the same save for a few more gray hairs.

Jake picked up the stack and walked over to the board. He lined the photos up, using magnets to hold them in place.

Warren Sommers. Rance Pruitt. Stephen "Rascal" Buchanan. Kyra Bardo. Then the silhouette of a faceless head that he'd drawn a giant question mark over.

"How does Buchanan figure in?" Meg asked. "Who is he?"

"Not sure yet. Just a lead I've got to chase down. I'll tell you more when I know more."

Meg pulled off the picture of Kyra Bardo. "You really think she would have been capable of killing that girl? Wouldn't that make her a target of King Rex's wrath more than anyone? I can't believe she'd be that stupid."

Jake took the photo from her. "Not directly, no. But I can't discount the theory that Kyra's negligence might have led to Adah's murder."

"Anything come of your interview with her?"

Jake put Kyra's photo back on the board. "She clammed up on me. She produced a slick lawyer who's been working for the family for years. Guy by the name of Alex Corvell. He's threatening to make trouble. I'm not scared of him. But it's something you should know. As far as Kyra, I know she had to be the one to procure that fake ID for Adah. She won't talk. I don't know who she's protecting now. Maybe just herself."

"What are you going to do about it?"

"I cut her loose," he said. "I don't have enough on her yet. Plus, I can't be sure we can keep her safe if she's in jail."

"Please don't say that. I don't even want to think about one of our people facilitating a hit on her. Are you sure you don't want her in custody? I get that it would ruffle feathers. But I'm willing to handle it. How do you know she won't just skip town? If she meddled in Adah's life without having the approval of Rex or Melva, I can't imagine they'll let that slide."

"I think the worst thing she could do right now is run. If she's managed to keep her dealings away from her grandmother, she should be safe enough for now. Not for long."

Landry frowned. "Just be careful. This thing feels ... I don't know. Sinister. Like there's a dark cloud forming over Blackhand Hills. If Kyra was involved, I can't see how this won't set off a civil war within the Bardo family. As much as I hate to acknowledge it, they're a necessary evil. As long as they don't go too far."

"I know. Trust me. I'm thinking of that."

"Good," she said. "Just tread lightly. What's your next step?"

"I'm waiting on Dr. Stone's post mortem. He should have it in a day or two. And I'm hoping there's good physical evidence from that poor girl's body."

"Okay. But I meant what I said. You look terrible. This one's eating you alive. Go home. Get some rest. Come back fresh Monday morning unless something blows up over the weekend. And pray nothing blows up over the weekend."

"I'm okay. Rex gave me a few things to chew over. I need to figure out my game plan there."

"I insist. Go home. At least for today."

"Look who's talking. What are you doing here this early on a Saturday?"

She smiled. "I promise. It's entirely boring. Going over budget reports. I'm meeting with the county commissioners first thing Monday. I mean, if you're going to be here. Maybe you could give me a hand."

Jake grabbed his jacket. "No, thanks. I surrender. I'll get out of here for a while."

"Oh," she said. "There's another reason I came looking for you. Gemma called me. She said you weren't answering your phone."

Jake picked up his cell. The battery died overnight. He figured he'd have at least a dozen missed calls or texts from his sister once he plugged it back in.

"Great. She's gonna let me have it."

"Maybe not. She was calling to let you know Virgil Adamski was released from the hospital late last evening. He's home now. She thought you might want to pay him a visit."

"Thank God. Yeah. I'll head over there now."

"You might want to grab a shower first. You smell bad."

"Virg won't notice." Jake smiled.

"Tell him I'm thinking about him. I'll have Darcy send something over from the department."

Jake promised he would, then headed out of the building.

When Jake pulled up to Virgil Adamski's place on Echo Lake, he saw a familiar face working out in the yard, raking dead leaves out of the flower beds.

Jake parked in front of the house. The driveway was filled with four other cars. Virgil had visitors.

"Travis!" Jake yelled. He had to do it two more times before Travis Wayne pulled his earbuds out. He put his rake against the house and raised a hand.

"Coach Cashen." He smiled.

"Virgil put you to work already?" Jake asked. He was a good kid. The son of his best friend Ben, Birdie's older brother. Though he was always glad to see Travis, it came with a pang of grief every time. Ben had been murdered a few years ago. The case would stick with Jake for the rest of his life.

"Yeah," Travis said. "Aunt Erica and Gemma asked me to come over and offer. I mean, I'm glad to do it."

"Good man. I'll let you get back to it."

"Actually, I wanted to talk to you about something anyway. Are you gonna be here for a while? I've got about a half an hour left before I'm done."

"I'll be here. Or I'll come find you before I leave. Is everything okay?"

Travis graduated high school last June. Since then, he'd taken some time to figure out what he wanted to do rather than jumping straight into college. Jake knew it worried Birdie. But from what Jake had seen, Travis had kept himself busy, working at the farm store and doing odd jobs around town like this one. At the same time, he understood Birdie's concerns. Travis was a star. A two-time state champion wrestler, with a high GPA, he'd been offered full rides at three different smaller colleges. He chose to hold off on all of them.

"Oh no," Travis said. "Everything's cool. I just wanted to run something by you."

"Okay. We'll talk." Jake gave Travis a good-natured slap on the back then walked up Virgil's sidewalk.

When he came into the kitchen, he saw another familiar face. One he hadn't seen in maybe twenty-five years. Vigil's daughter Crystal was loading the dishwasher. She rose and her face split into a wide smile when she saw Jake.

She looked exactly the same. Curly blonde hair and deep dimples in both cheeks. She had bright brown eyes and stood only four feet eleven.

"Jake! I was hoping I'd get to see you. You just missed Gemma."

Jake gave Crystal a hug. She smelled good. Jake laughed to himself. When he was in middle school, he had a small crush on Crystal. He remembered putting on cologne anytime Gemma brought her over after school. Crystal and Gemma would have been sixteen or seventeen at the time.

"You look great. How was your flight? How long are you going to be able to stay?"

Crystal pulled back from him. "Long. Exhausting. But I got here just before they wheeled Dad into surgery."

"How's he doing?"

Crystal scowled. "Ornery as ever. Bitches every time someone tries to help him. He's tried to kick me out three times just since he got home from the hospital."

Jake laughed. "So he's doing okay."

"Yes," Crystal said, her relief evident. "Everything went well. The doctors expect him to make a full recovery. As long as he doesn't try to overdo it and follows directions."

"Well, I'll see if I can help remind him of that. Where is he?"

Crystal pointed toward the living room. "We've got him set up in his recliner. He wanted to face the lake. Bill and Chuck are out there with him. He'll be glad to see you. Though he probably won't admit it."

Jake kissed the top of Crystal's head. "You're doing all the right things for him. And you know to call me if you need anything. I mean that."

Crystal teared up. Jake felt a stab of guilt that he hadn't been to see Virgil in the hospital after that first day. The Adah Lee case had swallowed his life for the last week.

"I know," she said. "And don't worry. You *will* hear from me."

Jake said a quick goodbye and went down the hallway to Virgil's living room. Just as Crystal said, Virg was propped up in his recliner. She had a TV tray set up beside him with a plastic water bottle and spirometer on it along with what looked like a half-eaten bowl of clam chowder.

"Jake!" Chuck said. All three men smiled when they saw him. Jake went up to Virgil and gave the man a quick hug. He stiffened, but didn't pull away.

"You look good," he told Virgil.

"Bullshit. I look like hell. I had my chest ripped open." Gemma had told Jake Virgil ended up having to have bypass surgery.

"Chicks dig scars, Virg," Bill said.

"Do they dig beer guts and surly attitudes?" Chuck quipped.

Jake took a chair next to Virgil. He really did look good, considering. The last time he saw him, Virgil's color was gray. Now he had a glow back in his cheeks.

"How's it going?" Virgil asked. "I'm sick of talking about my damn health."

Chuck and Bill laughed together. "Who the hell are you kidding?" Bill said. "He loves it. I think open-heart surgery was the best thing that ever happened to him. He's gonna ride the wave of this story all year."

"Shut it," Virgil said, but it was all good-natured. It warmed Jake's heart to hear it.

"Well, you gave us a bit of a scare," Jake said. "Tessa especially."

"They're coming over later," Bill said. "Tessa made some meals to put in Virg's fridge."

"It'll probably be enough to feed ten armies. And Crystal probably won't let me eat any of it. She's making me eat goddamn bean sprouts."

"You do what she says," Jake scolded him.

The ribbing died down. The men grew serious.

"How's it going, Jake?" Bill asked. "We've heard the nuts and bolts through the grapevine. You're in it with old Melva Bardo again, huh?"

"Yeah," Jake admitted. He filled the men in on what he could. Including the suspicion that his victim was Rex Bardo's secret daughter. He knew he could trust these three to keep it in the vault.

"Man," Virgil said. "You've got a real mess on your hands."

"I know. Meg's worried about this starting a Bardo civil war."

"She's right to be," Chuck said.

"So my question is," Jake started. "Any of you ever had any dealings with the Iron Voyagers MC? It's the one name Rex gave me when I asked him who'd be bold enough to try to retaliate against him through this girl."

Chuck scratched his chin. "I had a tussle or two with Buck Buchanan. Sounds like his kid inherited his president's patch. They've been making noise Buck never would have."

"That's pretty much what Rex said. Rascal Buchanan has taken over. He doesn't trust this tool knows how to honor the code they have."

"They don't go after families," Virgil chimed in.

"Exactly."

Bill whistled. "That's a tough one. You sure Rex isn't throwing this guy's name out just to get you to clean up a mess for him?"

"I'm not sure of anything. I'm taking a lot on faith here. And don't start. My eyes are wide open."

"Poor kid," Chuck said. "Sounds like she just got caught in the crossfire of something big. She should have just stayed over that hill."

"I think that's what Rex and Melva wanted. Until her old man started making plans for her future. It's bad out there. There's a faction of families who are pretty much forming their own cult inside the hill people. Rex said they were pretty fringe. They won't let their kids marry outside the group. A pretty malicious patriarchy from what I can tell. Adah wanted out. Melva wanted her under her roof. I think there could be a lot of kids at risk. I'm just not sure how much I can do about it."

"Then you got Rascal Buchanan acting stupid," Bill said. "Boy. I don't envy you this one, Jake."

"Any advice for dealing with the club?"

Chuck shook his head. "If this was twenty years ago, maybe. Buck was a reasonable man. I mean, for a thug. He never would have crossed Rex like this. Sounds like his son wants the Hilltop Boys to bring it to him."

"Rex pretty much admitted his crew blew up their club last year. They were planning on bringing some elements into the county Rex didn't want. That none of us would want."

"The devil you know," Virgil said.

"I'll keep my ear to the ground," Chuck said. "I still have a few contacts I can reach out to. See if there's something Rascal might respond to."

"I appreciate it," Jake said.

They spent the next half hour or so discussing more mundane topics like the fish on the lake and Virgil's predictions for the upcoming NHL playoffs.

Just about the time Virgil started to nod off, Travis poked his head around the corner.

"I'll let you rest," Jake told Virgil. "I'll see you soon."

He walked into the kitchen. Crystal had fixed Travis up with milk and cookies, which he scarfed down in less than a minute. She gave him a bag of leftovers to take home.

Jake said goodbye to Crystal, promising to stop by in a couple of days. Then he walked with Travis out to his truck.

"What's up?" Jake asked.

"I just wanted to tell you ... to thank you again. You know. For everything you've done for me. The last couple of years. In the wrestling room. On the side of the mat. All of it."

Jake hugged Travis. "You don't have to thank me. Everything you have you earned."

"Well, I know what it would have meant to my dad. That's all."

Jake felt a hard lump form in his throat.

"But," Travis started. "I wanted to tell you something else. It's been a long year since graduation. A good one. I've saved up a lot of money. Got my head clear. I just wanted you to be one of the first to know. I've been accepted to West Point starting this fall."

Jake was stunned. The lump in his throat turned into a boulder. He grabbed Travis and put him in a bear hug, lifting him off the ground.

"That's ... I don't even know what to say. I'm proud of you. Man. What does your aunt think about it all?"

He held his arms out, peering into Travis's face. The boy had tears in his eyes. Jake blinked fast, keeping them from forming in his own eyes.

"She doesn't know yet. I mean, she knew I was thinking about it. She hasn't said much. I think she's worried. About me having a military career. About me moving so far away. I won't get to come home much at first. It's just ... I know it's a lot for her. And she pretty much gave up her own life to come out here and stay with me. I don't want her to have to feel like she's obligated anymore. I want her to go do what she wants now."

"Your aunt has been doing exactly what she wants, Trav. I've never known her not to. But you should tell her. She'll be proud. Scared maybe. A little sad. But she loves you. This is good news. I promise."

Jake's phone buzzed with an incoming text. He expected it would be Gemma again. It was Birdie. He smiled.

"Her ears must have been burning." He read the text.

> Took a call from Stone. He couldn't get a hold of you. He pulled an all-nighter. He's got a few things to finish up, but will have news for us tomorrow morning. Meet at his office at nine?

Jake gave her a thumbs up then slid his phone back into his pocket.

"Tell her," he told Travis. "She's going to be happy. I'll be there with you if you want. Why don't you stop by for dinner soon?"

Travis smiled. "Yeah. That might be good."

"You got it," Jake said. He hugged Travis one last time. When he pulled away, he lost the battle. Tears filled his eyes as he turned his back and walked toward his truck.

FOURTEEN

Dr. Ethan Stone sat on the stool in the corner of his lab, writing on a notepad with one hand, smoking a Marlboro Light with the other. It was a county building, but this part of it had been his second home for over forty years. As Worthington County's Chief Medical Examiner, he'd developed the reputation of being one of the best in the state.

Birdie tapped on one of the double steel doors and waved to Stone through its round window. Stone tapped his ash in a coffee cup and waved them in.

Adah Lee lay stretched out on a metal examination table, bloodless, waxen, and held together by thick, black sutures from a standard Y-incision. Jake had never been squeamish. He wasn't now, but seeing her like that unsettled him more than he expected.

Stone must have seen it. "We can talk in my office if you're more comfortable. There's nothing more I need to do for her here."

"It's all right," Jake said. Stone went over to the table and covered Adah with a white sheet up to her chin.

"Thanks for meeting with us on a Sunday," Birdie said. "Do you ever go home?"

Stone smiled. "There's a reason I'm on my third wife." He snuffed out his cigarette in the cup and walked over to the table.

"She had a rough exit," he said. "Do you have any solid leads yet?"

"Some," Jake answered. "But a lot of it is going to depend on what you tell me."

Stone grabbed a tablet from the counter behind him. "I'll cut to it. Cause of death was strangulation." He pulled the sheet down a few inches, revealing Adah's neck. Her skin there was mottled and blackened in a thick band going all the way around.

"Classic signs," Stone said. "The contusion pattern, obviously. Broken hyoid bone. Swollen tongue. Broken capillaries in both eyes. Blood almost completely filling the whites of the left one."

"About what I figured, just from eyeballing her at the crime scene," Jake said.

"The second crime scene," Stone said. He pulled the sheet up, revealing her right leg. "Lividity pattern along her right side. Pooling the most around her right hip and right shoulder. She was lying in a fetal position for a long time. She was found on her back though."

"She was moved," Birdie said.

"Yeah," Stone confirmed. "You'll get more info from BCI's analysis. But I found blue carpet fibers in her hair. Some embedded in her right eyebrow. You gotta wait for the formal report from Ramirez, but I'd bet money those fibers came from the interior of a car. Probably the trunk."

"The killer panicked," Jake said. "There have to be a thousand better places in Blackhand Hills to stash a body where it would never be found. She was found within sight of a public walking trail. He threw some leaves over her but that's about it."

"Good guess," Stone said.

"What about her other injuries?" Birdie asked.

"They're extensive. She has abrasions, glue burns on her wrists, ankles, and across her mouth and cheeks. I'd say he used duct tape. Some of the blue fibers stuck to that too. Her arms and legs are all torn up and scraped. Probably from thorns or branches. I'd guess she tried to run at one point. If she were dragged, I'd expect to see most of the scrapes over her back, legs, and buttocks. They're not though. Wherever she was, she was running through thick, thorny brush. I gave Ramirez some samples of the tissue. She had a few thorns stuck in her hair."

"She wasn't fast enough," Birdie said.

"She was struck or dropped from some height," Stone said. "Skull fracture of the left temporal bone. No signs of any clotting or healing. I'd say that was done post mortem."

"What about sexual assault?" Jake asked, though he already knew the answer.

"Lacerations to the labia tearing inside the vaginal wall. Bruising to the vulva. So, yes."

"God," Jake said. "I hate to even ask. Were there signs of healing there?"

"There were."

"So she lived through it," Birdie said, her mouth a tight, bloodless line.

"What else?" Jake asked.

"Broken left wrist. The kind you get when you try to break a fall. She either fell or was pushed forward to the ground. And she fought. Hard."

It was the first bit of good news Stone gave them.

"Skin tissue under her fingernails," Stone said. "A strand of blond hair wound around her right middle finger that probably wasn't hers. Blood under her nails as well. Whoever did this, you're gonna want to look for somebody with fresh scrapes, probably on his face or neck."

"You got DNA," Jake said, hopefully.

"I sent everything to Ramirez. Semen samples as well. The works. You can never tell what'll show up, but I think there's a strong chance you're gonna have all the DNA evidence you could ask for."

"What about her blood?" Jake asked. "What's her type?"

"O positive. But the blood under her nails was B positive."

"That's something already, at least," Birdie said.

Stone walked up to the head of the table. He gently stroked Adah's hair back. "Poor kid. This one was brutal. I sense real rage from whoever did this."

"Someone who was trying to send a message," Jake muttered.

"Maybe," Stone said. "Or maybe somebody who knew her. Wanted to punish her. Or, you can't discount some random psycho. He kept hurting her even after she was dead. She has hairline fractures of the right occipital bone. Also post mortem. It could have happened when he dumped her."

"Or he punched her in the face," Birdie said.

"Distinct possibility," Stone said. "You'll want to closely examine the knuckles of any suspect you deal with. He could have broken his hand doing it. Or his thumb if he didn't know how to throw a proper punch."

Birdie put a hand over her mouth. She wasn't squeamish either. But the vibe in the room was downright oppressive.

"God," Birdie said. "She had nobody. She was all alone and looking for help. She found a monster instead."

"That's the gist of it," Stone said. "Preliminary tox screen was negative. BAC was zero. She wasn't on anything. She wasn't drunk. Didn't detect any of the usual prescription drugs either. I don't think this girl ever took so much as an ibuprofen."

"She probably didn't," Jake said. "She lived in a pretty remote, isolated area over Red Sky Hill."

"That's what Landry said. She was one of the hill people," Stone said.

"More than that," Jake said. "She was even more on the fringe. Undocumented. She never stepped one foot on our side of Red Sky Hill until the day she died."

Stone shook his head and clucked his tongue. "Tough, tough way to go out. Poor kid never really stood a chance. I wouldn't mind you keeping me in the loop on this one. She kind of has a way of getting under your skin, this girl. Haunts you."

"Coming from you," Jake said. "That's really saying something."

"Oh, I've seen a lot worse in my time. But something about this girl. You just wish you could have done something for her. Protected her. I don't know what it is."

Jake knew exactly what Stone meant. It's the thing that had settled over him the minute he walked into the room. There was a specter about Adah Lee. As if her life force hadn't yet left the air. As if every inch of her body was trying to tell him something. She was still asking for help.

"I imagine BCI will have findings for you in a couple of days," Stone said. "When I talked to Ramirez last night, he was saying the same thing. How this girl is one we're gonna remember."

"I appreciate it," Jake said. "And yes. I'll absolutely keep you updated."

"I don't even know what to hope for," Stone said. "If it was someone she knew. Someone who had it out for her specifically. That's one thing. But if she ran into some random psycho instead, a killing like this? He's escalated. The rush of it's gonna be like a drug. He's going to kill again. I can almost guarantee it."

Jake felt hollowed out. He didn't want to let his mind wander that far. But he knew Stone was absolutely right. It was difficult to know what to hope for. What would be worse? That someone Adah trusted could brutalize her in this way? Or that he had a murderous sociopath on the loose ready to strike again?

Jake's cell phone rang. It was Landry. He put up his index finger, gesturing for Birdie and Stone to wait for him. He walked out into the hallway.

"How bad is it, Jake?" Landry asked when he answered the call.

"Scale of one to ten?" Jake said. "Probably a twelve."

She let out an audible sigh. "Okay. Yeah. Okay. I'm going to need you first thing in the morning. I'm getting a lot of media inquiries. Word's getting out. We both know what happened the last time there was a murder thinly associated with the people over that hill. I don't want a panic or a lynch mob. But the pitchforks are already rattling."

"Anything I can do?" Jake asked, then instantly regretted it. He knew what she was about to say.

"I need you in the lion's den with me first thing in the morning. We'll hold a press conference. See if we can nip the rumors in the bud. You know the drill."

Dealing with reporters was one of Jake's least favorite things. Right up there with a rectal exam with no lube while on fire.

"Yeah," he said, not even trying to hide the disdain in his voice.

"Good. I knew I could count on you. Now go home. Get some sleep. Come back fresh-faced and in a good mood tomorrow morning. You're my wing man. Got it?"

"Yeah," Jake said again, then clicked off the call.

Fifteen

Far more members of the media showed up than Jake expected. The press room was standing room only plus a few reporters spilling out into the hallway. Jake and Sheriff Landry waited in a side room along with her media liaison, Neil.

"The less we say the better," Jake said. "Nothing about her cause of death. Nothing about what was found on her or her specific injuries."

"Of course," Meg said. "My bigger concern is trying to avoid inciting a panic. Do you have anything I can share that will calm anybody's fears that we've got some kind of serial killer running loose?"

Jake slid his hands in his pockets and rocked back on his heels, subconsciously stalling for a good answer.

"Jake?"

"You can say foul play is suspected. You can say you have every resource available working this case. You can say we have no reason to believe the community is at risk."

"Except we have no idea if that's true," Meg said.

Jake met her eyes. "Not really. But there's no point in putting that on record right now. Every lead I have so far points to this either being a domestic violence situation or retaliation against Rex Bardo."

"All right," Meg said, her tone one of resignation. "I'll do my usual tap dance and hope it gives us a little time."

"They're ready for you," Neil said. "They're expecting a brief statement, then I'll open it for questions."

"We shouldn't take any questions," Jake said.

"You're not going to be able to avoid it. And if you're really hoping to assuage public panic, you need to volley back some of the onslaught today. Gil Levy gave an interview to Channel 7 last night."

"He what?" Jake said. "The hell was he thinking?"

Neil rolled his eyes. "He was thinking he has freedom of speech. Ghoulish as it is, he probably likes having his name in the news."

"Just great," Jake muttered as Meg opened the door to the press room and walked up to the lectern. She adjusted the microphone, angling it downward. Even then, Neil kept a small, six-inch-high block hidden from view for Landry to stand on.

"Good morning," Landry started. "Thank you all for your patience. My statement today will be brief. There is an active investigation. You know the drill. There is a limit to the questions we can answer. But I'll do my best."

She cleared her throat and waited for the members of the press to settle.

"As many of you already know, a body was found off a hiking trail in Blackhand Hills State Park two days ago. For the sake of privacy of the victim's family, we've waited until we could inform them before making any kind of formal statement. But today I can share that the body has been positively identified as a seventeen-year-old Caucasian female. Her name was Adah Lee Sommers. She was a resident of the settlement on the northern valley over Red Sky Hill."

Murmurs spread through the crowd as she said the last bit. Jake knew that particular rumor had already started to fly. Meg made a downward gesture with her hands, hoping to settle the crowd.

"Do you suspect murder?" a female reporter shouted.

"Can you give us any idea what she was doing in Blackhand Hills?" another reporter shouted. Jake couldn't place the source of the question.

"Please," Landry said. "I'll take a few questions at the end of my statement. Let's play nicely, shall we? As I was saying, the victim has been positively identified. At this time, foul play is suspected and this is being treated as a homicide investigation. Detective Jake Cashen is heading that off. The victim went missing on April 11th. We are working through a number of leads and when I have more to share, I will. For now, I would ask you to respect the privacy of the people who live out there. I will not be disclosing the victim's address for obvious reasons. I'm afraid that's about all I can share. Detective Cashen?"

Jake stepped forward. "I'll just echo what Sheriff Landry said. We are investigating a number of leads and working closely with the Ohio Bureau of Criminal Investigation. You should have a photograph of the victim in your press kits. If anyone has any information or believes they saw the victim sometime between the evening of April 11th or after, I'd ask that you contact Crimestoppers or me directly. My number is also in your press kit or you can call the Sheriff Department's main line and your call will be correctly routed. That's all for now."

"As I said," Landry stepped forward. "I'll take a few questions."

The first round of questions were pretty standard. Meg handled them deftly. She repeated that the case was being handled as a homicide investigation. Yes, she was found by a family of tourists. No, she could not share the cause of death or answer anything about how the victim was found or what was found along with her.

"Can you share whether this was a sexual crime? Was she raped?" Karen Crandall asked from Channel 7. "We've heard reports from the person who found the body that her clothes had been removed."

"I'm not going to comment on any of that right now," Landry said. "You know the drill on that as well."

"Should the public at large be concerned that the killer will strike again?"

Meg squared her shoulders. "We have no specific concerns about that. I would, of course always advise the citizens of Worthington County to take precautions when walking or jogging. Use the buddy system. Stay in well-lit, well-trafficked areas. But that is, of course, general safety advice and common sense. The park service has assigned additional rangers to patrol Blackhand Hills and the Sheriff's Department is also providing additional manpower to carry that out. Basically, everyone needs to go about their lives as normal. There's absolutely zero reason to be fearful."

Mitchell Waverly, a reporter from Channel 2, stood up. Jake didn't know him well. He'd just transferred to the local station from Toledo.

"Detective Cashen," he said. "Can you confirm the rumors we're hearing that the victim, Adah Lee, was the daughter of Rex Bardo, head of the Bardo crime family, currently serving a fifteen-year federal prison sentence?"

To Jake, it felt like the air had been sucked out of the room. Beside him, he saw Meg's face turn white.

"Well," Jake started. "I don't comment on rumors."

"But you've heard that," Waverly said. "That's one of the leads you're investigating?"

"I'm sorry. I will not be speaking to rumors or the details of my investigation."

"That's all for now," Meg said, pulling the microphone toward her. "We'll update again when we have something else to share. The victim's information will be posted on the website along with the numbers members of the public can call if they have any information to share. Thank you."

Neil stood to the side, holding the door. Jake and Meg scooted out of the press room, ignoring the continued shouted questions about Rex Bardo.

As soon as the door shut, making certain they couldn't be overheard, Meg whirled around. "What was that?"

"I have no idea," Jake said, his blood heating up. The door from the inner hallway opened up and Birdie stepped through. She had likely seen everything on the television set up in the lounge.

"How do they know about the Rex Bardo connection?" Meg asked.

"Again," Jake said. "I don't have a clue. We've got a leak somewhere, obviously."

"No one knows about it from this office beyond the three of us," Birdie said. "I certainly haven't said anything to anyone."

"Jake?" Landry asked.

He shook his head. "I talked to Virgil, Chuck, and Bill. I'd swear on my life none of them would talk to the press at all, much less about this."

"Neil doesn't even know," Meg said.

"It has to be someone on the outside," Jake said.

"Warren Sommers and Rance Pruitt definitely wouldn't be talking to the press," Birdie said. "Can't imagine Bardo himself would. Or Melva for that matter."

Anger roiled through him. Jake knew of one other possibility. "Kyra Bardo," he said. "She's the only other person on this side of the hill who knows anything about it as far as I'm aware."

"But why?" Meg said. "Why in the world would she want that information in the public domain?"

"Adah's already dead," Jake said. "She doesn't have to protect her anymore."

"But Rex is alive," Birdie said. "There's no way he'd want that out. Even if it wasn't some kind of retribution against him, people will assume it was. That weakens him."

"Unless he wants someone to be scared he's out for revenge," Meg said. "Jake, where are you with this?"

"I'm gonna run down this Rascal Buchanan trail. I've got a line on a bar he hangs out at."

"Jake, be careful. Don't go alone."

"I'm not stupid and I don't have a death wish," Jake assured her.

"Do we need to reopen the investigation on the Murphy's Bar fire?" she asked. "Do you think that could shake something loose?"

"It won't help," Jake said. "And Rex isn't stupid either. He never came out and admitted he was behind that fire. The fire department ruled it was caused by faulty wiring. Rex's people will have covered their tracks three times over. And if I'm being honest, the Hilltop Boys did us a favor with that one. It kept the Iron Voyagers out of our backyard, at least for now."

"That's not making me feel better about any of this, Jake," Meg said. "What about Ramirez? How soon will you have the results of any DNA on Adah?"

"Hopefully within the week. Birdie, did you secure warrants to collect samples from Pruitt and Warren Sommer?"

"I did," she answered. "I thought we'd head out there tomorrow and try to collect them. But they'll know what we're up to by now. I wouldn't be surprised if they've both made themselves hard to find."

Before Jake could respond, his phone rang. The caller ID belonged to Mark Ramirez.

"This could be something," he said. He walked a few steps away and answered.

"Hey, Jake," Ramirez said. "I'm gonna send over a zip file with the crime analyst report on those two burner phone numbers you gave me."

"Can you give me the gist?"

"Well, like you expected, those phones only communicated with each other. I've got calls from Adah's phone to Kyra's phone and vice versa on the evening of April 11th, starting just after five p.m."

"Right when Adah was supposed to be at her party," Jake said. "Were you able to pinpoint the location of Adah's phone?"

"There's a map in the report I'm sending. It was in range of the tower on County Road Fourteen. Can't tell exactly what side of Red Sky Hill she was on, but that's the last location the phone was used. The signal goes down after that. I don't have it traveling anywhere else."

"It wasn't found on her body," Jake said. "So she either lost it or the killer dumped it before he moved her. But that could give me a good lead on where she was killed. Enough to get a team out there looking for it. Thanks, Mark. What about DNA? Do you have an ETA for me?"

"Soon," Ramirez said. "By the end of next week at the latest. Dr. Stone gave us a lot to work with."

"Good. Thanks. Keep me posted as soon as you hear."

"Always," Ramirez assured him.

Jake clicked off and gave Meg and Birdie the highlights.

"Good," Meg said. "Let's get a search team out there."

"I'll get it going," Jake said. "I'll meet up with Dave Yun in Marvell County tomorrow evening after I get the DNA warrants served. He's familiar with the bar where Buchanan's club hangs out. I want to be ready with Pruitt and Sommers's samples as soon as Ramirez has a report for me."

"Okay," Meg said. "That's something. I said the words, but I really don't think anybody out in that press room bought what we were selling about a potential serial killer. The sooner we can give a real answer, the better."

"Agreed," Jake said.

"Get on it," Meg said. "Get this solved, Jake. Quickly."

He eyed Birdie. He could sense she was thinking the same thing he was. Nothing about this was going to go quick or easy. He just hoped he'd get there before Rex Bardo reneged on his own promise. And he had to take another crack at Kyra Bardo. Fast.

Sixteen

At eight a.m. the next morning, Jake met the K9 team from the Columbus PD. The team would deploy four dogs: two bloodhounds looking for the victim's scent or human remains, two Labradors trained in electric storage detection or ESDs. If Adah Lee's cell phone was out there, Ruby and Bumper would find it. All paired with highly trained K9 officers who had produced incredible results.

Lieutenant Jerry DiSantos set up a command center under a tent at the base of Red Sky Hill. Earlier, Jake had let Melva know they were coming. He wanted no interference from her people or any of the other locals. They cordoned off a mile-long search area based on the zones Agent Ramirez mapped out from the cell phone data.

"How long do you think this will take?" Jake asked DiSantos.

"Hard to say. Sometimes ten minutes. Sometimes ten hours. Sometimes we never get lucky at all. But this is a fairly small area. If there's anything out there, human remains or cells, we'll find it."

Birdie pulled up in her cruiser accompanied by six other deputies in three marked patrol cars. One team would stay here with

DiSantos's team. One would stick to Birdie. Jake would take the other two up to Warren Sommers's compound.

"Keep your eyes open today," Jake instructed the deputies. "I've been assured we won't encounter any resistance. But I don't trust it."

"This place gives me the creeps," Deputy Denning said. "My dad used to threaten my brothers and me if we ever got as far as a mile from the other side of that hill."

"Don't believe every rumor you've ever heard," Jake said. "But ... still. Remember them. Mostly, there's just a lot of good people up there."

"You want me to bring Pruitt down here?" Birdie asked.

"No. Just get the swabs. If he truly doesn't have anything to hide, he should be more than willing to cooperate."

Birdie looked skeptical. "Jake, those people out there have been trained to avoid people like us since the day they were born. He's likely to try to refuse out of spite."

"Maybe," Jake said, checking his weapon. "Just make sure to tell him the harder he makes this, the more convinced I'm gonna be that he did something to that girl he doesn't want found out."

He turned to the group. "Keep your radios on TAC Seven. You won't hear from us unless it's an emergency and I call in the cavalry. Denning knows where we'll be."

Jake debated all night about how many crews to bring up here today. Truth was, he would have preferred an army. But he also knew the bigger the presence, the more disruption to the community up here, the less cooperation he was likely to get.

"All right," he said to Birdie. "Just be careful. And don't take any chances. If Pruitt puts up a fight, don't engage."

He turned to DiSantos. "You need anything else from me?"

DiSantos shook his head. "Nope. No offense, but I just need you to stay out of our way. Let the K9s and the handlers do their thing."

"Good enough," Jake said. He gestured to deputies Amanda Chaplin and Tim Broadmoor. They climbed back to their cruiser. Jake got in his car, hoping he could remember the way.

Ten minutes later, Jake rolled up to Warren Sommers's settlement. It looked deserted today. No clothes hanging on the lines. None of Sommers's sons were out in the fields behind the houses.

Jake got out. He waited for the deputies to fall in behind him. Then he walked up to Warren Sommers's front door.

"Sommers?" he shouted, pounding on the door. "It's Detective Cashen. I know you know I was heading up here today. This'll be quick. I'm not looking to start any trouble."

He waited. He heard movement inside, but nobody came to the door. Deputy Denning pointed to the house to the east of Sommers's, the one Isaac said his brother Elias lived in. The curtains on the front window snapped shut. The boys were watching.

"Sommers! Let's go. I have a warrant. I can come in whether you want me to or not."

Jake put a palm on the butt of his weapon, praying he wouldn't have to unholster it.

"Warren?" he called out one last time.

Just as he raised his hand to pound on the door again, it swung open. It was dark inside. It took a second for Jake's eyes to adjust, but Scarlett Sommers stood in the doorway wearing a flower print dress and an apron, her hair tied back under a yellow bandana. She looked like she'd been crying.

"My husband isn't home," she said.

"Mrs. Sommers," he said. "I'm so sorry about Adah. I wish there was something more we could have done."

Scarlett looked nervously behind her, then stepped outside, closing the door behind her. From the window to her left, he saw her youngest daughter, Zenni, peer out.

"You have to leave," Scarlett said. "I told you. If you're looking for my husband, he's not here."

"Where is he?"

"I don't know. He said he was going fishing over the ridge. He could be anywhere. He'll come back when he finds what he needs. Could be hours. More likely days. Maybe weeks."

Jake pulled a piece of paper out of his breast pocket. "Mrs. Sommers, this is a warrant. Warren's court-ordered to provide a DNA sample. It won't hurt. It won't take long. Just a cheek swab and I'll be on my way."

Her eyes widened. "Why would you need that?"

"Because your daughter's body was found with DNA from someone else under her fingernails. I need to rule your husband out."

She shook her head almost violently. "No. Warren had nothing to do with this. You're mistaken."

"If he had nothing to do with this, this test will prove that once and for all. I would think he'd want this resolved. I would think you would."

Scarlett's face drained of color. "Detective ... you said ... under her fingernails? What would ... did she ... my daughter? She fought?"

"Yes," Jake said, his tone sober.

Scarlett wiped her hands nervously on her apron. She looked to her left and her right, perhaps worried one of her sons would come out.

"Please," she said. "What ... can you tell me what they did to her? She was hurt very badly?"

It seemed an odd question to ask. She knew her daughter was dead. At the same time, he understood it.

"I'm sorry. But yes. Adah was beaten. She was ... it was violent, what happened to her. And I want to find out who did it. Do you understand? Whoever it was needs to be held accountable. That's my job. That's all I'm trying to do. I'm not here to hurt you or your husband. I'm on your side. Or more accurately, I'm on Adah's side."

Tears rolled down Scarlett's cheeks. "I wanted her to just stay home. If she'd have just stayed home."

She broke down, doubling over. Jake reached out and caught her by the elbows. She pitched forward and clung to the lapels of his jacket. He put his arms up and patted her on the back.

"I'm truly sorry. Whatever was going on in your daughter's life, she didn't deserve this. No one does. So will you help me? Will you tell me where I can find your husband?"

Scarlett immediately pulled back. She wiped her face with her apron.

"You really need to go. I can't help you. Warren didn't have anything to do with this. He couldn't. You're wasting your time."

"I don't think I am. I think you know more than you're telling me. I think you could help me if you wanted to."

"No. No. I can't. You have to go. Please go."

"You should listen to her!"

Two men approached from Jake's right. They were both the spitting image of their father. He guessed they were Warren's two oldest, Elias and Joseph. The taller of the two had a shotgun resting on his shoulder.

"Son," Jake said. "You need to put that away right now unless you want trouble you can't handle."

"I know my rights," he said. "And I know you have no business here."

"Except I do," Jake said. He held up the warrant. "Where's your father?"

The man spit on the ground.

"Elias," Scarlett said. "Just go back inside."

"*You* go back inside," Elias shouted, his voice like a thunder crack. It made his mother jump, then cower inside the doorway.

"Do what he says," Joseph said. "Get inside. Stay there."

Scarlett moved. She cast a distressed look at Jake, then slid back through the doorway and slammed the door. Jake heard a lock engage.

"You're done here," Elias said. "Warren's not here. He doesn't need to be. So get going."

Jake walked toward him and slapped the warrant against Elias's chest. He grabbed it from Jake, glanced at it briefly, then threw it on the ground.

Jake knew he had to follow the directive he'd given Birdie. He didn't come here for a fight. Not this time.

"You tell your father I'll be back," Jake said.

"You better bring more guns," Elias said.

"You threatening me?"

"Just making an observation," Elias said.

Jake gestured to the deputies. They stood in ready positions, hands on their weapons. They went back to their vehicles, keeping their eyes on Elias Sommers the whole time.

Jake started back down the trail with the deputies behind him. He got about a half a mile when he saw Isaac walking toward him on the road. Jake screeched to a halt and got out, leaving his vehicle running.

"Isaac," he called out.

"You shouldn't be here," Isaac said.

"You saw me drive up. You've been waiting. So what is it? What did you want to tell me?"

Isaac gazed at the ground. "Nothing. Just ... he isn't going to talk to you anymore. He told Ma not to either. Said he doesn't have to. That you can't make him."

"That's true," Jake said. "But I didn't come here for that. I'm here to get your father's DNA sample."

Isaac looked puzzled. "He'll never let you do that."

"He won't have a choice. I've got a court order."

Isaac smiled. "Won't matter."

"Where is he, Isaac?"

Isaac squinted at Jake, opening only one eye as the sun hit him in the face. "He's just gone. Took to the hills early this morning. He could be anywhere by now. If my dad doesn't want to be found, he won't be. He comes and goes as he pleases. I can't track him when he gets like this."

"When you see him, you tell him what I said. He can't hide from me forever. That DNA? I'm going to be able to find out pretty quickly if whoever killed your sister was related to her. If they were, then you're going to have cops crawling all over the place up here. Helicopters. Drones. We'll find him. We're good at this."

"It still won't matter," Isaac said.

"Don't you want me to find out who did this to Adah?"

Isaac looked at Jake, but didn't answer. Instead, he raised his hand in a silent wave, then disappeared into the woods.

Jake watched for a moment, waiting to see if Isaac would reappear. But he didn't. Jake turned toward the patrol car behind him and made a circular gesture above his head. He climbed in his car and headed back toward Red Sky Hill.

"I hope you had better luck than I did," Jake said when Birdie finally drove up to DiSantos's tent, pulled up alongside him, and rolled down her window.

Birdie frowned for a moment. Then her face split into a grin and she held up a plastic bag.

"Got it," she said. "It was like you said. Rance Pruitt was more than happy to provide a sample. He seemed pretty confident it'll clear him. Pretty smug, actually. Said Adah's finally gonna be found out for the whore she was."

"Lovely," Jake said. He filled her in on his failure at Warren's compound.

"Well," Birdie said. "I'd say that casts even more suspicion on him. What's your game plan?"

"First, we'll wait until Ramirez gets back to me with the DNA analysis. If it's a family match, that'll make it clear."

"Unless Warren's not her father and Rex really is. Then we're right back to where we started."

"Then I can justify coming in here heavier."

"Detective Cashen!" The shout came from behind him. Lieutenant DiSantos broke into a run as he came toward Jake. Birdie got out of her car.

Winded, DiSantos had to take a second to catch his breath. In the distance, Jake could hear a couple of the dogs erupt into a keening howl.

"They hit," DiSantos said. "About two hundred yards due west. Pretty thick brush down there. Lots of broken branches. A piece of red cotton snared on some thorny bushes."

"Adah was wearing a red cotton shirt under her overalls," Birdie said.

"Could be signs of a struggle. Probably blood on some of the branches. That's why the dogs are going nuts. And they found a smashed flip phone a few feet away from that. It was quick. The dogs were on it in about ten minutes. I think we found your crime scene."

"I'll get Ramirez on the phone," Birdie said. "He can have a crew out here in an hour or two. Do you have the area taped off?"

"Absolutely," DiSantos said. "Locked down tight."

"Good," Jake said. Birdie stepped away and got on her cell.

"It's a pretty large area," DiSantos said. "Ramirez is better at this than I am. But to my eye it looks like there had to have been a hell of a struggle."

Jake could picture it in his head and it made him sick to his stomach. Whoever found her, Adah had tried to run away. She was chased down. Hunted. She could never be fast enough. Then she had fought for and lost her life just yards away from the boundary line of the place she thought was freedom.

Seventeen

Detective Dave Yun, Jake's counterpart with the Marvell County Sheriff's Department, met him Tuesday evening at a coffee shop a mile down from the dive bar the Iron Voyagers were using as their temporary hangout.

"Thanks for doing this," Jake said. "I hope your wife wasn't too bent that you didn't come home for dinner."

Yun smiled. "Mila's a third year ER resident over at St. Albert's. She keeps rougher hours than I do."

"I didn't know that. Good for her."

"She was a nurse when I married her. As soon as the boys were in school full time, she started med school."

"Impressive," Jake said. He waved off a refill on his coffee. As it was, he'd probably be up until four in the morning.

"So," Yun said. "How sure are you that Rascal Buchanan could be your bad guy?"

"Not very. That's one of the things I wanted to pick your brain about. You know these guys better than I do. Bardo said there's a code. They don't go after family members. But Rascal's making up his own rules."

"He's right about that. Rascal's dumb and cocky. That makes him pretty dangerous."

"Rex said things were different when his old man was head of the club."

Dave let the server top off his coffee. "Buck was a mean son of a bitch. Don't get me wrong. But he was respectful of us. Knew we had a job to do. Same thing with the old-timers. Not so much with this younger generation. In Buck's day, they at least kept the even badder elements in check."

"Kind of like Rex," Jake said. "And I'm pretty sure that's what he had the Hilltop Boys doing when Rascal tried to encroach."

"And now he thinks Rascal retaliated by killing his kid."

"In a nutshell, yeah. Do you think he's capable of it?"

Dave considered the question, took a sip of his coffee, then set it down. "Honestly? Yeah. But here's the thing. A lot of people don't think Rascal really earned his patch. Including some of his own crew. So I think there's another possibility. One that only involves Rascal indirectly."

Jake sat back. "You think somebody just wanted to make it look like Rascal did this? Hoping that Rex would get Rascal out of the way for them?"

"Maybe," Yun said.

"Who?"

"Well, a lot of people think one of his own crew. Digger Rawlins. He was Buck's right-hand man. He's smart. More of a leader than Rascal. But like I said. Smart. Digger wouldn't be stupid enough to get his own hands dirty with this."

"And Rascal would."

"He is absolutely, exactly that dumb. Yeah."

"What are the odds he'll talk to us?"

Yun smiled. "Oh, I think Rascal's gonna put on a show. Pretend like he's not afraid of you. And he'll do it right in front of his whole crew."

"What else might we run into at this Cotter's?"

"Well, calling it a dive bar would be too much of a compliment. But Fred Cotter, he's well liked around town. He's not too happy that the Voyagers have taken over his place. But they've backed him into a corner. If he tries to push them out, they'll probably torch the place. With Cotter in it. I'm hoping he just sells the place and retires down south like his wife wants him to."

"Tough choice," Jake said. When their server came back and slapped their bill on the table, Jake threw down a twenty and slipped into his jacket.

"We can ride together," Yun said. "We'll take my car."

Yun picked up his campaign hat and slid it on. Jake was glad Landry didn't force her detectives to do the same. But he had his badge clipped to his belt.

Five minutes later, Yun pulled up to the bar. He wasn't kidding. From the outside, the place looked like the roof was about to cave in. The parking lot wasn't much more than a gravel bed with tall weeds poking through. But there were ten Harleys lined up on the side of the building.

Yun went ahead of him. It was so dark inside, it took a second for Jake's eyes to adjust. The smoke in the air almost choked him.

"Hey, Fred," Yun said to the man behind the bar. He was old, maybe Grandpa Max's age. He poured a draft beer and set it in front of the only other customer in the place. The back of the room was filled with Iron Voyagers, their hangers-on, and a few girls they seemed to be passing around.

Yun didn't have to tell him who Rascal Buchanan was. He sat alone at a table in the corner, holding court. One of the women sat on his lap. As Jake and Yun approached, Rascal slapped her on the rear end and said something to her. She looked Jake over, then disappeared deeper into the smoke-filled bar.

Yun grabbed a chair and sat at Rascal's table. He didn't protest. Jake took the other chair. Rascal snuffed a cigarette out right on the table, then lit another one. He had three empty bottles of Busch in front of him and was drinking from a fourth.

"You got a minute?" Yun said.

"For you? Sure." Rascal gave a sly smile and took a drag as he eyed Jake. "Who's your friend?"

Jake pulled out one of his cards and flicked it across the table. It landed face up in front of Rascal. He glanced at it but didn't pick it up.

"I've heard of you," Rascal said. It was hard to tell how old he was. He had long, scraggly dark hair. Clean-shaven but with badly pockmarked skin. His nails were dirty. He had tattoo sleeves down both arms and a few creeping up around his neck under his collar.

"I've heard of you too," Jake said.

"What do you want?"

"Just need to ask you a few questions. Easy ones. Then we'll be on our way."

"Everything okay, boss?" Another cut-wearing biker walked up to the table. Rascal's muscle, for sure. He had a dome-shaped bald head and probably weighed three hundred pounds, with a right arm as big as Jake's thigh.

"All good, Wolf. We're just having a conversation."

Wolf scowled at Jake and Yun, then lumbered off.

Jake pulled out a picture of Adah and put it in front of Rascal.

Rascal leaned forward to get a better look. "Am I supposed to know who she is?"

"That's question number one," Jake said.

Rascal pushed out his bottom lip, then slid the photo back toward Jake. "Never seen her. So whatever she's saying, she's lying."

"She's not doing any talking, Rascal," Yun said. "She's dead."

"Tough break," Rascal said. "Never seen her."

His eyes darted to the left when he spoke. He turned his head as he blew out smoke. Though Jake never claimed to read minds, it was the posturing of a liar.

"Second question," Jake said. "Where were you on April 11th from about six in the evening until the next morning?"

Rascal laughed. "You shitting me with this? We're done talking. Time for you to get the hell out of my face."

"Shouldn't be hard for you to answer," Jake said.

Rascal leaned forward. "I was sitting right here. Tell him, Fred!" he shouted toward the bar.

Fred Cotter looked scared. He turned his back and went into the kitchen.

Rascal laughed harder. "I mean it. Get the hell out of my face now, before you ruin my night." He picked up his beer, downed it, and slammed it on the table in front of Jake. Then he flicked his cigarette at Yun and got up from the table. His crew started laughing at Jake and Yun's expense.

Jake pulled a baggie out of his pocket along with two blue latex gloves. He snuffed out Rascal's cigarette and placed it in the baggie. Rascal turned and watched him. The smirk melted from his face. Jake picked up the beer bottle Rascal set in front of him and slipped that into the baggie as well.

"Pleasure to meet you," Jake said, holding up the baggie. Beside him, Yun couldn't contain his own chuckle as they walked out of the bar.

"We better get the hell out of here before Rascal and the rest of 'em decide to come back for his garbage," Yun said.

"You were right," Jake said as they slipped into Yun's car and hauled ass out of the parking lot. "He's incredibly stupid."

"You got DNA on your victim yet?"

"In a few days," Jake said. "And I'm expecting a lot of it. She had defensive wounds. Skin under her nails. Whoever did this sexually assaulted her. The rape kit was positive. You still think your boy back there was dumb enough to get his own hands dirty if he wanted to send a message to Rex?"

"Yeah," Yun said. "I do."

"Then I'll be able to rule him in or out pretty quick."

When they got back to the coffee shop parking lot, Jake put the evidence bag in the trunk of his car.

"You weren't really looking to question that knucklehead, were you?" Yun said. "That's what you were after from the get."

Jake smiled. "I was hoping. Everybody said he was dumb. I was just holding out hope he was *that* dumb."

"Glad you weren't disappointed," Yun said. "I'll get you an affidavit tomorrow morning. Lock up your chain of custody."

Jake shook Yun's hand. In the past few years, Dave Yun had become a valuable ally. He was a damn good detective, too.

"Let me know when you know," Yun said. "If you want, I can have some deputies keep an eye on him until you get your DNA back."

"Appreciate it," Jake said. He hoped Rascal wasn't stupid enough to run.

Yun and Jake said their goodbyes. Before he drove off, Jake sent Birdie a quick text, letting her know what he'd bagged. He didn't know what to hope for. If Rascal's DNA was a match, he didn't believe for a second that Rex would keep his promise and stay out of the mix. Then there would be a higher body count than just Adah. And someone else just as innocent might get caught in the crossfire.

EIGHTEEN

Jake's phone woke him out of a dead sleep at four a.m. He roused as he often did when startled, tight-fisted and swinging. It took him a second to orient. But he was just in bed. The cabin was quiet but for the dripping of a slow leak at the kitchen sink.

He fumbled with the covers and staggered out of bed, searching for his phone. He'd left it out in the living room inside his jacket pocket. He didn't get to it before the ringing stopped and it went to voicemail. Fishing it out, the phone started ringing again almost immediately.

"Birdie?" he said, his voice a hoarse whisper. He cleared his throat.

"Good," she said. "You're up."

"I am now."

"Get dressed. Run a comb through your hair. Then meet me at County Hospital. The ER."

Adrenaline raced through him. "What happened? Is it Travis?"

"No. God. Don't even say that. It's Scarlett Sommers. She came by ambulance with her daughter. She's hurt pretty bad. I got the heads-up from one of the nurses."

"How the hell did a nurse know to call you? You know what? Don't answer that. Maybe I don't want to know."

"You don't. Just get here." She clicked off the call.

Jake searched for the light switch. He sniffed under his arm. He needed a shower. He opted for deodorant and a wet comb through his hair. It took him no more than two minutes to throw on a pair of pants and a shirt. He grabbed his badge and gun off the kitchen counter and headed out.

He found Birdie pacing in the ER waiting room. Her face flooded with relief when she saw Jake and barreled toward him.

"What the hell happened?" he asked. "How did she get here?"

"We'll talk and walk," Birdie said, grabbing Jake by the arm. She led him toward the double doors leading into the trauma rooms. The guard on the other side waved and buzzed them in.

"They brought her in by ambulance about an hour ago. Head trauma, lacerations on her face, bruising on her abdomen and thighs. Two broken ribs. The right side of her face is all swollen. They're checking to make sure she doesn't have any bones broken there."

"Did Warren do this?" Jake asked. Guilt poured through him. Had her sons ratted her out for talking to him the other day?

"She won't say," Birdie answered. "But it's a pretty safe bet. I'd say he knocked her down. Doc thinks she hit her head on the sharp edge of something. Maybe a table. She's lucky she didn't break her neck. Then he kicked her when she was down."

"What about the girl?" Jake asked as they stormed down the hallway.

"She's fine. She ran out of the house, stole the keys to one of her brother's four-wheelers and managed to get Scarlett into it. She took her to Melva's. She called the ambulance from there."

"Is Melva here?"

Birdie shook her head. "Haven't seen her. It was just the daughter with her. She's scared out of her wits."

Jake and Birdie got to a curtained-off area. Scarlett Sommers lay on a bed, barely recognizable. Her fifteen-year-old daughter, Zenni, sat at her side with a tear-stained face. Deputy Chaplin was just walking out.

Jake took her aside while Birdie went in to Scarlett and Zenni.

"How bad is it?" Jake asked.

Amanda Chaplin sucked air through her teeth. "She had the shit beaten out of her. Doc said she was lucky one of her ribs didn't puncture her lungs. Her right wrist is crushed. She's gonna need surgery. There are treads in the wound. Doc thinks whoever did this was wearing steel-toed boots and stomped on her."

Jake's stomach churned. "This was her husband," he said.

"That'd be my guess. But she keeps saying she fell."

"There aren't any stairs in her house."

"Of course not. Nobody believes her. But if she won't tell anyone what happened, we're stuck. I know I'm not telling you anything you didn't already know."

"Thanks." Jake patted Chaplin on the arm. "I'll take it from here."

"I'll have my notes in your inbox before the day shift starts."

Jake thanked her again and walked behind the curtain. Scarlett Sommers stared at the wall. Zenni was at the head of her bed, smoothing her hair back. It was still caked with blood.

Jake couldn't help picturing Adah's body on Ethan Stone's exam table after her autopsy. Adah too had been brutally beaten. With the exception of also being strangled, Adah's injuries were pretty similar to her mother's. Not that it came as a shock, but this was proof that Warren Sommers was absolutely capable of violent rage.

"Mrs. Sommers," Jake said. "I'm sorry this happened to you. But I'm glad you're here. Zenni, you did the right thing, helping your mom."

"She's going to be okay. The doctor said they're going to have to fix the broken bones in your wrist, but that nothing else will need surgery," Zenni assured Scarlett.

"Scarlett, I need you to tell me what happened. If you don't feel safe in your own home, we can help you."

Scarlett turned her head and focused her one good eye on him. It was hard to look at her. Her pretty face was a ghoulish Halloween mask now. All bruised and misshaped. The right side was swollen and blackening.

"I don't need your help. I just need to go home."

"Did Warren do this? Was he angry that you talked to me the other day?"

She looked back at the wall.

"Scarlett," Jake said, raising his voice a bit. "If he did this to you, did he do it to Adah? He doesn't like disobedience, does he? Where is it going to end? When you're dead? When Zenni is?"

"Go away," Scarlett whispered. "I have nothing else to say."

"Why won't you help me if you won't help yourself? Or help Adah? If he did this to her ... if he did this to you, you need to get away from him," Jake said.

"Scarlett, we can find a safe place for you," Birdie said, taking the good-cop approach. "Somewhere where you can rest and recover your strength. No one else has to know where you are. There are people with experience in these kinds of things. You can be okay. Zenni too."

"Zenni," Scarlett said. "Pack up my clothes. Call Jeremiah. Tell him to come pick us up."

"You can't leave, Mrs. Sommers." The nurse walked back in. Her name tag read Stephanie. "You have a concussion. We're giving you IV fluids. The surgeon needs to come down and consult with you about your wrist. You'll need an operation so it can heal properly. A tetanus shot. Antibiotics."

"You can't make me stay," she said. "I know my rights. I'll be just fine. I can rest at home."

"Mom!" Zenni said. "Please listen to them. You weren't awake when I came in. You wouldn't wake up. I thought you were dead. Please let them make you better."

"Mrs. Foster can look in on me," Scarlett said, trying to sit up. She fell back against the pillow, groaning.

"Zenni," Jake said. "Why don't you and I step outside so the nurse can speak to your mother?"

Scarlett started to protest, but Zenni moved with purpose. Jake led her down the hall to the waiting room, out of earshot of her mother.

"Are you okay?" Jake asked. "Were you hurt too?"

Zenni shook her head. She looked so much like her mother. Pretty, waifish, deep brown eyes.

"Do you understand what's happening?" Jake said. "If your mother leaves without getting proper medical attention, she might not heal. She's hurt very badly."

"I know. It's never been like this before."

Jake sat back. This poor kid, he thought. She spoke softly, tentatively. He recognized a trauma survivor when he saw one.

"There have been other times," Jake said. A statement, not a question. "Zenni, what my partner said. It's true for you too. If you don't feel safe at home, we can help you. Take both you and your mother to a shelter. Somewhere you can talk to people who know how to deal with situations like this. You're not alone."

"She won't go. She'll never go. Adah tried to talk her into it. But she won't listen."

"What about you?"

"I'm okay. They don't pay attention to me. I don't make trouble for anybody. Not like Adah. She was always arguing with them. Always telling them why she thought they were wrong. Always running off. I wish she would have just stayed quiet some of the time."

"Zenni, did your father do this to your mother today? I need you to understand, if your mother won't admit to that, there isn't much I can do. There won't be any way to stop it from happening again. And it will happen again. I think you know that. I think that's why you realized you had to do something. What you did was brave. It was responsible. It was right."

She started to cry. Jake grabbed a tissue from a box on the table next to him. Zenni blew her nose into it.

"Is this the first time you've ever been on this side of Red Sky Hill?" he asked.

"Yes," she said. "I can't say I like it very much. It's loud. Everyone's in a hurry and rude. It's dirty. I don't like big cities."

Jake resisted the urge to tell her Stanley, Ohio was about as far from a big city as she could get.

"But no one's going to hurt you here."

She blew her nose again.

"Did you see it?" he asked. "You can tell me. I meant what I said in there. I'm trying to help your sister."

"She's dead. Nobody can help her."

"But I can make it so whoever hurt her can't do it to anybody else."

"You think it's my dad?"

"Do you?"

"He wouldn't kill her."

"Maybe he didn't mean to. Maybe it got out of hand. Maybe Adah was arguing with him and he went overboard. Like he did with your mom today."

Zenni's shoulders went up. She shrank further into her chair.

"She shouldn't have talked to you," she said.

"Is that why your dad got mad? Did your brothers tell him they saw her with me?"

Zenni nodded.

"Honey, I said if your mother won't tell me what happened, I can't do much. But you could tell me. If you saw what he did, it's okay to tell me."

"That other police lady said she could take him to jail. But you won't find him. He left again ... after."

"But you saw it. Do you think you could tell a judge what happened if I asked you? You were brave enough to get your mom help. This is another way to help her."

Something changed in Zenni Sommers. She straightened. Her eyes turned stone cold. Jake instantly realized he'd been wrong about her. She wasn't a waif. She wasn't meek. She might just be one of the bravest kids he'd ever met.

"Yes. My dad did this. He came in the front door. It was just us. Isaac was off somewhere like he always is since Adah left. My dad told me to go over to Joseph's. But I didn't. I just walked outside."

"What happened, Zenni?"

She looked down, shredding the tissue. "He yelled. A lot. Told her he was disappointed in her. That she'd betrayed him. That she needed to learn a lesson about obedience."

"Because she talked to me," Jake said.

"Yes. Elias told him. I begged him not to. But I knew this was going to happen. I asked my mom if we could go visit Miss Melva for a while. I knew she's been sad because of Adah. But my mom wouldn't go. She told me I couldn't go either. She didn't want to make my dad mad. But then she talked to you anyway."

Jake felt sick. He couldn't blame himself for what happened. Except part of him did.

"I went around the back and crouched down in front of the window. He took off his belt. Then ... he started. She just stood there. She didn't fight back. She didn't even put her hands up. Or scream. Or cry. She just ... went away in her head somewhere. Then he left. Just put his belt back on and walked out the front door. He's gone again."

Jake put an arm around her. Zenni let him. She cried into his chest.

"You don't have to go back. You hear me? You don't have to go back there. This is what Adah wanted to get away from, wasn't it?"

Zenni stared at the floor. "But if she would just have listened to him. Not made him mad. It's not hard."

"I'm sorry," Jake said. "You shouldn't have to go through this."

"I need to get back to her. I need to get word to Jeremiah. I need to go home."

Jake shuddered. "You want to go back?"

"I'll be all right. He won't come back for a while. And things will die down. She's never going to leave him. And I can't leave her there all alone."

"It's not your responsibility. You're allowed to want things for yourself, Zenni. I don't believe you're safe there. I can't let you go back."

"I'm not going back home. I'll stay with Joseph."

"He's next door. You think your father won't find you there?"

"I'll sign whatever you want me to sign. If you need papers. To come talk to my dad. Only, he's not going to show up for a while.

He knows you want to talk to him. He's gonna know that even more now. It will keep him away."

"Zenni ..."

She got up and started walking back to her mother's room. She disappeared just as one of the hospital social workers rounded the corner. Jake had worked with her before. Estelle Van Heusen.

"Hey, Jake," she said. "Was that the Sommers girl? I was called in for a consult. And I talked to Deputy Wayne on the phone."

"Do whatever you can. She just told me her father is the one who beat her mother. She saw the whole thing. He's a person of interest in the murder of the girl's sister. I do not feel she's in a safe home environment. I'll provide an affidavit if it'll help."

"It might," she said. "How old is she?"

"Fifteen."

"I'll do what I can. But it'll be hard to get an order to put her into protective custody if she's telling you she doesn't feel unsafe. I heard the tail end of your conversation."

"Just talk to her."

"For now, I'll coordinate with the mother's doctor. See if I can get permission for her to stay with her mom here if she's admitted."

"She's about to sign herself out AMA," Jake said.

Estelle rolled her eyes. "This is going to be a tough one. We've been alerted to those hilltop kids for years. There's a limit to what we can do."

"Sure, for the population up there in general. But I'm talking about *this* kid. A specific situation. When you see her mother's face, you'll know."

"Okay," she said. "Send me a copy of her statement when you've got it written up. I'll take it from here."

As Jake turned, Birdie came down the hall. Her face looked grim. She said hello to Estelle, then Estelle headed back to Scarlett's room.

"What are the odds Estelle will get Zenni and Scarlett into a shelter?"

"I don't know," he said. "At least Zenni's talking. If Warren finds out she talked to me ..."

"She admitted her dad was the one to do that to her mom?"

"Yeah."

"So then, it's enough to issue an arrest warrant. We just have to go find him and bring him in."

"Easier said than done," Jake muttered. He knew he had to trust the system. Trust Estelle. But it was going to be hard.

The sun was just coming up as he and Birdie walked out to the parking lot. Both he and Birdie got a text at the same time. She got to her phone first.

"Ramirez," she said. Jake pulled out his phone. Mark Ramirez texted that he was coming down to Jake's office early this afternoon. He had the DNA results from the blood, tissue, and semen samples found on Adah Lee.

NINETEEN

Mark Ramirez arrived in Jake's office at one p.m. He carried a file folder and a flash drive. Tossing the latter, Jake caught it one-handed.

"Thanks for coming down," Jake said.

"I've got another case over in Athens. Double homicide. Elderly couple. Wife had advanced Alzheimer's. Husband shot her then himself."

"God. That's a rough exit. Guy probably didn't think he had a choice."

"Yeah. I don't know what I'd do if it was Mila. I can't even think about it."

Birdie walked in holding a to-go bag from Papa's Diner. She'd picked Jake up a Greek salad and a couple of gyros for herself.

"You hungry?" she asked Ramirez. "I overbought."

Jake smiled. "Just like your mother. When we were kids, it

wouldn't matter what time of day I came over. She'd fix me a plate of food. And big food. Pot pies. Turkey legs. Lasagna casseroles."

"And half of the time, you and Ben were cutting weight. I used to feel so bad for you."

She set the bag down and pulled out four Styrofoam boxes. Then Birdie turned into her mother completely. She didn't give Ramirez a choice. She sat him down at the round table in the corner and shoved a giant gyro in front of him.

Jake sat at the table, with Birdie beside him. "So where are we?" he asked Ramirez, after taking a big bite of his salad.

Ramirez held a finger up as he worked to swallow his first bite. "God, that's good!"

"Spiros's specialty," Birdie said. She handed Ramirez a napkin.

Ramirez opened the file folder and pulled out a colored pie chart. "Most of this wasn't a surprise. DNA samples from your victim's rape kit, skin tissue under her nails, a strand of blond hair coiled around her left index finger. All of it came from the same person. Caucasian male."

Ramirez pointed to the pie chart. Jake and Birdie leaned closer to see it. Ramirez put his finger on the largest wedge, colored in red.

"Mostly Eastern European descent," Ramirez continued. "Little bit of Scandinavian. Scotland. Then a sliver from the Iberian Peninsula."

"So basically the same as probably two-thirds of the white males in the entire country," Jake said.

"Pretty much," Ramirez said. "I've got a geneticist from OSU working on it. So far, she hasn't been able to find any familial matches in the ancestry databases. Which just means his relatives haven't submitted anything to the commercial DNA services."

"What about CODIS?" Birdie asked.

Ramirez shook his head. "No hits there either. Whoever this guy is, he's never submitted DNA associated with any crime he's ever been charged with. Or doesn't have a record at all."

"What about the samples we gave you?" Jake asked. He'd been able to send off Rascal Buchanan's DNA along with Rance Pruitt's.

"No match to either of them," Ramirez answered, covering his mouth as he chewed.

"Honestly," Jake said. "I'm not surprised by that. Disappointed, but not surprised. So Pruitt's been telling the truth. He didn't kill Adah."

"Doesn't mean he had nothing to do with it," Birdie said. "Same with Buchanan. He could have ordered somebody else to do his dirty work."

"Maybe," Jake said. "I just ... I don't know. I really think if Rascal wanted to retaliate against Rex Bardo, he'd want to be the one. He'd get sick satisfaction out of violating her the way she was."

Birdie curled her lips in disgust. "We should do society a favor and castrate him right now. So we're nowhere again."

"Not exactly," Jake said. "It just means Warren Sommers moves back up to the top of the list of suspects."

"I thought you had a warrant for his blood?" Mark asked.

"We do," Jake said. "We just can't find him. He's gone to ground."

"Came back just long enough to beat the hell out of his wife for talking to us behind his back," Birdie said.

"Can you collar him for that?" Mark asked.

"Once again, if we could find him. I've got the other daughter's statement as a witness. I'll have the prosecutor file charges before the end of the day. Try to serve it on him. But he's too smart to show up when I'm there. We're going to need to come in heavy to properly search that area. We've got drones up, but there are miles of that land that's heavily forested. Too many places to hide, even from our eyes in the sky."

"He could disappear forever," Birdie said. She tossed a wadded up napkin on the table in front of her.

"We'll keep digging through the genetics," Ramirez said. "It's a long shot. But our analyst is good. Even if she finds some distant seventh cousin, she can zone in from there."

Jake shook his head. "These people have lived up in those hills for generations. Nobody's sending in DNA mail kits they bought off the internet."

"We'll keep at it just the same. And if you get Warren's blood, we'll fast track it. Same with any other suspect you have."

Jake took a sip of his soft drink. "What about Adah's DNA?" he asked. "Was there a familial relation between her and the suspect's DNA?"

"Lord," Ramirez said. "I probably should have led with that."

He took out another piece of paper. He ran his finger down a dizzying row of numbers. "Here," he said, handing the paper to Jake.

Jake read the bottom line. "Foreign DNA was excluded from paternity. So if it was Warren, that means he isn't her father."

"And no familial match to Adah on any other level," Ramirez said. "So you can rule her brothers out. Or half-brothers. It would have hit on her mother's side if it was one of them."

"That's something, I guess," Birdie said. "Do you think we can take this to Scarlett? Tell her we know her secret? Maybe it would make her more willing to talk?"

"Or make her clam up even more," Jake said.

"This doesn't prove Rex Bardo was Adah's father," Ramirez said. "It just proves Warren Sommers isn't."

"Should we pursue Adah's paternity?" Birdie asked. "Get a court order to test her samples against whatever's in the system on Rex?"

"No judge would grant it," Jake said. "Rex isn't a suspect. Let's just say he's got an ironclad alibi."

"You just gotta get a sample from Warren Sommers," Ramirez said.

Jake rubbed his eyes. His head started to pound. Every time he felt he was getting closer to the truth, it just wafted away like smoke. Nothing solid. Nothing he could grasp.

"I'm sorry this wasn't more help," Ramirez said.

"It's the only thing about this case that I know is true," Jake said. "It'll matter. I just don't know when."

"I'll leave all this with you," Ramirez said. "Thanks for lunch. I'll have to check out that diner the next time I'm down here."

Jake rose and shook Ramirez's hand. He sat back down hard, defeated as Ramirez closed the door behind him.

"What's the next play?" Birdie asked.

"I don't know."

Jake picked up the flash drive. He put it into his laptop and pulled up the full report. It was over a hundred pages of data. He paged through it. The only other item of real interest was the blue fibers they'd found in Adah's hair. Birdie read over his shoulder.

"The car," she said. "I'm assuming they ran it through FACID."
FACID stood for Forensic Automotive Carpet Identification
Database.

"Here it is," Jake said, pulling up the relevant portion of the
report.

Birdie squinted at the screen, then rattled off the relevant
paragraph. "Carpet matched to a Dodge or Chrysler. Model years
2012 through 2018. Dark gray. Most likely a Ram truck model but
it was also used in other Chrysler models." She straightened. "I
didn't see any actual cars up that hill. Certainly nowhere on
Warren's property."

"Doesn't mean he doesn't have access to one. We can start
there," Jake said. "Pull up every single model matching those
parameters in the state and find out who it's registered to. It's a
needle in a haystack. But at least with that, we know we're
looking in the right haystack. If we don't find anything, we'll
expand."

"Let me work that angle."

Jake's phone rang. It was a county government number.

"Jake Cashen," he answered.

"Jake, it's Estelle Van Heusen. You told me to get a hold of you if
Scarlett Sommers left the hospital."

He sat up in his chair. "I told you to call me if she *tried* to leave the
hospital. Why are you speaking in past tense, Estelle?"

"Don't shoot the messenger. I can't be everywhere at once. I'm
juggling a giant caseload, Jake. I told you I would do the best I
could. I did. Psych wouldn't put her on a hold. While I was doing
another consult, she bolted."

"What do you mean bolted?"

"I mean she signed herself out AMA and her nurse told me one of her sons showed up to take her home."

"She has serious injuries. They said she needed surgery on her wrist."

"I know. Listen, I wasn't happy about it either. But there was no legal cause to restrain her, Jake. You couldn't have done anything even if you were at her bedside."

He resisted the urge to yell at her that he damn well could have. He knew from a procedural standpoint, Estelle was right. It didn't make him feel any better.

"What about her daughter?"

"She apparently went with them."

Jake's anger bubbled over. He took it out on a pen sitting on his desk. He hurled it like a dart against the far wall.

"She's not safe, Estelle. You saw what Sommers did to his wife just for talking to me for thirty seconds. Zenni took her away from home. She gave me a formal statement. If Sommers finds out ..."

"Look, I know. We can open a formal case with child protective services. I'm working on that now. But it still comes down to the same logistical problem. What happens if our people try to go out there and talk to the family? I will not put them at risk."

"Yeah, yeah, I get it," Jake admitted. "Look, I'm sorry if I sound like I'm taking this out on you."

"You're frustrated. So am I. But our hands are tied. If you have an arrest warrant for the dad, serve it. Get him into custody. Then maybe I can get someone from CPS out there to do a home visit. If they don't like what they see, they can pull her. The kid, I mean. I don't know that we can offer much help for the mother if she's unwilling to take it."

Jake swore under his breath. He just prayed the next phone call he got wasn't someone reporting Scarlett or Zenni Sommers's death.

He ended the call with Estelle and filled Birdie in on it. Though she inferred the gist of it just from listening to Jake's end of the conversation.

"I'm worried," she said. "Warren's going to want to restrict Scarlett and Zenni's movements even more now. I won't be surprised if the two of them disappear next."

"I'm not going to let that happen."

"How are you going to stop it?"

"I don't know," Jake muttered. "I don't frigging know. But I know where to start."

He got up and grabbed his jacket off its hook on the wall. "I need to talk to Rex again."

"Do you want me to go with you?"

"No," he said. "It's gotta be just me. Rex and I have an understanding."

"Jake, your understanding with Rex is what I'm worried about. You can't trust him. One of these days, that relationship is going to get you into trouble."

"I know that. All of it. But I have to do this."

Birdie didn't look happy. But she knew better than to try to stop Jake.

"You keep in contact with me," she said. "I mean it. And I don't want to hear about you going back up that hill alone because of some *understanding* you think you have with Melva Bardo, either."

Jake smiled. He knew she was serious. She was worrying too much. But it was good to know Birdie had his back.

TWENTY

When King Rex Bardo walked into the private visitation room, he looked like someone had taken a hammer to the left side of his face. They were older bruises, yellowing. Most of the swelling had gone down. A crusted, black scab cut through his bottom lip.

"You gonna tell me I should see the other guy?" Jake asked.

"Can't," Rex said. "Last I heard he was in a coma."

"Do I want to know what happened?"

"Probably not."

"Does this have something to do with our last conversation?"

Rex didn't answer. He just kept those cold blue eyes focused on him.

"Fine," Jake said. "We don't have a lot of time. It took some doing to get space to talk privately for a while."

"I hope you came with answers," Rex said.

"Some. Not ones you're going to like. DNA came back on Adah. It wasn't the old man Warren Sommers tied her to. It wasn't Rascal Buchanan. At least not directly. And she had no familial relation to whoever did this to her."

Rex pulled a cigarette out of his sleeve. Jake came prepared. He pulled out a lighter and tossed it to Rex.

"You get what I'm telling you?" Jake said. "If Warren did this, he's not her father."

"Why don't you already know that? Whether Warren did this or not."

"That's why I'm here. It's time to cut the bullshit."

Rex took a drag on his cigarette.

"Listen," Jake said. "Things are getting bad out there. Warren Sommers has gone to ground. His family is closing ranks around him. They're protecting him. He lost his temper on Scarlett a couple of days ago."

Rex put his cigarette down. "What do you mean?"

"I think you know what I mean. I went out there to serve my DNA warrant on him. He knew I was coming and made himself scarce. I caught Scarlett alone. She came out and talked to me. She wanted to know about Adah. I tried to get her to cooperate. Tell me what she knew. Help me find her husband. She wouldn't. She was too scared. But her sons saw her talking to me. They alerted Warren. So he came back and taught her a lesson."

Rex's face hardened. "Is she dead?"

"No. But he busted her up pretty good. Concussion. Broken ribs. Smashed wrist. She took a beating worse than you did."

"How do you know all this?"

"Because of her other daughter, Zenni. She's braver than the rest of them. She put Scarlett in a four-wheeler and got her up to Melva's. She got her in an ambulance and she was taken to the hospital."

"Is she okay?"

"No," Jake said. "She's not okay, Rex. None of them are okay. I tried to get her help. To listen to me. I was working on setting up a safe place for her to go. But the minute I turned my back, she bolted and took Zenni with her."

Rex snarled. "Does that surprise you?"

"Actually, yes. She tried to cover for Warren. Wouldn't admit he's the one who knocked her around. But Zenni gave a statement. She witnessed the whole thing. She knows her father is dangerous. But she's back there. Under his roof. He's gonna know what she did. That she talked to me. If he's capable of hurting Adah that way, Zenni's probably next. Or Scarlett too."

Rex shook his head. "She'll never leave him."

"Do you love her?"

A muscle jumped in Rex's jaw. He never broke his stare. "No," he said. "I cared about her. Still do. But it wasn't love."

"If you care about her, it's time for you to help me. Really help me. You made me a promise that you'd let me do my job. But you're getting in the way of it."

"How the hell am I doing that? I'm here. You're out there."

Jake felt his anger rising. "Yeah. You're here. Quit pretending you don't have just as much influence over those men out there as you ever did."

"I have nothing to do with Warren or his followers. Nothing. They're into their own shit. You think I didn't try to get Scarlett out eighteen years ago? I wasn't gonna marry her. But I was going to help her. Get her someplace safe. Her and the baby if she meant to keep it. But she wouldn't leave. Not Warren. Not her sons. She will always go back to him. She'll never learn."

"I think they call that Stockholm Syndrome. She needs help. She can't leave him. She can't make the mental break. So the only way to help her now is by holding Warren accountable for what he's done. I have two warrants on him. One for his DNA. Now an arrest warrant for domestic battery. Zenni's statement gives me probable cause. I can't serve either of them if I can't find him."

"What do you want from me?"

"I'm going back up there. I have to. I've tried to play things your way and Melva's way. To respect what you have going up there. But that ends. Today. You need to get word to those boys up there. When I come, I'm going to come heavy. Heavier than they've ever seen. I mean to go everywhere I have to to find that asshole. So you make sure to get the word out. Nobody gets in my way. And standing on the sidelines isn't enough. Your people need to help keep the peace while I go do my job. And I think you know where Warren could be hiding. You know that land."

Wrinkling his nose in disgust, Rex shook his head. "I can't help you with that. I told you. I have nothing to do with those freaks."

"Except your people were there way before his were. You've been up there for a hundred and fifty years. So you tell me where to find him. I know he's gone to the place where your people disappear. And that's a problem for you as much as it is for me. Someday you or somebody else you care about might need to go there. Except you can't. Not while Warren's people have control over it."

Rex sat back and snuffed out his cigarette. Jake knew his dilemma. Rat Warren out, and he'd reveal one of the most valuable secrets the Hilltop Boys had. And he surely wouldn't want to run the risk of Jake stumbling across any of his boys' different operations.

"Where is he, Rex?"

"I don't know."

"That's a lie. You want him out. And you can't do it yourself. Can you? So help me. Christ. Help Adah."

"Nobody can help Adah," Rex said, bitterly.

"You wanna make it so she died for nothing? Is this thing so important to you it's worth denying her justice?"

"Maybe I don't need your version of justice."

"The hell you don't. If you didn't, your people would have taken care of Warren and his followers long before this. I don't know why you haven't. I don't care. I'm not interested in causing trouble for peaceful people, Rex. And I know most of them up there just want to live their lives, raise their kids. Survive. But this is different. He's hurting kids. Those girls are being abused. Used just to breed. I can put a stop to it. But only if I know how to find Warren."

"I. Don't. Know!" Rex shouted.

"Maybe not," Jake said. "But you know where I should look. Tell me. Then let me do the rest."

"It'll never be enough," Rex said. "Those people are entrenched up there. They're armed."

"Since when have you ever been afraid of that? And it's not your neck on the line. As you pointed out. You're here. Safely removed from it."

Rex pointed to the fading bruises on his face. "This look safe to you?"

"Like you said, I should see the other guy."

Nothing. No response. "You can't handle it!" Jake shouted. "You want to sit there and pretend you're in charge. You want people to keep on fearing King Rex. But you can't deal with the war in your own backyard. I can."

Rex's face melted into a sly smile. "Don't presume to know what I can and can't handle."

"Great. So prove it. To me. Make sure my people can get in and out of there. They don't have to know it was you. You just have to point me in the right direction and have your men stand down. Clear the field for me. That's what I'm asking."

Rex went stone cold. Jake could hear his own voice echoing off the concrete walls.

"If I do that," he said. "Then you have to do something for me."

"I am doing something for you. I'm solving your problem. And I'm figuring out who killed your daughter."

"She might not be mine."

"Sure. Right. You can keep telling yourself that. But even if she wasn't, you're probably still the reason she got killed. Raped and killed."

Rex finally flinched. But he recovered quickly. "I haven't lied to you about any of this. Not once. But you have."

"What are you talking about?"

"Somebody helped her," Rex said. "Somebody gave Adah a phone. She was running to something. Wasn't she?"

How the hell did Rex know about Adah's cell phone?

"Don't hide behind your active investigation crap. You've already told me more than you're probably supposed to. You've been selective in what you've shared. So I want to know who Adah was talking to. Where was she planning to go?"

"Ask your mother," Jake said. If Rex didn't know, it meant Melva still hadn't put it together that Kyra was involved with Adah. If they did, Kyra might already be dead or missing. But neither of them could fathom it. They'd never been betrayed before by a member of their own family. Not one as close as Kyra. Rex hand-picked her to run things from the outside.

"I'm asking you. You want me to trust you? Then tell me the truth. All of it."

"Rex, I'm still trying to put all of that together," Jake said. "That's the truth." And it was. From a bird's-eye view, anyway. "But none of that matters. Right now, Warren is the only thing that matters. He killed Adah. You know it. He had the motive, the means. She defied him. Rumors were already spreading that she was your daughter. It doesn't even matter if they're true. It only matters that Warren believed it. He's the enemy. Whoever was trying to help Adah ... I believe they were truly trying to help her. So let's focus on the bad guy here. There's no doubt to either one of us who that is."

Rex squeezed his eyes shut. "I can't promise your safety."

"I'm not asking you to. I'm only asking you to make sure you don't put us in more danger. And I'm asking you to point me in the right direction. You let me handle the rest of it. Let me find Warren and fix your little problem."

Rex's eyes snapped open. His pupils went to pinpoints. It reminded Jake of those clips he'd seen of bald eagles zoning in on their prey while they readied for an aerial attack.

"We're not done," Rex said. "You and me. When this is over. You owe me the truth. All of it. For now, go back up there. You'll have the help you need. Though it might not be what you're expecting. It will get ugly up there. Not even I can stop it."

"I just need a clear shot," Jake said. "Give me a fighting chance to bring Warren out alive."

"He might not let you take him alive."

"I'm betting he will. I'm betting his need to keep his power will trump everything else. He doesn't want to be martyred."

"Maybe," Rex said. "You got something to write on?"

Jake pulled a small pad out of his pocket and handed Rex a pen. It took him a full minute. But he drew a crude map and slid the pad back to Jake.

"Keep your eyes open," he said. "And bring more men than you think you'll need."

TWENTY-ONE

For ten generations, this had been a place to hide for outlaws, both Shawnee and white men. Before that, the Clovis culture and Paleo-Indians. Rough terrain, natural forests, and over a thousand acres that remained mostly untouched going back to the Paleolithic era.

Then the Scotch and Irish settlers came. Among them, even Jake's ancestors through his grandmother's line. It was the reason Melva Bardo still considered him family in some ways.

At six a.m., Jake rolled in with two Humvees and a cargo van. Six members of the Worthington County Sheriff's SWAT team and six SWAT members from Marvell County, who had teamed up and trained together. They set up a command post in Melva Bardo's backyard. As Birdie began to strap on her tactical vest, Jake felt a flare of fear go through him. He walked up to her, pulled her aside out of earshot of the others.

Jake looked down at Birdie's well-worn beige desert combat boots. He knew it should put him at ease. She knew what she was doing.

Yet his instinct was still to keep her behind, protected, out of the fray. "I'm sure you've handled some shit in those boots," Jake said.

Birdie looked down and smirked. "A bit," she said.

"Listen," Jake said. "The two teams are going to do the entries for the target locations. We're on the outside perimeter watching their backs. If Sommers isn't there, they'll take point for the cabin in the woods. It's up to you if you want to go or hang back here at the command post." He hoped she'd jump at the offer. He knew she wouldn't. And he knew he couldn't make her.

"Are you kidding me?" Birdie said. "Other than that old jarhead Grady, I have more experience out here than both teams combined. Just stick by my side. I'll get you through this in one piece."

Jake smiled. She wasn't wrong. As much as it irritated him at times, she was mostly never wrong.

"We're set, Cashen," SWAT team Sergeant Tim Grady said as he walked up. Grady was a combat-tested Marine before joining the Sheriff Department. He single-handedly modernized the SWAT team, securing grants and getting surplus military equipment from the feds.

Grady checked his headset. Jake did the same, then tightened the straps on his Kevlar helmet. "We are working off secure tactical Channel 7. Radio check on Tac 7," Grady said. Both teams gave Grady a thumbs up.

The brilliant crimson sun peeked out over Red Sky Hill, true to its name. First light. Time to go.

"Don't do anything stupid," Birdie chided Jake.

"Like what?"

"Like try to be a hero."

He waved her off. The SWAT teams loaded up in the Humvees and cargo van. This would be the easy part. Melva put the word out they were coming. They would drive in, taking a winding, overgrown track that snaked past Warren Sommers's compound.

As they made their way, they had an audience. It seemed every resident of the hilltop came out to watch what was about to happen. Cold eyes stared at the convoy as they weaved their way through the settlements. It was probably the first time this many cars had driven back here. Or any cars at all. They were used to riding all-terrain vehicles. Several of those lined the trail, their drivers keeping a close eye on the procession.

Jake knew they were armed. All of them. He took it on faith that Rex, through Melva, had gotten through to these men that they were to stay out of any action that was to come.

"It's eerie," one of the SWAT team members piped in on the radio. It was. As they crept deeper and deeper through the woods and the valley, Jake kept thinking how easy it would be for them to mount an ambush.

The lead Humvee called out, his radio scratching through, "Thirty seconds to target, no signs of snipers or ram vehicles."

At each point, Jake found himself holding his breath. And he thought of Birdie. He wondered if any of this triggered memories she wanted to forget. She never really talked about her time in Afghanistan. She'd lost people. He knew that. Ben had told him. She'd been one of only two survivors of a convoy heading into Kandahar. They were ambushed, came under heavy fire, and the lead Humvee hit an IED.

He wanted to ask her if she was okay. But she was in the van behind him. He wouldn't bring something like that up over the radio.

Finally, they reached Warren Sommers's encampment. The houses looked empty. They had to know Jake was coming. Though Warren's little enclave segregated themselves from the other settlements closer to the hill, word would still have gotten around.

"Stop here," Jake said into his radio. He got out and walked up to Sommers's front door. Jake was able to obtain a no-knock search warrant due to the likelihood of weapons.

Grady's team flanked Jake, guns drawn. The Marvell team split off to clear the other houses.

Jake waited as they got into formation. Deputy Matt Bundy was ready with the ram. Jake felt every muscle in his body tense. Even though he knew the odds were long that anyone was still inside.

Deputy Stuckey, the point man, tried the door handle. The door swung open. It was dark inside. "Police search warrant!" Stuckey called out.

Jake waited as the team went in. The Marvell County team did the same thing at Elias and Joseph's houses on either side of their father's.

No answer. Unlocked doors. After a few agonizing minutes, the teams came out. The answer was the same. All three houses were cleared. No occupants inside.

"This guy," Jake muttered. "He knows we're coming. He knows how this is going to end."

Birdie walked back from the rear of the house. She walked up to Jake. "I'm worried Warren Sommers is planning his suicide by cop."

Jake shook his head. "I don't know why, but I feel like that won't be his style. That doesn't mean he wouldn't want to martyr one of his kids."

Jake scanned the tree line. "Where are you, Isaac?" he whispered.

"Christ," Birdie said. "You're right. If Warren knows Isaac talked to us, he'd make the perfect sacrificial offering if this thing goes sideways."

"All right," Jake said into his radio. "We're heading through the woods down to Conner Creek. Stick to the map you got. There should be a trail about a half mile east. Assume every tree has eyes."

He resisted the urge to caution them not to shoot anything unless they absolutely had no choice. He didn't need any trigger-happy mistakes. But he knew these men and women were well trained. Only they'd have to do the rest of this on foot.

The teams spread out. Team One led by Sergeant Grady would go directly to the cabin. Team Two would take a slight flanking formation toward the target to avoid any chance of friendly crossfire. Team Two would gain control of a bluff overlooking the cabin. The teams took a slow, steady pace through the woods, all while looking for ambush points, tripwires, or traps. Team Two would radio as soon as they secured the bluff overlooking the cabin.

The woods were thick. A mix of old hardwoods and a few pines that could have been at least a hundred and fifty years old. A drone would have been useless here. The forest floor was covered from above. The old hickory and oak trees would make perfect cover if shots rang out. Birdie stayed on Jake's right as the SWAT teams went ahead.

Jake's heart thundered in his chest as they slowly advanced. Jake never would have found the little log cabin without Rex telling him where to look. The trees around it were overgrown. The roof sinking inward. But it looked sturdy enough to provide shelter in a harsh winter. With enough supplies, someone could stay out here for months. Maybe longer.

Jake knew what it was. One of the hilltop secrets. But he knew there would be others. Rex had only provided a partial map. There could be places like this dotted all along the hillside and deeper into the woods. Jake had to trust Rex was right. That this was the place Warren Sommers would go.

"Team Two in position. The bluff is secure, nothing moving around the target." The radio call came from Lieutenant Haskett, from Marvell County SWAT. Jake's head jerked to the left as he heard the unmistakable sound of a pump-action shotgun racking a round. Then another, that sounded like a semi-automatic handgun chambering a round. There was no doubt now that the cabin was occupied. Through the trees, Jake could see the front door and a window about fifty yards away.

Sergeant Grady made a silent gesture to two of the men. They would carefully take positions to the east and west of the sound.

"Don't be stupid," Jake whispered to himself. "Don't make me have to light up these entire woods."

Jake took a beat to steady his nerves, then called out. "Sommers! I know you're in there. Let's take care of this the easy way, all right? There are more of us than there are of you. I don't want anyone getting hurt."

He heard laughter coming from inside the cabin.

"Warren!" Jake yelled. "I've got a warrant for your arrest. Do you understand? You're out of places to hide. This is happening. It's over."

From the corner of his eye, Jake saw the barrel of a shotgun slide by a window on the side of the cabin.

"You gotta be kidding me," Jake muttered.

"Drop your weapons and come out with your hands up," Jake said. "This doesn't have to get ugly."

As he spoke, three members of the SWAT team took crouched positions on the north side of the cabin. Just below where the shotgun barrel appeared, then disappeared back into the window.

They would give him a small amount of latitude. But when it was time to act. It would be Grady's call.

Jake nodded to him. The team sprang into action. First, they shot knee knockers into the window. Immediately after, a teargas canister went through the same, now broken window.

Jake covered his ears against the noise. Birdie was gone. She ran to the left, covering the cabin's front door.

Jake drew his weapon. They heard coughing and shouting from inside the cabin. But nobody came out. Grady's team advanced.

Jake followed Birdie. There was only one way in or out of the cabin.

Desperate shouts. There was chaos inside that cabin. Coughing, furniture knocked over, breaking glass. Then the front door burst open. Elias and Joseph Sommers staggered out.

"Let me see your hands! Walk toward me, down on the ground," Jake shouted.

Birdie took the first man into custody, Elias. She sprang into action, driving him down, pressing her knee into his back. As one of the SWAT team members covered her with his Benelli M4 , Birdie got cuffs on him.

Two other officers tackled Joseph and did the same. The team moved the two men to a secure area and searched for weapons and asked if anyone else was in the cabin. No response. Jake kept his eyes trained on that door.

Jake turned toward the cabin door. Warren Sommers walked right out on steady feet. His eyes were red and watering, snot was running out of his nose, but he stayed upright.

"Hands!" one of the officers shouted. "Get down!"

But Warren only had eyes for Jake. He smiled. Raised his hand. It was empty, but he formed his fingers into a gun and pulled an imaginary trigger. Jake slowly rose to his feet and faced Warren Sommers. From Sommers's right, two SWAT officers tackled him to the ground.

Sommers didn't cry out. Didn't flinch and never lost eye contact with Jake. He went rigid on the ground as they jerked his arms backward and slapped on cuffs.

TWENTY-TWO

Warren Sommers looked smaller somehow as he sat in a chair against the wall in interview room one. Jake left him there for almost an hour. He was angry. He couldn't come at Sommers with rage. Because Scarlett and Zenni Sommers were missing. If Sommers had killed Adah, nothing would have stopped him from exacting vengeance on the other women in his family who he believed betrayed him.

Birdie called him on his cell as he was about to walk into the room to join Sommers.

"What've you got?" Jake answered.

"Still looking," she said. "Joseph and Elias Sommers are in custody. Charged with obstructing official business and assaulting a peace officer. So far, they're keeping their mouths shut tight. But we're deeper in the valley. Ten more houses about a half a mile northwest of the Sommers's encampment. Denning and Bundy are doing a thorough search of every building on Warren's property. I'll let you know what they come up with."

"Dammit," Jake said. "Zenni and Scarlett could be anywhere."

"Melva's people are cooperating," she said. "The second you hauled Warren out of here, the whole vibe changed. People are coming out of the literal woodwork. Somebody's going to know something."

"Any sign of Isaac?"

"Not yet. I'm hoping when word gets to him his father's off the reservation, he'll come out, too."

"Good. Keep at it. But don't let your guard down. I'm not going to breathe easy until all of our people are back on the other side of the hill."

"Same," she said, then clicked off.

Jake walked into the interview room. Warren kept his back to the wall, his eyes narrowly focused on Jake.

"You've been read your rights," Jake said. He slid a single sheet of paper across the table. "Here's a written copy. If you understand it, sign it."

Warren slid the paper back, unsigned. "I understand my rights. One of which includes not signing a damn thing."

"Fine," Jake said. "Please be aware this entire interview is being recorded. So, for the record, you have the right to remain silent. Anything you say can and will be used against you in a court of law. You have the right to an attorney. If you cannot afford an attorney, one will be provided for you. Do you understand these rights as I've stated them to you?"

Sommers stayed still as granite. Jake sat in the chair across from him. It could be a long day.

"Do you know why I brought you here?"

Warren's scowl deepened. "You brought me here against my will. I do not consent to being questioned."

"I don't need your consent. I need probable cause. Which I have. You're under arrest for domestic assault. I have a witness statement. I know you beat and kicked your wife. You broke her ribs. Gave her a concussion."

"I have nothing to say about that," Warren said. "You got your facts wrong. Scarlett will tell you."

"I'd love to ask her again. So why don't you tell me where she is?"

Warren rubbed a thumb on the table but clamped his mouth shut.

"If you're so sure Scarlett will back up your story, give me a chance to interview her. Where is she?"

"I don't keep my wife from doing or saying anything she wants to. If you can't find her, then she doesn't want to be found."

"Like you? I found you easy enough. I think people are tired of you, Warren. I think your neighbors don't want to hide your sins anymore. They're not afraid of you. As we speak, I've got deputies out there taking statements from people who know you. Know what you're capable of."

"Is that supposed to bother me? Make me afraid? I've done nothing wrong."

"I think you have. In fact, I know you have."

"I think you're a bigot. I think you think you're better than me. You judge the way I live my life. Only I don't answer to you. I answer to God alone."

"Oh, but I do judge the way you live your life. When you hurt other people, then you answer to me." Jake leaned forward and got in Warren's face. He knew he needed Warren Sommers's anger. He wanted him enraged. Jake had dealt with too many of his kind. Insecure, evil men who believed they were in control. Who thrived off having power over people he thought were weaker than him.

"This isn't your show anymore," Jake said. "You have no power here. Your sons are turning on you. They're talking to my deputies. Jeremiah folded the second I put you in the back of my car. When he watched you get hauled off in handcuffs. He started to cry. Started to beg for mercy."

Warren slammed a fist on the table.

"Adah was never afraid of you, was she? Did you beat her too?"

"I never touched that girl. She was born rotten. Her soul already decayed before she came out of the womb."

"You gonna tell me you tried to save her?"

"Of course I tried to save her. For her mother's sake, if not for her own."

"By beating her down? Forcing her to abide by your wishes? And you were gonna marry her off to a man three times her age. To be raped by him?"

"There is no rape within the confines of a sanctified marriage," Warren spat.

"Sorry," Jake said. "The laws have changed a bit. Consider this your introduction to the twenty-first century."

"Whatever happened to Adah was God's will, not mine."

"Are you going to tell me you were acting as God's instrument? Yeah. I've heard that one before. I'm not interested."

Warren finally broke Jake's gaze. He stared at the wall.

"Scarlett and Zenni," Jake said. "Where are they? If you want to help yourself, let's start there."

No response.

Jake set a leather portfolio on the table. He took out a thin file and opened it in front of Warren. It contained blown-up, color photographs of Adah's body as it was found, and the snapshots he'd taken of Scarlett Sommers's battered face in the hospital. He started with Scarlett.

"Was this God's will?" Jake asked, thrusting a close-up of Scarlett at him, her eye swollen shut. "She's what, five foot two? You outweigh her by easily a hundred pounds. Wasn't really a fair fight, was it?"

Warren shoved the picture back at Jake. Undeterred, he pulled out one of the worst of Adah as she lay staring skyward, her neck grotesquely bruised.

"Did God want this for Adah?" Jake asked. "It wasn't God's hands that wrapped around her neck and choked the life out of her. Those were yours, weren't they?"

Warren's eyes flicked to the photo. He showed no emotion.

"She was raped," Jake said. "I'm pretty sure incest is against God's will, too. Was this you trying to save her soul, Warren? Last I checked, lust was a deadly sin. So is murder. Who's going to save your soul? Because there's only one place rapists and murderers go. There's no salvation for you. I mean ... since you're only concerned about God's judgment."

Pure hatred distorted Warren Sommers's face. He slapped a hand on the picture of Adah then crumpled it up and threw it at Jake. Jake dodged at the last second and the paper ball fell harmlessly to the ground.

"Tell me where Scarlett and Zenni are," Jake said. "If you're worried about your own soul at all, that might be a good first step."

"I owe you nothing. My soul isn't in jeopardy."

"See, that's where you lose me," Jake said. "Guys like you. You like to spout your platitudes about how only God can judge you. Then you say crap like that. How do you know your soul's not in jeopardy? I mean ... that kind of means you think you have divine powers. That you presume you know what God thinks about you. To me, if I was God, I don't think that'd help your case."

"I have nothing else to say to you."

"That's fine," Jake said. "I've got plenty more to say to you. Another thing about guys like you. You like to prey on people you think are weaker than you. Women. Children. Does that make you feel powerful? Godlike? Doing this kind of thing to them. Making them cry. Bleed. Beg you to stop."

No response. But Warren started to sweat. His breathing got heavier. His nostrils flared.

"Is that what Adah did? She ran for her life. I know that. I'm sure she screamed. Begged you ... her father ... not to hurt her. She probably prayed, too. Did you kill her while she was praying?"

No response. Just tightly clenched fists.

"Ah," Jake said. "You want to take a swing at me?"

Jake opened the door to the observation room next door. Sheriff Landry and Lieutenant Beverly sat against the wall, out of view of Warren. Jake unclipped his gun from its holster and set it on the table. Landry silently mouthed, "Watch it." Jake winked at her, shut the door, then faced Warren.

"Go ahead," Jake said. "Take your best shot. It's just us here."

Warren rose to his feet. His face had gone purple with rage. Jake could almost taste his fury as if it thickened the air they breathed.

He took a step toward Jake.

"Tell me where they are, Warren? Tell me what you did to Adah?"

"You can go to hell."

"I suppose I'll meet you there," Jake said. "I've talked to the prosecutor. If you're convicted, they'll seek the death penalty. I won't make you any promises, but the best way you can help yourself now is by telling me what happened. Tell me where I can find your wife and other daughter."

Jake's cell phone rang. It was Landry. He let it go for a second, but it kept on ringing. Keeping his eyes on Sommers, he picked it up.

"Yeah?"

"You should know," she said. "Deputy Wayne just called. They've found the wife and daughter. They're safe. The other brother, Isaac. He'd taken them to another remote cabin. They were hiding out. But in the process of looking, the team found nine other minor children who appeared to be abused or neglected. They're securing the scene so CPS can come in and take them into protective custody."

"Got it," Jake said. "Thanks."

Warren took a step back. Though he couldn't have heard Landry through the phone, some of the rage seemed to have left him. He sat back down.

"It's over, Warren," Jake said. "That was my boss. Ten kids, including your daughter, are being taken out of there. You'll never get them back. You'll never get any of it back."

Warren Sommers's entire body began to quake. "You can't do that."

"I actually can. As soon as we sort out who hurt those kids, there will be more arrests. There's nobody left for you to try to control. You're going to prison whether you cooperate with me or not."

"You have nothing," Warren said. "Nothing but threats."

Jake went to the doorway leading to the hall and opened it. "Deputy Chaplin? I'm ready for you now."

A moment later, Deputies Amanda Chaplin and Jordy Holtz walked in carrying a collection kit.

"You're going to let this woman swab your cheek. I've got a court order allowing it. Which means we're taking those samples with or without your cooperation. I'll strap you down if I have to. If you really believe you've done nothing wrong, then this shouldn't matter to you."

Warren stayed rigid. When Chaplin and Holtz approached, he didn't move.

"I need you to open your mouth," Chaplin said, ready with the swab.

Warren glared at Jake, but seemed to know he had no other cards to play. He opened his mouth.

"We've got this," Chaplin told Jake.

"See you later, Warren," Jake said. "You get to stay with us for a while."

He turned his back on Warren Sommers and walked away.

TWENTY-THREE

Four days later, Judge Cardwell set a bail too high for Warren Sommers to come up with. Sommers represented himself at his arraignment on the domestic assault charge. It was still an open question whether the prosecutor would take that case to trial. On a first offense, it would normally be pled out. Odds were, not much would come of it. But it would buy Jake the time he needed to get the DNA results back. When Jake left the office that Friday afternoon, he at least felt like he'd finally made real progress in solving Adah Lee's murder.

By Sunday afternoon, he looked forward to a normal family dinner where he could pretend like anyone named Sommers or Bardo didn't exist.

As he put on clean clothes and got ready to head up to the big house where Grandpa Max lived, someone knocked on his front door. He looked out the window, puzzled, then swung the door open. Travis Wayne stood there wearing his varsity jacket, some new patches having been sewn on.

"Looks nice," Jake said, tapping the state champion letter on the left breast. "Took you long enough to get it."

"I didn't have anybody to sew it on." It caused an unexpected twist of Jake's heart. It was a thing he and Travis had in common. They were both orphans by the time they graduated from high school.

"What's up?"

Travis looked toward the hill. "Gemma invited Aunt Erica and me to come up for Sunday dinner. I think she knows what's up?"

"Who? Gemma or Erica?"

"Gemma at least. Did you tell her about my West Point admission?"

"I didn't tell anybody," Jake said. "You asked me not to. But maybe this will be a good opportunity for you to do it. You can't keep her in the dark forever. And her reaction might surprise you. She'll be worried. But she'll also be proud, Trav. She's allowed to feel both."

"I know." Travis looked down at his feet, shuffling them. "I think I'd still like it if you were there. She trusts your opinion. She likes that you're still around for me."

Jake smiled and put a hand on Travis's shoulder. "I'll always be around. You never have to worry about that. So let's go. Grandpa Max makes chili every third Sunday. It's about the only thing he can still manage with his eyes as bad as they are."

It was warm enough to walk, but it had rained the night before. The trail up the hill was nothing but mud. Jake had Travis climb into his truck and drove them on up.

Birdie's car was already there. "I told her to drop me off at your place," Travis explained. "Told her I wanted to talk to you about something."

Jake put the car in park. Poor Travis had no clue. Birdie could practically read the kid's mind by now. Teenage boys weren't that big a mystery. Though she'd never said a word to him, Jake could guess that Birdie already knew what he was up to. This could be an interesting dinner.

"Come on," Jake said. "I'm telling you. It's not going to be as bad as you think."

When they walked in the front door, he could hear Gemma yelling her usual threats to Grandpa not to burn the damn kitchen down. He responded with his usual belligerence.

"Don't tell me how to run my own kitchen! I've been doing it since before you were even a gleam in your daddy's eye. And you sure didn't get your cooking skills from your mother. The only meal she knew how to prepare involved a takeout menu."

"Stubborn old mule," Gemma muttered.

"Screeching old crow!" Grandpa yelled back.

It could go on like that for a while. Jake sent Travis into the den where he knew his young nephew Aidan would be. Travis made it two steps before shouting in delight.

"What the hell!"

Jake's other nephew, Ryan, walked out into the living room. Jake shared Travis's surprise. Ryan was a sophomore at Putnam College. He wasn't supposed to be home for break until later in the week.

"Surprise!" Ryan said.

Jake went to him and pulled Ryan into a hug. "You're looking good." He was. Each time he saw Ryan, he looked more and more like a grown man. He'd gained some weight. Bulked up with muscle in a way he never could while cutting weight. Now, he wrestled more at his natural weight. And he was solid as a tank.

"When did you get in?" Travis asked. He and Ryan embraced with a slap on the back and their own handshake.

"Early this morning," Ryan said. "Couple of my profs canceled classes for Monday and Tuesday. I think they wanted to start their own break early, too."

Travis and Ryan disappeared into the den. Their laughter filled the house. Jake went into the kitchen to see if he could defuse any bombs about to go off.

Gemma stood at the butcher block island, slicing homemade bread. He kissed his sister on the cheek. Her nose was covered in flour. Her dark hair piled high on her head but for a few wayward wisps around her face.

"Did you know he was coming?" Jake asked. He reached for a slice of bread and got his hand slapped away.

"No," she said. "Little shit just woke me out of a dead sleep, all smiles and smelling like a locker room."

Her words were harsh, but Jake detected a twinkle in Gemma's eyes. Good for Ryan, he thought.

Birdie sat at the table, rolling silverware into napkins and sliding them to each chair. He sat across from her and helped.

"Hey, Gramps," Jake said. "Smells amazing, as always."

The old man grumbled his thanks. But there was no talking to him when the man was seasoning his chili. He was of a singular focus. Anyone who tried to interfere would end up with a ladle-shaped welt on the side of their heads.

"Glad you're here," Jake said. "I think we both need a break from the hilltop."

"I wanted to tell you," Birdie said. "I got a call from Estelle Van Heusen. She was able to get Scarlett and Zenni into Jenny's House. They'll be able to stay there at least until Warren's domestic case gets resolved. And she's working with a pro bono lawyer to get a protection order in place so he can't come near them."

"What about the others?" he asked.

"Estelle said five more came down from the hill. Two women and three boys under the age of six. And they're starting to talk. No matter what else happens, Boyd Ansel thinks we might be able to charge Sommers with trafficking."

Gemma wielded a kitchen towel with the speed and precision of a bullwhip, catching Jake on the shoulder.

"Ow!" he protested.

"You know the rules. No talking about work. Either of you."

"Since when?" Jake said, grabbing a piece of bread as Gemma set down the plate. She scowled at him, but didn't abuse him any further.

"Since I said so," Gemma said, but she had a smirk on her face. "It's too good a day. We're all here. Birdie and Travis too. The sun's coming out. Grandpa's in a good mood."

Birdie caught Jake's eye. He read the question in her expression. How could you tell?

"Soup's on!" Max called out. Jake got up and intercepted the chili pot before his grandfather tried to walk the thing to the table.

Two seconds later, the boys stampeded into the kitchen, their heavy footfalls sounding like thunder. Aidan tried to pull out his chair.

"Animals!" both Grandpa and Gemma called out in unison.

"Wash your hands," Gemma said. The boys lumbered over to the sink and did as they were told.

Jake smiled. Though she'd brain him if he said it out loud. With age, Gemma was getting more and more like Max.

With all manners attended to, Gemma started scooping chili into the bowls and passing them out. Ryan reached forward and grabbed the serving dish in the middle of the table. Gramps had shredded some cheddar cheese. Ryan sprinkled some over his chili.

The table grew silent as the boys' hunger won out over their chatter. Jake found himself starving, too.

"This is delicious," Birdie said. "Max, you're going to have to give me your recipe."

Jake caught Gemma's eye. It was the third rail of Max's kitchen. Nobody would get his chili recipe until the day they put him in the ground.

Grandpa grumbled instead of answering. Birdie laughed to herself. She was in on the joke.

The conversation turned to normal things. Jake told Grandpa he'd work on mending his fence on the north end of the property. The thing was in perpetual need of repair.

"Have the little squirt help you this year," Grandpa said, pointing his spoon at Aidan.

"He's looking forward to it," Gemma teased.

"When's your spring break start, little man?" Jake asked his nephew.

"Day after Easter," Aidan said with a mouthful of chili.

"Perfect," Jake said. "Have your mother drop you off at my place by eight. Wear the grubbiest clothes you have. Jeans. No sweat pants. Long sleeves. And your boots. Not the shoes you wear to school."

Travis asked Ryan about his team at Putnam College. They were young. Developing. But Ryan was emerging as a leader.

Finally, as Travis scraped the last bit of chili from his bowl, he cast a glance at Jake. Jake gave him a silent nod. Now or never.

"Aunt Erica," Travis said. "Since we're all here, there's something I've been meaning to tell you. I ... don't freak out. I know what I'm doing."

Erica set her spoon down. She flicked her gaze toward Jake. He folded his hands in his lap and turned his attention to Travis.

Travis stood up and pulled his crumpled acceptance letter out of his pocket and handed it to Birdie. Jake felt a flutter of vicarious nerves for the kid. He hoped he was right about her reaction.

She read the letter, her face betraying nothing. Then she let out a breath and set the paper on the table, smoothing it out.

"What's he on about?" Grandpa asked.

Jake cleared his throat. No sense in pretending he was in the dark. If Birdie was mad, maybe he could draw her fire first.

"Travis got into West Point," Jake said. "Fall enrollment."

Grandpa sat straighter in his chair. "Well, that's a thing, isn't it?"

Birdie slowly closed her eyes and took a few meditative breaths. Then she looked at Travis.

"Are you sure this is what you want?"

"I'm sure," Travis answered. By the silence at the rest of the table, Jake guessed Ryan already knew Travis's plans. Same with Gemma. She sat next to Birdie and put a hand over hers.

Birdie teared up. She wiped her face with a napkin. "You're a young man, now. I don't know how it happened. But your dad would be proud of you. Your mother would be a nervous wreck. But she'd be proud, too. You've worked pretty hard."

"Yeah," Travis said. "But ... are you?"

Birdie let out an uncharacteristic sob. Jake felt like he had a tennis ball in his throat. She got up from her chair, tossed her napkin on the table, and came around to Travis. She grabbed him in a hug.

"Of course I'm proud. And terrified. But I love you. If this is what you want."

Gemma got up from the table and started clearing plates. It was too late though. She couldn't hide her own tears. Jake slapped Ryan on the shoulder. Then the two of them got up and carried the rest of the dirty dishes into the kitchen.

"I take it you knew," Jake whispered to his sister.

"Ryan told me," she said. "Jake, should we do something? Try to talk him out of it?"

Jake leaned in and kissed Gemma's cheek again. "We absolutely should not. We support him. And we sit in the front row clapping and cheering our faces off when he graduates."

"Okay. Yeah. You're right. But ... ugh. How did these babies get so big so fast?"

Later, after Gemma served rice pudding for dessert, Jake found Birdie on the covered back porch. It looked out over a small ravine. It had started to drizzle again.

"My grandmother had him build this back here," Jake said. "She liked to watch the deer grazing."

"I remember," Birdie said. "She brought me out here a few times. Had me help her fill her hummingbird feeders."

It struck him sometimes how long their families had been intertwined. He'd forgotten Grandma Ava had babysat Birdie sometimes when she couldn't have been more than three or four. She'd find her things to do while Jake and Ben, a couple of seven-year-olds, kept themselves out of trouble and out of her hair in the woods.

"You okay?" Jake asked.

"Nope. Not even a little. But I will be."

He looked at her. He never thought about it much, but the way the light hit her, she looked strikingly like her own mother. Judith Wayne had become something of a surrogate mother to him after he'd lost his own. She was pretty. Always tan. Liked to wear her hair in ponytails tied with colorful scarves.

"You already knew, didn't you?" Jake said.

Birdie gave him a secretive smile. "Yeah. A few months ago. I went into his room to empty his garbage. He had the application pulled up on his laptop, already filled out. I figured if he wanted me to know, he'd tell me."

"You've been good for him," Jake said. "I know you didn't sign up for this. Raising a teenage boy all by yourself. You mean everything to him. You know that, right? I think if you asked him not to go, he'd withdraw."

She turned to him. "But I'd never ask him that. I couldn't. It's gonna rip me apart, but I know it's what he wants. And I think he'll make a good officer. I just wish I could protect him from the hard parts."

"The hard parts will be what makes him good."

"Yeah. I suppose so. I'm glad he told you. I'm glad he looks up to you and knows you're there."

Then she came to him. Birdie was always so tough. So capable. But for a few minutes on Grandma Ava's porch, she cried into Jake's chest as he held her.

TWENTY-FOUR

Opened in 1987, Jenny's House had helped hundreds of women and children escape abusive homes, giving them shelter and a safe place to stay while they recovered and got back on their feet. It was named after Jenny Gerard. A young woman who was murdered by her husband after decades of abuse in 1981. Her sister and parents founded it, purchasing a 4,000 square foot Victorian farmhouse in a remote area in Navan Township. You couldn't see it from the road. It didn't show up on any maps. Had no internet presence. It operated through word of mouth from social workers and other health care workers trying to save whom they could.

Not even Jake was permitted to enter the premises. But he communicated with Mariah McDonal, the current director of the home. So when Isaac Sommers reached out to Jake, asking for information about his mother and sister, Jake could only agree to meet him at a truck stop not far from Red Sky Hill.

It was only when Jake walked in that he realized this was the place Kyra Bardo had told Adah to run to. Maybe it was fitting that Isaac came here now, too. He seemed even smaller, skinnier, grubbier as he walked through the door, looking nervously for Jake. His shoulders sagged with relief when he saw Jake wave to him from the back of the diner in a booth against the wall.

At two o'clock, the place was mostly deserted save for a couple of truckers getting coffee refills at the counter.

"Thanks for coming," Jake said as Isaac sat down. "Did you have trouble finding the place?"

"Not really," Isaac said. "I have ... I've been staying with a friend who lives just down the road."

"So you're out," Jake said. "You're not going back?"

When the server came, Isaac ordered a water and a BLT and fries at Jake's insistence. The boy downed the water like he'd been walking in the desert for a week. The server came back and Jake asked her to just leave the pitcher.

"What's your plan, Isaac?"

"I don't think I can go back. My brothers are mad at me."

"Joseph and Elias are still in custody. Joseph tried to assault an officer. Elias resisted arrest. They'll be out in a day or two, I'm sure. But they aren't in a position to give you trouble at the moment."

"They know I talked to you. They blame me for Warren being where he is."

"Warren beat the crap out of your mother. He's going to be charged for that. He may have to spend a few months in jail. And he'll have to submit to home visits by a social worker. There've been several more arrests up and down the valley. A lot of kids were pulled out of there based on the shape they were in."

"That's what I wanted to talk to you about. I mean ... it's one of the things. There's been a lot of rumors. Lies and rumors. But there's one girl. Her name is Rachel Clayton."

Isaac pulled out a small, creased color photograph of a pretty girl with red hair and freckles. She looked to be about sixteen or seventeen, though it was hard to tell. She was skinny like Isaac. Her eyes held that haunted look that could make her seem older than she probably was.

"Nobody's seen her since the raid," Isaac said. "I think she may be one of the girls your people took out. Her dad was sometimes worse than mine. But she never gave hers any trouble. She's a good person. She stays out of trouble. And I was hoping you could tell me where she is."

Jake didn't have all the names of the whisper kids taken into custody from the hill committed to memory. But it was certainly plausible she was one of the ones saved, especially if she looked like she'd been abused.

"I'm assuming she's a minor?" Jake asked.

"She's seventeen. Same age as Adah was the day she died."

"Was she a friend of Adah's? Do you think she'd know anything about what happened to her?"

"I don't think so. And no. Rachel stayed away from Adah. I told you. She never caused trouble."

"Is she your girlfriend, Isaac?"

The server brought Isaac's food. He wolfed down his fries and gulped another full glass of water.

"Rachel," Jake prodded him. "Is she your girlfriend?"

"She ... we're ... she was promised to Luke Redfield. He's old though. More than sixty, I think. He's got a wife but she's old too. She never gave him kids. So ..."

"So Rachel's supposed to fix that," Jake said, not hiding the disgust from his voice.

"Can you just tell me if she's okay? If you know where she is? She's one of the reasons I was hiding out in the woods that first night you came. If my father and Rachel's father knew we were seeing each other, it could have been bad for her."

"Isaac, I think it's time for you to tell me exactly what you know about what happened to your sister. Did you ever hear your father threatening to do her harm?"

Isaac slumped down in his seat. He pushed his plate away.

"Isaac," Jake snapped. "Your dad can't hurt you anymore. Neither can Rachel's dad." He took out his phone and pulled up the names of the men who'd been arrested during the raid. Sure enough, Harlan Clayton was on the top of the list alphabetically. He was currently sitting in the Worthington County Jail, awaiting his own arraignment on domestic battery and child endangerment charges.

"Harlan's in custody," Jake said, turning his phone so Isaac could see Clayton's mugshot. "Child Protective Services will probably place his minor children in foster care. Do they have a mother up there somewhere?"

"No," Isaac said. "She died from cancer a few years ago. Harlan was ... I don't know for sure ... but the rumor was he was going to marry Zenni in a couple of years."

"Zenni? Your sister's fifteen years old, Isaac!"

"I know. I know. I don't want that for her. My mom didn't want that for her. Neither did Adah. She told me that. She said she was never going to let Warren hurt Zenni. She was going to figure out a way to get her out, too. She asked me to go with her. I just couldn't. I had my reasons to stay."

"Rachel," Jake said. "You didn't want to leave her behind?"

"No," Isaac said, his voice barely more than a whisper. "So that's why I need to know. Where is she? Can I see her? Talk to her?"

"I'm sorry," Jake said. "Rachel's still a minor in the eyes of the law. I can't disclose where she was taken. But I can tell you she's safe. She's being taken care of. I don't know what's going to happen. If she has no mother, no other relatives that could take her in ..."

"I could take her in," Isaac said. "I'm going to be twenty in two months. I can get a job. Find someplace to live. I'm not going back there. I can't. Not now."

"That's good, Isaac. And if I can help you in any way, I will. That's a promise. But I also need you to do something for me. I believe your father killed your sister. Is that what you believe as well?"

Isaac covered his eyes with his hand. He looked like he was holding back tears. Then he sat straighter, clenched his jaw, and looked Jake in the eyes.

"I think so. I think Warren knew what Adah was planning to do. I don't know if he overheard her talking, or if Adah flat out told him. But yeah. I know what Warren can do. I've seen it. He's hurt my mom so many times. I tried to stop it. I swear. I tried to protect her."

"I think you did all you could," Jake said. "And you're a kid, Isaac. I don't care that you're almost twenty. You're just a kid yourself. I'm going to need you though. Did you ever see Warren hurt Adah? Did he ever hit her?"

"He ... he used a belt on her sometimes. All of us. He locked her in her room. A few times, he wouldn't let her eat as punishment for raising her voice to him. For being disobedient. I'd sneak food to her through the window. Zenni would too."

"Did you ever hear him threaten to kill her?"

"I don't know. I don't know if he said kill. But he was always saying a day would come when she'd have to pay for her sins. That she'd be judged. Then he'd hurt her again."

"There may be a trial, Isaac. In court. I'll need you to say these things in front of a jury. Do you think you can do that? Do you think you can write down the things you just told me? You said you wanted to help Adah. This is the way. The only way left."

Though his face held no expression, Isaac nodded. "I'm not going back. I think my brothers will end up staying there. Do you think Warren will ever come back?"

"I don't know. Not if I can help it. If we can prove he killed your sister, then no. And if he's convicted, he may get the death penalty. She was hurt very badly, Isaac. For a long time. I'd like to tell you she went peacefully and suffered no pain. But I don't believe that."

"Neither do I," Isaac said.

"It's never going to be the same up there. That I can promise."

"Can you at least give Rachel a message from me?" Isaac said, his eyes wide and hopeful. He pulled a folded envelope out of his pocket. It was sealed but the envelope was thin enough Jake could see dense handwriting on notebook paper inside of it.

"I can do that," Jake said. "If she wants to get in touch with you, she can do that. Your friend. Is there a phone number she can call to get in touch with you? That I can?"

Jake pulled a pen from his pocket. Isaac took it and scribbled a phone number and address down on a napkin.

"You can walk there from here," Isaac said. "I don't know how long I'll stay there. Just until I can make enough money to get a place of my own."

"I might be able to help you with that, too. I think I know a few people who could use somebody who's good with his hands. Who doesn't mind a long, hard day of work."

"I can fix things," Isaac said. "Build stuff. I'm good at it. I built a couple of the cabins with my brother."

"I'm sure there are plenty of construction jobs around here that pay pretty well. You could learn a trade. Build a life for yourself if you're willing to put in the work."

Isaac nodded eagerly.

"Good," Jake said. "Be available. Don't run off without telling me where I can find you."

Jake took out a business card, wrote his cell number on the back, and handed it to Isaac.

"What about the girls?" Jake asked. "Your mother and Zenni. I'm afraid I can't tell you where they are either. Not yet. But if you'd like me to get a message to them too, I can. Do you think your mother might know more about how Warren planned to hurt Adah?"

"I don't know. I doubt she'd ever say. My guess is the first chance she has to go back to him. She'll do it. He's in her head. She does whatever he says. Adah hated it. I guess so do I."

"Okay. Well, I think it'll bring her some comfort to know that you're okay."

"I can take care of Zenni too," the boy said. "Just give me a little time to save some money. She can stay with me. They'll let her, won't they? If Warren goes to jail. If my mom says it's okay. And I think she will. I think she thinks Zenni is probably a lost cause, too."

"Maybe," Jake said. "It'll help if you have a steady job and your own apartment. So make that your priority."

Isaac rose. He seemed determined. He gave Jake's hand a respectably solid handshake. As he walked back out of the truck stop, Jake had a feeling the kid might just make it. If it was within his power to help ensure it, he would.

Jake made his way back to his car. With a few more hours left in his shift, he had to sift through the statements the women and children from the hill gave. There weren't many. Most of them were reluctant to talk. Still terrified. Still suffering the effects of long-term abuse.

When Jake walked into his office, Birdie nearly ran into him, coming out the other way. She grabbed his shoulders. "I was just about to hunt you down," she said. "Get in here."

Puzzled, Jake brushed past her. Mark Ramirez was sitting perched at the edge of Jake's desk, his expression grim.

"What do you have?" Jake asked. It could only be one thing. The DNA.

"Sit down," Ramirez said. "This won't take too long."

Ramirez already had papers spread out on the table at the back of the room. Jake saw Ramirez's familiar colored pie charts.

"Labs are back," he said.

Jake felt his heart skip a couple of beats. He sat in his desk chair and swiveled it toward the table. Ramirez grabbed a paper off the top of the stack.

"We ran your suspect," Ramirez started. "Warren Sommers."

"And?" Jake said, impatiently.

"I'm sorry, Jake. There's no match. It wasn't Sommers's DNA on Adah Lee."

He heard the words. Understood the words. But it took a couple of seconds for him to process the words. Not Warren's DNA.

"Not the blood, the semen, or the skin under her nails," Ramirez continued. "All three of those samples came from one man. We know that. But it wasn't Warren Sommers."

Birdie sank into her own chair, looking as shocked as Jake felt.

"What about the family?" Jake asked. "Were you at least able to tell if it was a familial match? One of his other sons, maybe."

"No," Ramirez said. "I told you last time. Adah wasn't related to the person whose DNA was on her. And neither was Warren Sommers. It's somebody else."

Jake felt like a trap door had opened beneath him, leading to a bottomless, dark pit. Nothingness. No answers. No leads.

If Warren Sommers was innocent, then Jake was back to square one.

Twenty-Five

"You slept here again last night, didn't you?"

For a second, Jake thought he was dreaming. The light from his office window stabbed through, burning his eyes. But the voice he heard didn't match who he thought it was.

"Gemma?" he croaked.

His sister stood in his office doorway, one hand on her hip, the other holding a paper bag and a large Styrofoam cup of steaming coffee.

Rolling her eyes, she barged into the room and set the food and coffee on the table. She set out what looked like a wrapped bagel and a fruit cup.

"Eat," she said. "I came to your place this morning. When you weren't there, I figured this was the next most likely place. You can't keep doing this."

Jake wiped the crust from his eyes. His shirt and tie were crumpled. He felt stubble along his jawline. But the food smelled too good to turn down.

"Thanks," he said. She had a way of making him feel like a seven-year-old. In a lot of ways, she'd kind of raised him from that age forward.

"Can you make me a promise?" she asked.

"Depends," Jake said, past a mouthful of food. The egg and cheese bagel was delicious. Homemade from Hole Lotta Love, a new breakfast place near Gemma's house.

"Come by the bar tonight. I've got shrimp baskets on special. You always like those. I want to see more of you. Gramps does too. I don't like those shadows under your eyes. I don't like how you get when you're working a case like this."

Jake put the bagel down. "Gem, there hasn't been a case like this. And you know I can't talk about it with you."

"You don't have to. You always take the ones involving kids the hardest. Why wouldn't you? Anyone would. Can you at least tell me if you're anywhere close to wrapping this one up?"

He felt the heavy weight of Adah's murder settle over his shoulders again. "I thought I was. But no. Not really."

"Good morning!" Birdie walked in carrying two cups of coffee and another brown paper bag filled with something that smelled heavenly. Seeing what his sister put in front of him, Birdie laughed.

"Great minds think alike, I guess." Birdie pulled out fresh donuts, also from Hole Lotta Love.

"I'll leave you two to it," Gemma said. She went to Jake and hugged him. "I mean it, though. You have to eat. Come by the bar. I'll save your booth for you. At least let me make sure you've got good food in you today. You think better on a full stomach."

She put a hand on Birdie's arm as she passed her to walk out the door. "You too, Birdie," she said. "You look too skinny."

Birdie waited until Gemma had disappeared down the hall. Then she turned to Jake and wrinkled her nose. "You stink."

He lifted an arm and sniffed under it. She had a point.

"Did you get anywhere last night?" she asked.

"Not really. I was so damn sure this was Warren."

"Me too. He had the motive and opportunity. And it's not like he hasn't acted guilty from the beginning. He hasn't made his hatred of Adah a secret."

"If it wasn't him, I'm still thinking it had to be someone from his little enclave."

"Who?" Birdie said, taking a seat on the opposite side of the table. "It wasn't any of her brothers. We know that based on the DNA. The only other person who seemed likely was Rance Pruitt. DNA ruled him out, too."

"It could have been someone acting on Warren's behalf."

"Again. Who? From what we've seen, his own sons were the closest to him. Nobody else comes close."

"I feel like I'm just banging my head against the wall."

"Me too," Birdie agreed. "So now what?"

"Now that we've broken up a few of those families, maybe enough time has passed so that some of the wives might be willing to talk to us more. Warren's not a threat right now. With any luck, he never will be again."

"Come on," Birdie said. "We'll be lucky if he does ninety days for domestic assault. Bastard that he is, his record was still clean up until now."

"Only because he's avoided law enforcement his whole life. And I'm working with Boyd Ansel. If we can get some of the others to make a statement against him, we can charge him with child endangerment. Maybe even human trafficking."

"What a mess." Birdie sighed. "It won't be easy. Some of those women seemed brainwashed to me. It's going to take a lot of time to break through all of that."

"Can you start?" Jake asked. He went to his desk and pulled out a clean shirt and tie. There was a mirror on the wall near the door. He finger combed his hair. He could wash up in the bathroom across the hall. He kept travel toiletries in a bag under his desk for this very reason.

"Where are you headed?"

Jake turned to her. "I need to talk to Kyra Bardo again. Maybe if she realizes Warren's innocent of this, she might be more willing to cooperate."

Birdie looked skeptical. "I don't trust her, Jake. You shouldn't either."

"I don't."

"I mean it. That woman is like a black widow spider. And she turns your head."

Jake whipped around. "What?"

"She knows it."

Jake turned back to the mirror and tied his fresh tie into a Windsor knot. He needed a shave, but this would have to do. He didn't want to waste any more daylight.

"You're seeing things," he told Birdie.

"I know. That's my point."

"Birdie, I've got to convince Kyra that her best bet is to help me. Her family will turn on her when they find out about her involvement with Adah. I don't know how she kept it under wraps until now. She might know something. I need to know everybody she told about this plan of hers. I need to know every conversation she had with Adah."

"I don't disagree. I just don't see how today will be any different. Alex Corvell isn't going to let you near her."

"You're right about one thing. Kyra and I ... there's some kind of connection. It's not the kind you think. It's more her knowing that I have a relationship with Rex."

"Which will backfire someday," Birdie snapped.

Jake didn't want to argue with her. She sensed it. She put her hands up in surrender.

"Will you follow up with some of the families we pulled out of there? See if anyone might have talked to Adah in depth. If they saw her with anyone they didn't recognize. If she might have told them what she was planning or if there's anyone else over that hill who might have wanted to do her harm."

"I can do that," Birdie said. "I'll see you in a few hours." She still had a scowl on her face when she walked out.

B y the time Jake got to Kyra's trailer at Bardo Excavating, Alex Corvell's BMW was already parked out front. Jake had no choice but to message Kyra he was stopping by. She called her bulldog right away. He hoped what he'd told Birdie turned out to be true. That she'd be more willing to cooperate now that Warren Sommers was off the hook.

Jake didn't knock. He didn't have to. Corvell swung the door open and made a sweeping gesture with his arm, inviting him in.

"Corvell," Jake grumbled.

"Detective Cashen," he responded. "Hope you're having a fine morning. Though I'm afraid to tell you you made this trip for nothing. My client has nothing to add to your previous conversations."

Kyra sat behind her desk. She looked far less cocky than the last time he saw her. She wore a black suit with a jacket a size too tight. She had the top button open, revealing a tight black bodice underneath that barely covered anything. Jake darted his eyes away.

"What do you want?" Kyra asked.

"I'll make this quick. Just an update. Warren Sommers didn't kill Adah Lee. We know for sure."

Corvell stood with his arms crossed, looming next to Jake. Kyra's eyes flicked to her lawyer. When she looked back at Jake, he could swear some of the color drained from her face.

"Did you hear what I said? Sommers is innocent. He didn't kill his daughter. None of the DNA found on the victim matched his."

"Why are you telling me this?" Kyra asked.

"You know why."

"This is impossible. Your tests had to have been wrong," Kyra said. She rose from her desk.

"They're not. It doesn't work like that. Warren didn't do this. Someone else did. It wasn't her brothers. It wasn't the creep Warren wanted to marry her to. It doesn't look like it was anyone who lived on the other side of the hill, Kyra. I don't think she was followed that night. I think she was picked up by someone who knew where she was going to be and when. So that's why I'm here. You knew when and where she was headed."

"I don't have anything to add," Kyra said.

"And you don't have to answer another question," Corvell said. "Thanks for the update, Detective. But we're done here. Unless you plan on charging my client with something, there's nothing more to say."

"You sure about that, Kyra?"

"And you'll address all further questions to me, Detective."

Jake ignored him. "Fine. No more questions. Just listen. Kyra, Warren's innocent. There's no mistake. So whatever happened to that girl, I believe it happened because of you. Because of what you ordered that girl to do. I can't stop that from getting out. Not anymore. Rex will know. And there's something else. I told you Warren's DNA wasn't found on her. But it's more than that. Warren's DNA wasn't a match for being Adah's father, either. They weren't related. He's not her father. You know what that means."

She went pale. She cast a nervous glance toward Corvell. It made Jake wonder whether Corvell knew Adah could be Rex's before he agreed to defend her. Certainly, he knew now. The rumors were all over the internet. Landry's office had been hammered with questions about it ever since their press conference. Corvell worked for the Bardos. If Kyra had kept that little detail from him before he got entangled with her, she was playing an even more dangerous game than Jake realized.

"Nothing worked out how you wanted it to," Jake said. "But you can help me now. What do you think's going to happen when other people find out you were the last one to talk to Adah?"

"Enough," Corvell shouted. "You can leave now, Detective."

"You think he's helping you?" Jake addressed Kyra, but pointed at Corvell. "You think this jackhole has your best interests at heart? As soon as the family finds out your involvement, the money's going to dry up. The only reason he's even here is because he thought you were the up-and-comer. That's over. You'll be out. The family will close ranks against you. How fast do you think it'll be before he turns on you, too?"

"Leave!" Corvell's voice boomed.

"Jake, please," Kyra said. "I'm not responsible for what happened."

"Don't say another word," Corvell said. "I mean it, Kyra."

"He's not helping you," Jake said. "If anything, he's making me more inclined to issue a warrant for your arrest for obstruction of justice. Who do you think you're protecting? Adah's killer? Certainly not yourself."

"This is harassment," Corvell said. "I'm not afraid of you and neither is she."

"No, but I know who you're really afraid of, Kyra. I've kept your secrets, but that's over."

"Stop it!" she shouted. She had a wild look to her. She seemed afraid of Corvell. Was Corvell starting to realize he might have backed the wrong horse? Would he sell her out to Rex to save his own skin? As soon as he thought it, Jake knew the answer. Of course he would. Kyra wasn't dumb enough not to realize that herself.

"All right," Kyra shouted. "All right. But not here."

"Fine, my office then."

"Absolutely not! I will not allow it."

"It's okay, Alex," she said. "Jake's right. I want to help find whoever did this to Adah. It's the least I can do now." She walked around her desk.

"You are not leaving this office without me," Corvell said.

"I think she is," Jake said. Thank God for it. It meant Kyra had finally opened her eyes. Corvell wasn't someone to be trusted. He was shrewd enough to see why Kyra could be considered damaged goods with Uncle Rex.

"I'll talk to you later, Alex," Kyra said. Corvell's face turned purple. Jake thought he might actually try to physically restrain Kyra. He moved in between them as Kyra opened the door and made her way down the short steps to the parking lot.

"See you later, Corvell," Jake said. As he stepped out, Kyra had already let herself into the passenger seat of Jake's car. He turned back one last time to wave at Alex Corvell. The man was fuming. He raced to his own car, ready to follow behind.

TWENTY-SIX

She looked smaller somehow. Girlish. It had been sometimes hard for Jake to see Kyra Bardo for what she was. She was strong. Smart. Cunning. An unlikely successor to King Rex's empire. But of all the Bardos of her generation, Kyra was the natural born leader. Her two older brothers, Kyle and Knox, had been disappointments. Too much like their father, Rex's good-for-nothing brother, Floyd.

At this moment, though, sitting at the table in the interview room, Kyra looked her age. She was only twenty-seven.

"You can't think I wanted harm to come to that girl, Jake."

"I don't." He sat across from her. "But I just can't understand why you took that big a risk with her safety."

"It didn't seem like a risk. Far less risky than me charging in there trying to drag her out. I knew she wasn't safe there. She knew she wasn't safe there. I don't know why Warren's DNA wasn't found on her. But he's the one who openly threatened to kill her."

"She told you that?"

"Yes." Jake wanted to throttle her. It didn't matter now, but Kyra had never directly admitted that to him before.

The door behind him opened. Sheriff Landry poked her head in. "Jake. I need to speak to you for a moment."

"This will just take a second," he told Kyra. "Just sit tight."

Landry looked pissed as he closed the door behind him.

"What are you doing?" she asked.

"What does it look like I'm doing?"

"Her lawyer is down in my office raising hell. You can't question her without him in the room."

Jake held a piece of paper in his hand. "This says I can."

He'd gotten Kyra to sign a written waiver of her Miranda rights. She gave him specific permission to question her without Corvell present. Landry read it over.

"I still don't like it. I'll tell you who else won't like it. Boyd Ansel."

"So give him a copy of that waiver. I'll get it on video too."

"Jake, you know how this goes. Even if Kyra Bardo cooperates and gives you actionable information that leads to your perpetrator, Corvell's going to argue it's the fruit of a poisonous tree. Any judge will be hard-pressed to disagree with him."

"I don't know what to tell you. I know what I'm doing. You can ask Kyra yourself if it'll make you feel better. She doesn't want him in the room. She's made that clear. So I need you to let me go do my job."

Landry bit her lip. "I hope you know what you're doing."

"I do," he answered, but in his head, he thought, "Me too."

Kyra sat with her head resting on her arms when Jake walked back in. She straightened.

"Sorry," he said.

"She thinks you're making a mistake in talking to me."

"She's just making sure you're doing it of your own free will. Corvell's making some noise."

Kyra looked at the large mirror on the wall beside her. She wasn't dumb. She waved at the mirror, knowing full well Landry was probably watching everything from the observation room behind that wall.

"My name is Kyra Bardo. I'm here of my own free will. I'm talking to Jake because I want to. I know my lawyer is here. I want him to wait outside."

Jake tried to suppress a laugh. "Nice."

"Where were we?"

"You were telling me how you couldn't believe Warren didn't kill Adah. And you were telling me for the first time that she told you he threatened to kill her."

"Because you already knew it. You thought Warren did this too. You didn't need me to confirm it."

"Yeah. I did. And what I needed was for you to tell me every damn thing you know about Adah. Every detail. Not pick and choose what information you wanted to dole out."

"I'm sorry. I was trying to help her. I swear to God."

"I believe you. But I need to know everything, Kyra. Who you talked to. What your arrangement was. She called you that night. What did she say? What did you say?"

"There wasn't any other number on her phone but mine, was there?"

"I'm the one asking the questions."

"No. I know. But I told you the truth. There was no one else Adah was afraid of besides Warren. She was running from him more than anything else. She knew if she stayed in that house, he would have forced her into a marriage she didn't want. One where she'd be abused."

"See, you didn't tell me that either, Kyra. I found that out from one of her friends. Do you see my problem? What else aren't you telling me?"

"Nothing!"

Jake pulled up a picture on his phone of the driver's license found on Adah's body. "You did this," he said. "You procured this for her. From whom? I want to know everyone who knew you were helping Adah. Anyone who might have known where she'd be the night of April 11th."

"That won't help you," she said, pushing the phone and photo away.

"Tell me anyway."

"Look, you're not stupid. You know how these things work. The good ones, anyway. I have a contact. Some guy on the dark web who's done work for us over the years."

"What kind of work?"

She rolled her eyes. "Getting me a fake ID when I asked for one."

"A name."

"I don't know his name. Not his real one anyway. And I don't know where he lives. He could be in Thailand for all I know. You think there's some guy in a trench coat in the alley? Come on. There are ways of getting things done if you have enough money. I do. I knew Adah would need documentation. So I made a call and got it."

"You gave him her picture."

"And that's all. My contact never even knew her name. Or what this was for. He just did what I asked. I don't even know for sure he's not a she. His handle is Prometheus. I mean, how stupid is that? He has a particular skill I needed. That's all."

Jake knew she was telling the truth. But it was just another frustration. Another dead end.

"So who else? You gave her the phone. You got her an ID. You met with her how many times?"

"A handful. I was visiting my grandmother one day and Adah was there, helping her make butter, of all things. When Melva stepped out, Adah came to me. She asked me what it would take for her to leave. And would I help her? I told her no at first. But then later, my grandmother was talking about how worried she was about Adah. That things were getting difficult with Warren and the faction on the north side."

"Do you think Melva was trying to ask you without actually asking you?"

"No. Not really. I just knew the rumors about who Adah was. And I liked her. She was smart. Savvy. And I just didn't want her living the life Warren was carving out for her."

"Plus you were hoping to score points with Uncle Rex."

"Yes. Okay? Yes. I thought if I could get her out in secret, help her build a good life where she'd be safe, it would be good for both of us."

"You want me to believe Melva didn't know any of this?"

"No! I swear. No. She might have tried to stop me. But I don't think she realized how dire Adah's circumstances were. Adah hid it from her. Along with some of the bruises. She didn't want to start some kind of war between Melva and Warren's people. She was afraid if that happened, her father would keep an even closer eye on her. Not let her come to Melva's at all. I think she was right. I think that's exactly what would have happened. So I took the initiative."

"And Adah trusted you," Jake said, his voice flat.

"Yes. More than that. Jake, she begged me. She told me things I don't even think Melva knows. How violent Warren was. How it was more than just her. There are dozens of girls up there. Warren wanted to basically pimp out and force them into marriages with old men. So they would bear them children."

"Why wouldn't she just go to Melva with that?" Jake asked.

"I told you. Adah was smart. She understood the politics of it all. She was worried about what could happen if Melva's people tried to interfere. People could get hurt. Her friends. Her mother. Her sister."

"But she was willing to abandon them all? Leave them behind with you helping her?"

Kyra looked away. Jake had the strongest sense she wasn't telling him everything.

"What was the plan? You weren't going to just let her come live with you."

"No. I was working on getting her somewhere far away. That part I've already told you."

"She would have needed more than a driver's license. She'd have needed a social security card. Money."

"I was getting all of that."

"You and your dark web guy."

"Yes."

"Who else? Did you have a family lined up to take her in?"

"Again, I was working on it. Alex knows a family in Nebraska. He did some work for them a long time ago. I was going to send her there as soon as she got away from that place."

"Alex," Jake said. "You're saying Corvell was in on your plan?"

"Not all of it. Just the part where he was going to help me find her a family to stay with."

"Did he know who Adah was to you? Who she could be to Rex?"

She didn't answer at first.

"You think he couldn't have figured it out on his own?" Jake asked. "Are you telling me you asked the Bardo family lawyer to help a probable secret member of the Bardo family and he didn't know who she was? You put him in as much risk with Rex as you put yourself."

"I didn't know what Alex knew or suspected. We didn't discuss it. I asked him for help with this girl. He didn't ask questions. He never would. He just did what I instructed him to."

"How the hell could you be sure he wouldn't just turn around and go to Rex behind your back?"

"It wasn't supposed to be like this! We were gonna get her out. Get her safe. Then nobody, not even Rex, would have had a problem with it."

"Where did you discuss all of this?" Jake asked. "You and Corvell. By phone?"

"No. Never. Only in person. At his office."

"Christ, Kyra. You're telling me Alex Corvell knew you were working on getting Adah away from the Sommers family? Did you tell him the day she reached out to you?"

"Yes," she said. "So he could get in touch with the family in Nebraska. So they'd know when to expect Adah. And he was going to figure out how to get her there."

Jake felt his blood run cold. "He knew. Kyra, how dumb are you?"

"Screw you, Jake. This is a family matter. It's always been a family matter."

"You have withheld crucial evidence from me. You're telling me someone else knew Adah's plans? Knew where she was going to be. And you didn't think to mention it?"

"Because Warren Sommers killed her! Because of the risk to me in dragging anyone else into this."

"Bullshit. You were afraid of making Melva and Rex angry. Of retaliation. You got in over your head and Adah paid the price."

"Alex didn't kill Adah. What possible reason would he have had for that? He's been our family lawyer for twenty years, Jake. I would trust him with my life. Take his DNA too, for God's sake. He's got nothing to hide."

"Except now you finally understand he's not working for you, Kyra. He's been trying to cover his own ass from the beginning. And if he knows you crossed Rex and Melva, you think he's gonna stand by you when they decide to deal with you? There's a damn good chance he's sold you out already."

Kyra shuddered. "Help me, Jake. I swear I was only trying to do the right thing by Adah. I never wanted anything bad to happen to her. I thought she was out. I thought she was going to be safe. And you're right. When my uncle finds out ... God. You can't tell him. Please. I'm begging you. You don't know what they're capable of."

Jake stood. He felt sick to his stomach. All Kyra's lies. Her false promises to Adah. He thought she was stronger, smarter.

"Jake, please," Kyra sobbed. She came around the table and threw her arms around him, pressing her body against his.

Jake took her wrists and tried to untangle her from him. She knew they were being watched. What was this performance for?

"Help me," she whispered. "You're the only one who can now." She cupped his face in her hands. Her desperation, her fear, stirred something in him. She was truly scared. He knew she had reason to be. God. How could she have been so reckless?

Jake grabbed her wrists again and tried to pull her away. She dropped her voice low so no one but Jake could possibly hear her.

"I'll do anything," she said. "Do you understand? Anything. Just please, help me."

There wasn't much that shocked Jake anymore. But that did. He peeled her off of him, but not before the door opened and Birdie stood there, seeing the whole thing.

TWENTY-SEVEN

K yra made an awkward step away from Jake. Birdie's eyes bored into him.

"I need you to stay available," Jake said to Kyra. "If you try to leave town, I'll issue a warrant."

"I'm not going anywhere," she said. She turned her body sideways to avoid running into Birdie as she left the room.

Jake turned to the mirror, assuming Meg was still behind it. "Don't let Alex Corvell leave the building. He and I need to have a conversation."

"So do we," Birdie said to Jake. "But not here." She turned on her heel and walked back to their office. Meg came out of the observation room at the same time Jake stepped into the hallway.

"You heard it all?" he asked her.

"Enough. Jake, that woman should be in jail until we get this sorted out. I think she's still lying to you or withholding something."

"Maybe. I think it's highly likely Corvell's been giving her bad advice to protect his own ass. I need to find out everything I can about him."

"You actually expect him to tell you anything today?"

"No. But I can make sure he knows he's under fire."

"He's still in my office. I'll get him down here. Give me ten minutes."

Jake wanted to just wait in the interview room and avoid Birdie altogether. He knew she'd come charging back in here if he didn't deal with her now. When he walked into the office, she was fuming. Pacing near the table, her lips pressed into a hard line.

"What the hell was that?" she asked.

"That was me doing my job. Kyra's cooperating now."

"She's still playing you. She practically threw herself at you. And you ..."

"I what?" Jake snapped.

"You're attracted to her and you're letting it cloud your judgment."

He grumbled. "Birdie, I don't have time for this. To be honest, I don't even know what *this* is. You're seeing things that aren't there. I don't need a lecture."

"You need something. You've given Kyra Bardo a pass. I don't think you're capable of thinking clearly where she's concerned. You've got this warped connection to Rex. But that I get. He's useful in his way. But I see the way this girl looks at you. Today? I saw the way you looked at her."

"Stop. Just ... stop. You're acting ..."

"Do not!" she shouted. "Do not try to gaslight me. I'm telling you. Kyra is more connected to this than you realize. I can sense it."

"So can I," he said. "But this is still my case."

"Are we partners or not?"

He felt a headache coming on. "Yes, but ..."

"The thing about partnerships, it's give and take, okay? It's your job to have my back and me to have yours. Part of that is me calling you out when I see you doing something you shouldn't."

"Okay, so how do you want me to handle this? What am I doing that you'd do differently?"

"I'd park Kyra Bardo's ass in jail until this case is solved."

"If I do that, she'll shut down. But more than that, she wouldn't be safe. She knows Melva and Rex are going to view her as a problem that needs to be taken care of."

"Right. Their problem. Not yours."

"We're going to have to agree to disagree. We can fight about this later. Right now, I've got Alex Corvell sitting in the interview room about to have an aneurysm. He might also just turn into my number one suspect."

"Why? What possible motive could Corvell have for killing that girl? He's worked for the Bardos since before Adah was even born. He's got to know Rex thinks she was his kid. He'd have to be seriously crazy to harm her in any way."

"I know," Jake admitted. "But Kyra admitted Corvell knew she was in touch with Adah that night. He knew where she would be and when. So it's worth pursuing."

"All right. We agree on that."

"Did you get anywhere with the other women from Warren's little compound?"

"Nothing. Nobody knows anything or they're just not willing to talk about it. They need more time."

"Keep on it," he said. "Now let me go do this."

Birdie seemed placated for now. He knew it wouldn't last long. He knew she was dead wrong about how he handled Kyra Bardo.

Alex Corvell refused to take a seat in the interview room. Jake ignored it and sat at the end of the table.

"You know I don't have to do this," Corvell said.

"You're gonna tell me you came here as a courtesy to me?"

"I came here to tell you whatever my client told you won't be admissible in court. I came here to tell you to expect a formal complaint about the way you've conducted yourself, Detective."

Jake couldn't help himself. He laughed. "You do what you have to do, Corvell. And I'll keep doing what I have to do."

"Which is what?"

"Have a seat," Jake said.

"I'd rather not. I don't plan to be here long."

"Fine. I need to know where you were on April 11th from say five o'clock to noon the next day."

Corvell's face changed. He seemed surprised by the question.

"An alibi? You expect me to produce an alibi?"

"It'd be a start."

"You can go to hell."

"What do you have to hide or lose?" Jake asked. "I mean, you're gonna tell me you had nothing to do with what happened to Adah. So just answer my question and we can put this thing to bed. You can go on with your life."

"I didn't kill Adah Lee."

"You were trying to help her. Just like Kyra."

Corvell stood mute. Only the fire in his eyes told Jake what he was thinking.

"Look," Jake said. "Kyra's done with you. She's talking to me now of her own free will." He slid Kyra's waiver across the table to Corvell. He scanned it. His scowl only grew.

"You coerced her."

"No. See, Kyra is smarter than you. She knows she had nothing to do with what happened to Adah. So she knows the best way to help herself is to help me figure out what *did* happen to her. So I asked her to tell me everyone who knew about her plan to get Adah out. It was only you. You were there when Adah reached out to her. You were going to help her put things in place. Get her to this family in Nebraska that *you* set up for her. You knew where Adah was. You knew when. So right now, that makes you a person of interest. Unless you can convince me otherwise. A good way to do that is to tell me where the hell you were when she went missing."

Corvell smirked. Finally, he pulled out a chair and sat. "Or what?"

"Or … I'm going to walk across the street and get a warrant to search your office, your phone, your computers, your home, your car. Oh, also your blood, and a cheek swab. See, Adah fought hard. Though she lost the fight for her life, she won the fight to help me identify who killed her. Warren Sommers wasn't a match. Whoever hurt her wasn't related to her."

"You're grasping at straws," Corvell said.

"I don't think I am. And I think the easiest way to remove yourself from my list is by providing a DNA sample. Right now. It'll take me five minutes to get someone in here to collect it."

"Absolutely not."

"Fine. I'll get a warrant. You want me to show up at your house? Upset your wife? Or maybe show up at your office. I don't think that would be good for business."

"We're done here," Corvell said, but he didn't get up.

"I don't get it. You're acting like a man who has something to hide."

"And you're acting like a man who doesn't understand the Bill of Rights."

"Where were you, Corvell? You know I'll succeed in getting those warrants. Your DNA and your cell phone activity won't lie. So get ahead of this now, before it ruins your reputation."

"You're a real piece of work," Corvell said. "You've been tripping all over yourself since the second you got this case. You let Warren Sommers make you his bitch. You made things worse for his poor wife and daughter. And you're about to become the Bardo family's least favorite cop. That's gonna matter."

"Where were you?"

"I wasn't anywhere near Red Sky Hill."

"Great. Prove it."

"I'll do you a favor. Just the one. I was out of town meeting with a potential new client."

"Who?"

Corvell smiled. "You know I can't tell you that. It's privileged."

"It's convenient. So tell me where?"

"Columbus."

"You spent the night?"

"It got late. We had some drinks with dinner. I didn't feel comfortable driving home."

"You stayed in a hotel?" Jake asked. He grabbed the pad of paper in the center of the table and slid it down to Corvell. Corvell slid it back.

"I didn't stay in a hotel. I slept in my car."

Jake raised both brows. "You want me to believe you spent the night in your car?"

"I don't care what you believe. You wanted an answer. I gave you one."

"Where did you have dinner that night? What restaurant?"

"McClain's Steakhouse. I recommend it. Their prime rib is the best I've ever had."

Jake took the pad and wrote down the name of the restaurant.

"Do you have a receipt? It was a business dinner. You'd expense that. So show me the record and we can be done with this."

Still smirking, Corvell rose. "I don't owe you anything. Get your warrants, Detective. Beyond that, I've got nothing more to say to you. I've probably already said too much. As far as my client, if I find out you talked to her again without me present ..."

"You might want to check and see if Kyra even still is your client. To me, she seemed pretty dissatisfied with your representation."

Corvell lifted his middle finger and flashed it at Jake on his way out of the room. A moment later, Birdie and Landry walked in. Of course they'd been listening too.

"Get those warrants, Jake," Landry said. "I think every word out of that scum's mouth just now was a lie."

"I'll have them written and signed by the end of the day," Birdie said. "I already put a call in to Judge Cardwell's clerk. She gave him a heads-up not to leave the building until I get there."

"Good work," Landry said. "I trust you two have worked out your differences?"

Jake met Birdie's eyes. She turned to Landry. "Nothing to work out, Sheriff. We're all on the same page." With that, she left the room.

Landry hung back. "You okay, Jake?"

"I'm fine."

"Don't let Erica be right," Landry said. "Are you certain you can be objective where Kyra Bardo is concerned?"

Jake hardened his jaw. "Yes."

"Good," she said. "So go nail Corvell to the wall if he did this to that girl."

TWENTY-EIGHT

Four hours later, with his warrants in hand, Jake showed up at Alex Corvell's law office. He'd sent everyone home except for one assistant who tried to bar entry into Corvell's personal office space.

"You can't do this," she said. "Those files are protected by attorney-client privilege."

"I'm not after the files," Jake said. He turned away from the woman and directed the rest of the deputies he brought with him to secure Corvell's desk computer.

"There are sensitive files on that laptop!" She'd identified herself as Jane Timmons. She wore readers at the tip of her nose, secured with a jeweled chain hanging by her ears. Jake guessed Ms. Timmons was used to successfully bullying Corvell's clients and court personnel. She had that look about her. Stalwart. Scowling. She probably kept Corvell on a tight schedule as well.

"Ms. Timmons," Jake said. "You've been instructed to cooperate with us. I know you understand the significance of a court order.

You don't want to stand in my way. You're not protecting your boss, believe me."

"You listen here," she said, pointing a finger right in Jake's face. "I will not have you disrupting this entire practice. I'm not afraid of you or your court order, Detective. I will not compromise client confidentiality either. You can take me to jail if you have to. But I'm not letting you into this office."

She tried to physically bar the entryway. With a look from Jake, three female deputies, Amanda Chaplin, Molly Darwin, and Anne Schmidt, moved in. "I don't want to have to do this," he said. "But if I have to bodily remove you, I will."

Jane Timmons gripped both sides of the doorway and stared Jake down.

"Mr. Corvell has entrusted me to protect his clients. I'll do whatever I have to."

"So will I," Jake said, exasperated. With a gesture to the deputies, they moved in and lifted Ms. Timmons off her feet and put her in handcuffs.

"Park her over there," Jake said. There was a long wooden bench in the front entryway. "Don't let her move."

Schmidt and Darwin stood on either side of her. Ms. Timmons lifted her chin in defiance. But at least she was contained for the time being.

Jake watched as the deputies conducted a thorough search of Corvell's office. He'd sent three more deputies to Corvell's private residence in Arch Hill. He just hoped in the precious hours since he'd left the interrogation room until now, Corvell hadn't done anything stupid like destroy evidence.

Jake spotted a shredder underneath Ms. Timmons's desk in the anterior office. It was nearly full. "Pack that up as well," Jake ordered.

It would take the team almost three hours to wrap things up at the office. Jake trusted them to do what needed to be done. Birdie called. He'd sent her to oversee the service of the warrant on Corvell's residence.

"You doing okay over there?" Jake answered.

"Not exactly. The idiot won't answer the door. The place is huge. Has to be something like eight thousand square feet. No way we're going to just boot this door in. I'm going to have to call the SWAT guys in and let them use their toys."

"Where's Corvell?"

"Haven't seen him. But his Beemer's in the driveway. We saw someone peeking out through one of the front windows. But it looks like we're going to have to smash in the front door."

"I'm on my way," Jake said. "I'll be there in ten minutes."

He clicked off the call and walked over to Jane Timmons. "Do you have a key to your boss's residence?"

Her expression dripping with contempt, she turned her head away from him.

"Look," Jake tried again. "We don't have to have all this drama. If Corvell has nothing to hide, then you don't have anything to worry about."

"I read your warrant," she said. "It says nothing about turning over any house keys, even if I had them. You'll have to take that up with Mr. Corvell himself."

"Right. Fine," Jake said. He waved a dismissive hand as he walked away from her and got into his car.

B irdie wasn't exaggerating. Corvell's house was huge. A sprawling, three-story colonial situated behind a locked gate. The deputies had gained entry through it so Jake was able to drive right up.

Corvell had stables behind the house. Four black horses grazed in the pasture on the east side. He found Birdie at the front door, shouting through a bullhorn.

"We're coming in," she said. "I'm counting to three, then this door is coming down, Corvell."

She had the team ready behind her, carrying the big ram and a Halligan tool. Jake really hoped it wouldn't come to this. So far, everything about Alex Corvell read guilty. The only blessing was that no members of the media had picked up on this lead. Though that probably wouldn't hold true for very long.

Birdie got to two before the massive black double doors swung open. Corvell stood there wearing the same expensive suit he had on earlier that morning.

"Great to see you again," Jake said as he pushed past him along with Birdie and the crew.

The foyer ceiling went up all three stories. A double winding staircase led to the second floor. Working for the Bardo family had apparently been lucrative. Jake couldn't help but wonder, why the hell would a guy like this risk it all on some whisper girl?

"Alex?" A pretty blonde woman came down the stairs. She wore a pink robe and her hair was disheveled. She looked either slightly drunk or like she'd been asleep until a minute ago. It was after six p.m.

"Don't worry about a thing, Deirdre," Alex said. The woman floated down the stairs and went to Corvell's side. He put an arm around her. Jake noticed the massive rock on her finger.

"Who else is home?" Jake asked.

"No one," Deidre Corvell answered. "It's just us."

"You have any pets? Dogs?"

"Just Beatrice and Bethany. They're corgis. They wouldn't hurt a fly. They're both in their bedroom upstairs. Second door on the right."

"That's enough," Corvell snapped at her. "You don't have to say anything more to them."

It was going to be a long evening. Ramirez from BCI sent four members of his team to assist. The house ended up having twelve bedrooms, fourteen bathrooms, and two kitchens. Corvell kept a home office on the second floor overlooking the horse pasture and stables. Most of what they collected came from there.

They ended up carrying out twelve boxes. Clothing. Shoes. Four cell phones. Two computers. Corvell had six cars in the garage. Each one was swept for evidence. To Jake's eye, none of them had blue carpeting. There were no Dodge Rams or Chryslers in that garage. Though that didn't mean everything.

Corvell and his wife stood in the foyer the entire time. She crumpled against him. Neither of them said anything more.

By the time it was over, the sun had already set. Jake was dead on his feet. He wanted a shower and his warm bed. But Birdie persuaded him he needed something else more.

"Come on," she said. "I'm buying. Spiros has moussaka on special tonight. Tessa promised me she'd set two plates aside. She's open for another hour. I already told Gemma you'd be too beat to head to Sips but she made me swear to get you fed."

She was right about everything. The smell of Spiros's cooking perked Jake up immediately. They took a booth near the back and Tessa busied herself putting enough food in front of them to feed half the department.

"Do you think we'll find anything in that mess we collected today?"

Jake spread butter on Tessa's homemade bread. That alone would have been enough to fill his stomach.

"I don't know. Corvell's cocky, but he doesn't strike me as stupid. Ramirez's people will scour those phones and computers for anything he's tried to scrub since Adah's murder. That might tell us the most interesting story."

"They'll let anybody in here!" a familiar voice boomed behind Jake. He turned and smiled. Virgil, Chuck, and Bill walked in together. It was good to see Virgil on his feet. His color had gone back to a rosy glow. He'd lost weight, but wasn't haggard like the last time Jake saw him.

Besides Birdie, Jake, and the Papatonis behind the counter, the Wise Men were the only other patrons in the diner. It was well past normal dinner hours so Jake wondered if Tessa hadn't given these three a heads-up that Jake was coming.

"Moussaka for all of you?" Tessa shouted. Bill gave her a thumbs up. Then the trio took the table next to Jake's booth and slid it over close.

"You look good, Virg," Birdie said.

"Thanks, honey," he said. Somehow, out of his mouth, it didn't seem condescending, just warmly affectionate. Birdie leaned over and gave Virgil a hug.

"Heard a rumor," Chuck said. "Corvell's on your radar?"

Jake caught Birdie's eye. "Now, how the hell did that get to you already?"

Chuck tapped his temple. "Nothing gets by these old ears."

"Seriously, how?" Jake asked. "The only people who should know that are working inside the department. Who's talking?"

"Don't worry," Chuck said. "Nobody you gotta worry about."

"How well do you know Corvell?" Birdie asked. "Any dealings with him during your tenure?"

Bill reached for the bread basket on Jake's table. Two seconds later, Tessa came out with a fresh basket. She slapped Bill's hand and gave the other basket back to Jake.

"Corvell's been around forever," Bill answered. "But I can't say we ever crossed paths much. I mostly dealt with public defenders. But I had some cases overlap with some fed stuff out of Columbus. I can tell you Corvell's price tag was too steep for most of the suspects I dealt with."

"Same here," Virgil said. "There was a murder case I was involved with. Suspect had a rich daddy. Corvell represented the kid. He ended up getting an acquittal. It was a shaky case to begin with. I gotta say, I didn't mind dealing with him. He was respectful. A straight shooter. None of that bluster you usually get."

"That's odd," Jake said. "He's been nothing but bluster since I started dealing with him."

"He's just protecting the golden goose," Chuck said. "Word is he decided to hitch his wagon to Rex's niece."

"Maybe that wasn't such a good idea," Birdie muttered.

The conversation drifted to more mundane things. Virgil's physical therapy. The upcoming varsity wrestling team. Travis's West Point plans.

Sated and full to bursting, Jake got up and paid the bill for both tables. Birdie and the others protested, then thanked him. Jake was looking forward to a good night's sleep. He and Birdie would have their work cut out for them in the morning, sifting through the fruits of his warrants on Corvell. Ramirez promised the DNA results in a few days.

"You heading home or back to the office?" Birdie asked as they walked out to the parking lot together.

"Home," he said.

"I'm surprised. I'm also glad. But if you want to dive back into it now, I'm game."

"First thing in the morning is soon enough. You've put in as many hours on this thing as I have. We'll take a break. Get some perspective. Come back fresh in a few hours."

Birdie looked down at the ground. Things were a little awkward between them. This was the first time they'd had a minute alone together since Jake finished with Kyra.

"Look," Birdie finally said. "I'm not sorry for what I said earlier. About you and Kyra Bardo."

"There is no me and Kyra Bardo."

"No. I know. At least I hope I know. It's just ... this one seems different somehow."

"What do you mean?"

"It's just a lot. Those kids up there. We're both worried about how and where they're going to land. And I don't like how you let the Bardos in."

"In?"

"Don't pretend you don't know what I'm talking about. I just need you to promise me something."

He had a feeling he might regret what he was about to say. "I can try."

"I need you to listen to me a little more when it comes to them. This whole thing ... it just doesn't smell right. Okay? I'm worried they're using you to play off each other. You know I've been worried about that since day one. And I'm not at all convinced Melva's been telling the truth. Certainly not Kyra. And now with their family lawyer involved ... I don't know. It just feels like there's a bomb about to go off. I just don't want you getting hit by any shrapnel, you know?"

"I know. And I appreciate it. With any luck, we'll have some answers soon."

"And if we don't? If Alex Corvell turns into another dead end? What then? Because right now, I have a strong suspicion this case is going to go cold. And I also have a strong suspicion that maybe Kyra wants it that way."

"I got it," Jake said. "And I am listening. I promise."

"Good," she said. "So go get some sleep. You look like hell and you smell even worse. I told you that like twelve hours ago and you were overripe then."

Jake laughed. He was glad things seemed easier between them. She was right. If they were going to be real partners, they would have to learn to work through their differences. And he would have to learn to trust her judgment as well as his own.

As he climbed into his car, he watched Birdie walk to hers. She smiled back at him.

Jake felt good as he drove home. It was full dark now. The giant owl that lived in the tree just behind his cabin hooted as he parked and got out. He could smell rain in the air. It was coming. He made a mental note to check Grandpa's pole barn in the morning before work. He'd patched a hole in the roof but it had been dry for the last two weeks. A fresh rain would be a good test.

Jake tossed his keys between his hands as he walked up the porch. He unlocked the door and went inside.

He was exhausted. Barely able to put one foot in front of the other. Though he was tempted to just climb into bed, Birdie's multiple warnings about how badly he smelled played in his mind. He tossed his work clothes in the laundry room and stepped under a hot shower.

He lathered up and let the water run down his face and chest. It felt good. Started to clear his head. Bed would feel even better. He was just beginning to rinse off when he heard a loud, insistent knock at the front door.

Jake stepped out and toweled off. The knocking got louder. Jake threw on a pair of drawstring sweats and grabbed his gun. Still dripping, he opened the door. Kyra Bardo stood there, her eyes swollen from crying. Before Jake could say a word, Kyra practically fell into his arms.

"Jake," she said. "Everything you said was right. Please. I have nowhere else to go."

Twenty-Nine

"You can't be here," Jake said. He'd never seen her like this. Looking small. Scared. Her makeup smeared.

"I can't be anywhere else, Jake. Please let me come inside."

"Kyra ..."

"Please! I mean it. I have nowhere else to go. It's over for me now. Corvell got the word out that I'm cooperating with you. Just like you said he would. The family knows."

"What do they know?"

"Everything. That I tried to help Adah behind their backs. Alex probably cooked up some story to make me out to be the bad guy."

"You're his client. He made a point all day about protecting confidentiality when I served my warrants."

"The family is his client. When I cut him loose, everything changed. Please. It's cold out here. It's going to rain. Can we just talk? You don't want to risk anybody seeing me here, either."

Jake looked past her out into the yard. She'd parked her car on the side of the house, shielded by two large maple trees.

"I can't help you, Kyra."

"Yes, you can." She stepped forward, daring him to block her path. She put her hands on his bare chest. She was so cold. He found himself taking a step back and letting her inside. She was right about one thing. It wouldn't be good if anyone saw her here. Which was exactly why he should have slammed the door in her face. Only he couldn't.

Jake shut the door. Kyra moved past him and sat on his living room couch. She buried her face in her hands and started to cry again. Was it an act? Was this everything Birdie had been warning him about?

"What did you think was going to happen?" he said, rubbing his still wet hair with his towel. "You've been in over your head since the beginning. Melva had her reasons for not just getting Adah out of there herself."

"You don't get it," she said, letting out a bitter laugh. "Rex has been playing you. Playing everyone. And he's had help. My help."

Jake walked away from the door and took a seat in the chair opposite Kyra. "You better explain what you mean. You're talking out of both sides of your mouth."

"I know I made mistakes. Big ones. And I know if it wasn't for me, Adah might still be alive. I did what I thought was right. And I don't know that I would change anything now if I could go back in time. I didn't know any other way of helping her. How could I know Alex would betray me like that? He knows the family too. In some ways, better than me. I have no idea why he'd be involved with putting Adah in harm's way."

"How sure are you that Corvell couldn't be trying to hurt Rex for his own reasons? Or you? Maybe it was Corvell who wanted to send some kind of message to your uncle. I don't care what it is. I only care that I find out who killed her."

Kyra came to him, kneeling on the floor at his knees. "I want that too. God. Jake. If I could switch places with her, I would. Soon enough, that's probably what will happen to me anyway."

"Have they threatened you?"

Her head shook with ironic laughter. "You still don't get it. You still only see what we want you to see."

"So tell me the truth. For once in your life, be straight with me. I can't help you if I don't know the truth."

"The truth?" she said. "God. Jake. Wake up! Kids were being hurt out there. Women and children. In Melva's backyard. And she did nothing about it because of some stupid, generations-old creed that the people on the other side of that hill are a kingdom unto themselves. An outdated pact that she's been too stubborn to break. So *I* tried to do something about it. I wasn't going to stand by and let those kids be sold into some barbaric sexual slavery right under Melva's nose. Adah bought into it too. She made me swear not to tell Melva how bad it was for her. And I agreed to it. Not because I was stupid or reckless like you want to believe. But because I am the only one holding this family together. Me, Jake. Not Rex. Certainly not Melva."

She was almost manic. She knelt there on her knees in front of him. Her scent, her vulnerability. All of it drew him to her. It was some magic web she spun and he felt himself getting tangled in it. He would be if he wasn't careful.

"Jake," she whispered. "Melva isn't strong like she wants people to believe. Like she wants *you* to believe."

"What are you talking about?"

"Christ," Kyra said. "She's eighty years old. She's survived two bouts with cancer already. The second one, not even my Uncle Rex knows about. She refuses to go to doctors anymore. After her last cancer scare, she was supposed to continue to get bladder scans and do a round of maintenance chemo. She won't do any of it. She refuses treatment for her high blood pressure. She's a ticking time bomb. She's sick, Jake."

"You're certain Rex doesn't know any of this?"

"He's willfully ignorant. And my grandmother is a skilled liar. They need me, Jake. I told you. I'm the only thing holding it all together. Rex isn't in charge. That's an illusion. A fiction like the Wizard of Oz meant to keep people intimidated. Even you. And I'm the one helping to perpetuate it. Because it has served me. But if I go, this whole thing crumbles. That's bad for the family and even worse for you. No one else can do what I do. What my uncle could have done until he messed it all up by getting himself convicted. You think my father could keep the wolves at bay? Or my idiot brother, Knox? No. It's me, Jake. Me. Look at me. You know it. Alex Corvell knows it. You think he was just hedging his bets by helping me? He's smarter than that. So are you."

He hoped she was lying. But it had the ring of truth. She looked up at him with those striking blue eyes. She was beautiful. Probably one of the most beautiful women he'd ever seen.

"I was going to end it," she said. "My way. Adah was just the first. I was making plans to get all of those kids out of there. Put a stop to Warren's bullshit. I swear to God. I wasn't going to let any of it stand. It all just turned on me. If Alex turned on me, then you're all I've got, Jake."

She ran her hands up his thighs. For a moment ... just an instant ... he let her. Dark thoughts flashed through his mind. Like a devil sitting on his shoulder ... or in another part of his anatomy ... he knew he wanted her. He knew how easy it would be to just give into it. His eyes went to the swell of her breasts. Her lips parted. He knew she'd taste like honey.

He didn't move. He didn't say anything. But maybe something in his eyes betrayed the war raging within himself. She moved, sliding her hands further up. She leaned over him and pressed her lips to his.

The devil inside him rose up. She did taste like honey. Some deep part of him knew they would fit. She was all the things he wasn't. If he was noble, she was pure sin. His desire clawed at him. He felt it pulling him down. Irresistible ... almost.

"Stop!" he shouted. Grabbing her wrists, he stood and held her away from him.

"Jake ..." His name escaped her lips as an invitation.

"Just stop it," he said. He felt like he'd shattered something inside him. It left him shaking. Almost disoriented. But all at once, he knew himself again. "You can't be here. This won't work."

"You want me just as much as I want you."

"Kyra, I swear to God ..."

She jerked her wrists out of his hands. "Fine. I'm sorry. I shouldn't have done that. I just thought ... Jake ... I meant what I said. I don't have anywhere else to go. Something bad is going to happen to me. What good will any of this be if I'm dead? Is that what you want? You can't stand there and tell me you don't understand. You know what my family is capable of. You know they won't let this slide."

She was right. This wasn't a game. She'd betrayed Rex. Betrayed Melva. And because of her, Adah paid the price.

"You're resourceful, Kyra. You'll figure it out."

"This *is* me figuring it out. Right now, you're the only person in the world who doesn't want me dead. You're the only one who can help me. Please. Let me stay here until I can figure out some things. Just tonight."

He still felt the devil trying to claw its way out. "That can't happen. This can't happen."

"Jake, I'm not going to survive the night. There was someone watching my house. I know if I try to go to get on a plane or even a bus ... they'll be there."

"You can't stay here," he said, growing angry.

"Then where?"

Dammit, he knew she was right about the Hilltop Boys. Rex would have to send a message, make an example out of her. But he couldn't have her here.

"Son of a bitch," he muttered. Then he charged past her, threw on a shirt and a pair of shoes and grabbed his keys.

"Did you bring a bag?"

She'd gone still. "It's out on the porch."

He took her by the arm and led her out his front door.

THIRTY

He hadn't been back here since the end of fall. It showed. The yard was a mess again. He'd have to come up and spend a day tidying up out here. Cutting back some fallen tree limbs. Clearing the trails in the woods behind the house. He pulled up to the garage, fished for the remote in his center console, then parked inside.

"Who lives here?" Kyra asked.

"Don't worry about it. No one."

He cut the engine and closed the garage behind them. It took him a second to find the right key on his chain. The door stuck a bit, not having been opened in over four months. He put his shoulder into it and took Kyra through the laundry room.

"It's freezing in here," she said. The kitchen was dark. The whole house was. Jake went to the thermostat. He kept it at fifty-five degrees. He turned it up to sixty-eight and held his breath for a second. When the furnace kicked over, he felt relief.

Kyra found the light switch and flicked it on. Frank's kitchen was clean, the way Jake left it. He checked the traps in the pantry and under the sink. No sign of any unwanted guests.

Kyra walked through the kitchen and out into the sunken room Frank used as a den. She found the light switch there too and wandered over to the built-in bookshelves where Frank kept most of his awards, medals, and photographs. Kyra picked out two frames. Jake unhooked the side door key from his chain and tossed it on the table.

"Frank Borowski," Kyra read. "He's a cop?" She had Frank's plaque from when he retired as a detective.

"Was," Jake said.

"Is this you?" Kyra held a framed photograph. It was Frank in his younger days. Coach Borowski. It was a picture of the two of them. Jake was eighteen years old and holding up his state championship medal. Frank coached him to a win at the Ohio State High School wrestling tournament.

"It was a long time ago," Jake said.

"He lives here?"

"Not anymore," Jake said. "Frank's gone and he isn't coming back. I just keep an eye on his house. It'll be mine someday. He left it to me in his will."

"He's not dead?"

"No. He's just … gone. But you should be safe at least for tonight. Nobody will think of looking for you here. The pantry's stocked with non-perishables. There's meat in the freezer. I pay for the gas and electricity. The water's on a well. There're three bedrooms down that hallway. Take your pick."

"But you'll stay with me tonight?"

"No. That's not happening, Kyra. Not tonight. Not ever."

She smiled. "Never is a long time, Jake."

"Not long enough," he said under his breath. "But as I said, nobody will think to look for you here. Just don't do anything dumb. Don't use the phone. Don't bring anyone over here. Where's your cell?"

She took it out of her back pocket. Jake grabbed it from her. She'd been smart enough to put the thing in airplane mode. But he took out the battery and handed it back to her.

"Just for a day or two," he said. "Until you figure out what to do."

"How am I supposed to do that without my phone?"

"You're resourceful. You'll figure it out. But I mean it. Don't talk to anyone. Don't screw this up."

She sat in one of the kitchen chairs. "Thank you. This will be fine. I'm grateful. Really."

"Give me the keys to your car. I'll figure out something to do with that."

"Don't bother. It's a rental."

Jake inhaled sharply, ready to lecture her. She put up a hand.

"Don't worry. I paid cash. Used a fake name."

"Fake ID, I suppose, too. So why didn't you just keep on going?"

She eyed him, but didn't answer.

"Fine," he said. "It's late. I'm beat. You don't need a grand tour. You'll find your way around. Just do what I say. I'll check back tomorrow."

Kyra gave him a salute. She rose, giving him that tempting look again. Jake didn't give her the chance to follow through with it. He turned his back on her and left through the garage.

He only got about four hours of sleep. At six a.m., Jake knew Landry would already be headed to the office. He planned to meet her when she got there. He thought about calling Birdie too. But there would be time for that later. He was only in the mood for one lecture.

He parked in his usual spot behind the Public Safety Building. Gauging it perfectly, Landry was already walking in, carrying two cups of coffee. Both for her. Jake got to the door before her and held it open. Landry stopped short, giving Jake a puzzled look.

"Why do I feel this is a bad omen?" she said.

"I just wanted the chance to talk to you before things get going this morning."

Raising a skeptical brow, she walked in. Jake followed close behind. He got to her office door before her and took the keys she juggled along with her cups of coffee. Jake opened her door and flicked her office lights on.

"Can you at least let me get my coat off?" she asked.

Jake took a seat in front of her desk and waited for Landry to settle. She had a stack of unopened mail on her chair. She tossed it on the desk and sat down with a great sigh.

"Kyra Bardo came over last night," Jake started. Meg froze as she was about to peel the lid off one of her cups of coffee.

"She just showed up," he continued. "Pretty freaked out. Scared she wouldn't live until morning now that Corvell was putting the word out about her involvement in Adah's disappearance. She thinks the family will retaliate against her."

"She should have thought about that before she bungled this whole thing and put that girl in harm's way."

"She knows that. She asked for my help. She asked for a place to stay."

Landry rolled her eyes and sunk deeper into her chair. "For the love of God, Jake. Do not tell me ..."

"She's not at my place. I wouldn't allow it. But I took her somewhere safe. Gave her a place to hide out until ..."

"Until what?"

"Until I button up this case. Until I have a chance to talk to Rex again. I don't know."

"Talk to Rex again? And say what? Please don't put a hit out on your niece who I'm hiding from you?"

"I'm making it up as I go."

"No kidding," Meg said. "Jake, is Erica right about you and this woman?"

"What?"

"Don't play dumb. You know what I'm talking about. You know I saw you with her in that interview room. You want to lie to me now and say you're not attracted to her?"

Jake popped to his feet. He paced for a second then gripped the back of the chair and faced her. "Yeah. She's a smoke show. Objectively. But my head's clear here."

"Let me guess, she tried to come on to you last night."

Jake almost denied it, but realized there was no point. "Yeah. She did. But it didn't go anywhere. I told you, my head's clear."

"It's not your head I'm worried about. You're a guy, Jake. Your kind aren't that hard to figure out. So where is she?"

"Maybe you shouldn't know that," he said.

"Believe me, I sure as hell don't want to know any of this. But here we are. Where is she?"

Jake hesitated. It wasn't even about protecting Kyra from Meg or Meg from Kyra. He had more than one reason for keeping up Frank's house. In the back of his mind, he thought maybe someday he or someone he cared about would need a safe place to be. Taking Kyra there last night could make that impossible now. There was still an old bomb shelter under Frank's pole barn no one knew about though. He planned to keep it that way.

"She's at Borowski's old house," he finally said.

"Are you serious? That place hasn't been sold?"

"How could it be? Frank's a fugitive. He's not dead. It can't be sold without him signing a deed over to someone. I've kept it up on my own. Just in case."

"In case what?"

"I don't know. In case I need it. In case he comes back. In case ... this! If something like this happened and I needed to stash someone. Or myself."

She put a hand up in surrender. "You're right. I probably shouldn't know. Forgive me if I have the urge to brain you right now. Do you understand the position this puts me in? If something goes wrong and she ..."

"Nothing's going to go wrong. This is me. Not you. I'm not trying to hide anything. If I were, why would I even come here and tell you about it?"

"I don't know. Right now, I don't know anything where you're concerned. Jake ..." She steepled her fingers under her chin and closed her eyes, collecting herself.

"Yes, you do," he said. "Nothing's changed."

She snapped her eyes open. "That's what I'm afraid of. Jake ... I've always had your back. Given you the benefit of the doubt. But you know what they said about you when you got kicked out of the FBI."

"I didn't get kicked out," he snapped.

"Right. You resigned just ahead of that. You know full well what I'm talking about. You were accused of sleeping with your CI and jeopardizing a case."

"It wasn't true."

"Then there's Bethany Roman. Do I really have to remind you how bad that could have gone? You slept with a reporter covering a case you were working on. I've never told you about all the fires I had to put out for you over that."

"And I told you. I didn't know she was a reporter until ... after. And I've never let my personal life compromise my job. I never will. This isn't that. This is just me keeping a material witness to a murder case from floating belly up in the damn river."

"All right!" she shouted.

"And I sure as hell resent the insinuation that I—"

"I said all right," Meg repeated.

Jake relaxed his shoulders. His head throbbed from grinding his teeth.

"I'll go out on a limb with you. Again," she said. "And I agree we can't have Kyra Bardo ending up dead. But I really hate how you're going about this. You should have arrested her weeks ago. I went along with your decision not to pursue that. Don't make me regret it. I think she should be in a jail cell right now. That's how she can be protected."

Jake shook his head. "Except you know it wouldn't work like that. She'd be a sitting duck in there. You knew that weeks ago too."

Meg gave him a reluctant nod. "What a mess. Jake, for the love of God, get to the bottom of this. Quickly."

"I'm trying," he said quietly.

A soft knock on Meg's door gave Jake a chance for a getaway. Birdie poked her head in. She could, no doubt, read the tension in the room as she looked from Jake to Sheriff Landry.

"Hey," she said. "I've got some stuff to go over with you if you're ready to get to work. I spent the night studying Alex Corvell's financial records. There's something I think you should see."

Meg waved Jake off. "Get to it. Brief me before lunch with whatever you've got."

"Thank you," Jake said.

As he walked out of Meg's office, Birdie eyed him. "Should I ..." she started.

"No," Jake said. "You shouldn't. Not now."

She gave him a tight-lipped nod as they walked back to their office.

THIRTY-ONE

"Everything came back quick," Birdie said as she closed the door to the office. "Ramirez is really coming through on this one."

Jake looked at her. Birdie looked more disheveled than usual. Bits of her hair had come loose from her ponytail. Her eyes were red and puffy. He could see in the trash can she'd already gone through three Styrofoam cups of coffee.

"You okay?" Jake asked. He stopped short of telling her she looked terrible. He'd been around too many women in his life and knew better.

"Yeah. Fine. Why?"

"Did you get any sleep last night?"

"Not really. Mark couriered over the banking and credit card statements on Corvell's business and personal accounts. There's a lot to go through. I've been working on the bank accounts. I printed out statements on those along with the credit cards for the last three months. Figured we could start there and work our way back."

She handed him a thick file folder. Jake flipped it open. They were credit card statements. Birdie had separated them into two sections, Corvell's business and personal cards.

Jake sat at the table and poured his first cup of coffee. They'd need another pot soon.

"What did you want to tell me?" Jake asked.

Birdie came to the table. She held two sheets of paper with long columns of numbers. She'd used pink highlighter on several of the lines.

"Here," she said. "Corvell's got two business accounts. One's his general operating fund. He draws a salary for himself. Another one for his legal secretary, Jane Timmons."

"She's the one I met at his office. A real joy."

"He also pays a few independent contractors. Process servers. He's got two accountants. One he uses as an expert witness. The other is for his personal and corporate bookkeeping. His records are meticulous. So far, I haven't been able to find a single transaction that doesn't match up for his incoming and outgoing expenditures."

"What's the other business account?" Jake asked.

"See, that's where it gets interesting. He's got an Interest on Lawyer's Trust Account. An IOLTA. He's required by law to keep it. It's a protected fund where client payments go. Retainers before he's earned out the hourly. Client settlements. That sort of thing. He only deposits billable hours into the general fund. But those are for services already invoiced. Everything else has to be held in trust. Say he gets a big settlement on behalf of a client. The bulk of it goes into the trust account until he pays himself back for any costs he incurred on behalf of the client. Court costs. Expert witness fees, that kind of thing. Then he pays out the client's portion and deposits his percentage into his general operating fund where he pays his salary and whatnot."

"Do you have names of the independent contractors he's paying?"

"Still working on all of that. Jane Timmons is sharp. She codes everything based on who the client is. It won't be hard to match everyone up. It'll just take some time."

"Okay," Jake said. "So what did you find that was so interesting?"

"Here," she said, placing the two sheets of paper in front of him. She'd written GOP on one paper, IOLTA on the other. "General operating fund, lawyer's trust."

The data entry was dizzying. Jake's vision started to go blurry. He held the pages out.

"Maybe you need readers, old man. You're pushing forty, aren't you?"

Jake scowled at her. "I've got eyes like a hawk."

"Right. Well, anyway. Then there's this." She set a third sheet in front of him that she'd labeled Personal Checking. Once again, she'd highlighted one line in pink. Jake squinted to read it.

"April 12th," he read. "Deposit going in for fifty grand to the personal account."

"Right," she said. "Cash. But if you look at the two business accounts, there's no match. The money didn't come from either one of those accounts. He deposits fifty grand into personal checking, only I can't figure out the source."

"It could be anything," Jake said.

"That much cash?" she said. "Figures like that are pretty common in his two business accounts. He's getting multiple five- and six-figure deposits into the trust account when things settle or he gets a fat retainer from a new client. Or an old one. But there's no other deposit that big going into his personal account. If you look several months back, his banking activity is pretty regular and methodical. He pays his bills on time. He pays off his wife's credit card every month. He takes a salary every month, exactly the same amount. Thirty thousand dollars."

"Birdie, he's got millions sitting in those business accounts. What's the big deal about fifty k?"

"I know. But he never takes bonuses. This fifty grand just pops in there the day after Adah Lee's murder. I've been over everything, Jake. There's no source for it. Like somebody just handed him a wad of cash."

"Maybe he already had it on hand. In a safe or something. Who knows?"

Birdie sat down and rested her head on her palm. "I know. I know. But I'm telling you, this deposit is most definitely outside his normal pattern. And the timing is weird. Just plop. As soon as the bank opens the morning of April 12th, he shows up with a wad of cash."

"It's thin," Jake said. "But I'm not saying it's not strange."

"This alone isn't enough to nail him," she said. "I get that. But my gut tells me it's related."

"Keep at it," Jake said. He went back to the file with the credit card statements. He reached over and grabbed his notebook, and flipped through it. It took him a minute, but he finally found the right page.

"McClain's Steakhouse," Jake said.

"What?" Birdie asked.

"McClain's Steakhouse. That's where Corvell said he was the night Adah went missing. His alibi."

Jake went back to the credit card statements. He flipped through those until he found the right time frame.

"He said he was meeting a new client," Birdie said. "So I'd expect if he used a card, it would be the Amex. That's the one tied to the general operating fund."

Jake scrolled down. "Nothing," he said. "No charges to any restaurants the night of Adah's murder. But ..."

Jake's heart started to race.

"What?" Birdie said. Jake handed one of the statements to her.

"He's using his personal Visa card to get gas here in Stanley at four p.m. The Sunoco on the corner of Radley and County Road Seven."

"That's only about a mile and a half from his residence," she said. "Adah was last seen at what, four thirty?"

"Yeah." Jake was puzzled. There were more charges after that. A food delivery service at seven thirty that night. Another designated as online shopping at ten, then another at eleven thirty. Jake would be able to coordinate those purchases with the activity on Corvell's phone or laptop when the full forensics report came in.

Jake reached for his cell phone and hit Mark Ramirez's personal cell. It was almost eight o'clock. Ramirez would either be on his way into the office or out on the road headed to another crime scene. He answered on the first ring.

"Hey, Jake," he said. "I was just about to call you."

"You in yet?"

"I've been in. Got to the office just after six. I've got preliminary data on Corvell's cell. I knew you'd need that quick."

"You're reading my mind, Mark. I need to know one thing," Jake said. "Can you tell me where Corvell's phone was from three p.m. April 11th to three p.m. on the 12th?"

"It was on and it was moving," Ramirez answered. "He made a couple of calls to his wife after five p.m. on the 11th. Got some incoming texts from her. Some from Jane Timmons. He called the courthouse in Columbus at nine a.m. on the 12th. But all of these calls were made in Worthington County. He bounced around a little. Probably driving. But after four forty-three on the 11th, he's hitting the tower on Bailor Road in Arch Hill Township. That's the tower closest to his residence. He doesn't move after that. Not until eight thirty the next morning. Then he hits the tower closest to his office and stays there until six p.m. that day."

"Thanks," Jake said. "You're sure you're not seeing any movement near Red Sky Hill?"

"Nope. His phone, at least, doesn't hit anywhere near it. I'm working on the full report. I expect to have it to you within forty-eight hours. You're moved to the front of the line. DNA just got delivered to the lab. Results on that might take a day or two longer. Blood type came back though. Corvell's B positive."

"Same type as the samples taken off Adah Lee," Jake said.

"Same type as roughly ten percent of the people in the US alone. Don't jump to any conclusions on that just yet. I'll call you the second I have anything definitive."

Jake thanked him and clicked off the call. He relayed Ramirez's report to Birdie.

"He lied," she said. "He wasn't in Columbus. He was here. Jake ..."

"Don't," Jake said. "Not yet. We still have a few big fat questions that need answering."

"There's a large sum of money that goes into his account within hours of Adah's murder."

"Which doesn't make sense if Corvell hired somebody to kill her. I'd expect to see a withdrawal, not a deposit."

"Unless it's a finder's fee," Birdie said. "Somebody paid Corvell for the information on where she'd be and when. So even if the DNA doesn't match his, he's not cleared. Not even close."

Something nagged at Jake. He left the table and stood at the whiteboard. His hierarchy of suspects was mostly cross-hatched lines through every name. Rascal Buchanan, no DNA match. Warren Sommers. No match. All of Adah's brothers. No match. Corvell was the only lead left.

"What's the matter?" Birdie said. "Why that face? We're closing in. I can sense it."

"Yeah. It's just ..."

"Just what?"

"Corvell lied about his alibi," Jake said.

"Guilty people usually do," Birdie said.

"But it took us what, ten minutes to check it out? Corvell's not stupid. He knows I'd get phone forensics. The credit card statements. Why give me an alibi at all? Why not just tell me to pound sand? He knows I couldn't compel him to tell me a damn thing. But he volunteered that."

"He's cocky," Birdie said.

"He is. But he's a criminal defense lawyer."

"On white-collar crimes," she said. "He's not out there defending murderers, Jake."

"But he helps Kyra Bardo. Gets his hands dirty while she's trying to help Adah. Kyra says she didn't think Corvell knew who Adah could be. Maybe she's wrong. Maybe he always knew."

"Kyra never said she told him that, did she?" Birdie asked. "She was keeping the family secret. Maybe Adah was just some girl to him. He didn't know he'd be kicking up this particular hornet's nest by killing her himself or delivering her to someone. Maybe you should ask Kyra about that."

"He knows now," Jake said. "It doesn't matter anymore what Kyra did or didn't tell him. Christ, we had that reporter put it together at that press conference two weeks ago. Maybe Corvell didn't know beforehand. But he's covering his tracks now. I just don't know exactly from whom yet."

Jake got quiet. Birdie noticed. "What aren't you telling me?" she asked.

"I put Kyra somewhere safe. She asked me for help and I gave it. I've already talked to Landry about it. I don't need another lecture."

Birdie considered his words. She didn't look happy, but neither did she look about to launch into a temper-fueled speech.

"Okay," she said.

"Okay?"

"Okay. I trust that you know what you're doing. For now."

Relief flooded through him. Jake realized he didn't like being at odds with Birdie one bit.

"Good," he said.

"So what's next?" she asked.

"We wait for a callback from Ramirez. And we keep sifting through these records."

He left the last task unspoken. He prayed nothing happened to Kyra Bardo in the meantime.

THIRTY-TWO

Nothing cleared Jake's head more than hard manual work. With the spring thaw finally settling in, Jake set about fixing the northwest corner of Grandpa Max's fence. Long ago, he kept at least six goats, twenty chickens, and even his grandmother's two ponies out here. Now, with his eyesight going and Grandma Ava long gone, he didn't use this pasture for much. Jake had tried to convince him for years to just let him tear the fencing down. The old man wouldn't hear of it. So Jake would come out here at least twice a year and repair fallen boards and touch up paint.

"You ever heard of a level?" Grandpa Max shouted. His voice pulled Jake out of his thoughts. He'd been focused on Alex Corvell. The only motive Jake could glean for Corvell's actions was greed or revenge. But fifty thousand dollars didn't seem like something that would be worth the bother for someone in Corvell's tax bracket. And why cross Rex Bardo at this stage of his career?

Jake and Birdie had spent all day Friday combing through the full cell phone and the digital forensics reports Ramirez sent over. It left Jake with more questions than answers. Corvell was in town, conducting business as usual the day Adah went missing, the day after, the week leading up to it, and the week after.

"Jake!" Grandpa shouted again. "That post is rotten. Just replace it."

Jake squeezed his hammer. "You shouldn't have come all the way down here, Gramps. The trail's still slick from yesterday's rain."

"You need to get a brush hog through there," Grandpa said. "I've been on you about that for a month."

"I'll get to it. I promise."

Grandpa Max guided his hand along the fence until he walked right next to Jake. "You always did like coming out here," he said. "Your grandmother always knew where to find you when you were in a mood, sulking off when that girl messed with your head or you didn't like something Coach Borowski told you. Or even just the way the wind blew."

The girl in question had always been Anya Strong, Jake's first and only girlfriend through high school. Long ago, he thought he might marry her. But when the time came, Jake took the first opportunity he could to get as far away from Blackhand Hills as he could.

"I'm not sulking," he said.

"The hell you're not. You barely said anything at dinner last week. You haven't been up to the house in days. And you're out here wailing on those nails like they personally offended you."

Jake put the hammer down, smirking at his grandfather. He couldn't fault the man's observations.

"Plus," Grandpa said. "You come out here when you're trying to figure something out. Make some decision and you're too stubborn to listen to anybody else's advice."

"I do not," Jake said, though once again, Grandpa Max was right.

"You wanna talk about it?" Grandpa asked.

"Not really. It's just this case."

Max perched himself on a tree stump just inside the fence. "Figured. It's not good for your soul to deal with those hill folk. Your grandmother always said that the whole valley was haunted. Filled with ghosts and bad spirits."

"You really think she believed all that? Grandma was practical."

"Oh, I think she believed it. I think she knew there was a damn good reason her great-grandpa took his family the hell out of there. Rex Bardo shoulda done the same thing."

Jake let out an ironic laugh. "So you heard about that part of it, too?"

"That the girl was his daughter? Everybody knows it now. Poor thing. Seems to me she never really had a chance. You gonna be able to keep that bastard who raised her locked away?"

"First, it's not for sure that Rex was her father. That hasn't been determined yet. Second, I hope so. Sommers isn't talking. But he hasn't hired a lawyer either. He's not doing anything in his own interests. He thinks the system is rigged against him so he seems to just be lying down."

"Well, I don't imagine he's gonna fare too well in prison if that's where he ends up. Good riddance."

Jake didn't want to admit it out loud, but he thought the same way.

"You've talked to him, haven't you?"

"Warren? I wouldn't call it much of a conversation."

"Not Warren," Grandpa said. "I'm talking about King Rex. You've been to see him."

Jake turned away from his grandfather and rested his arms on the top of the fence, looking out at the woods. He could see a doe just through the trees. She had twin fawns trailing behind her, probably less than a week old.

"Yeah," Jake said. "I've been to see him."

"It's going to get bad again, isn't it?"

"What do you mean?"

"You don't remember how things were the last time. When there's in-fighting among the Bardos, it's bad for everyone. Before Rex's father, his uncle was in charge. Melva's brother. Carl Knox was as bad as they come. But worse than that, he was stupid."

"Rex inherited the family business from his father, who got it from his father before that."

Grandpa shook his head. "Not at first. When Rex's great-grandpa died, there was a family war. Uncle Carl tried to get in Rex's grandpa's way. It got bad. Some shootings. Couple innocent people got dead over it. It would be a bad thing for this town if that started up again. Though I figured we were always headed that way the second Rex got locked up."

"I didn't realize you knew so much about the Bardo family history. You've never brought it up before," Jake said.

"Never saw the point. I'm only saying it now because you can feel it. Like it's in the wind. You need to know what you're up against."

"You sound like Virgil and Bill."

"This was all before their time, too. I'm talking sixty years ago. But I remember. Hell, I'm probably one of the last around here who still does. I just don't wanna see you get hurt. There were ... a couple of cops got shot last time. Earl Davies and Syd McCardle. Syd was one of my dad's best friends. Carl tried to send a message. Shot 'em while they were just sitting there in their patrol car outside the old spark plug factory out on County Road Three. That place burned down fifty years ago. Just the smoke stack is left."

Jake knew the place. And he'd seen Davies's and McCardle's names engraved on a memorial plaque outside the Sheriff's Department. He never really knew their story. He only knew they were the last two Worthington County deputies killed in the line of duty. It sent a cold chill through Jake. As if their ghosts had been summoned. He tried to shake it off. Maybe it was some of Grandma Ava's DNA working inside him.

"Thanks for telling me," Jake said. "It's something to think about."

"That's all I'm saying. Just ... be extra careful. This one just feels different. If Rex lost his child, he's going to want someone to blame. Someone to punish. That feeling doesn't go away easy."

Grandpa's voice trailed off. Someone to blame. Someone to punish. Max more than anyone knew what it was like to lose a child. But in Jake's father's case, there had been nobody to blame but his own diseased mind. Grandpa's words seared through him. The only punishment and blame Max Cashen could have delivered for the loss of his son was to himself.

"I don't mean to spook ya," Grandpa said. "I'll leave you to it. Finish that section before the rain rolls back in. I can feel that too."

So could Jake. He watched as Max held the fence as he made his way back up to the house.

Monday morning, when Jake parked in the lot and headed into the Public Safety Building, he saw Mark Ramirez's silver sedan parked in one of the visitor spots. There was only one thing Ramirez could be here for.

"Jake!" He turned. Birdie had rolled in just behind him. She saw Ramirez's car too.

"Come on," Jake said. "Better not keep Mark waiting."

"I wanted to talk to you about something," she said. "I pretty much made my eyes bleed looking over Corvell's office and cell phone reports."

"He never moved. Never left the county," Jake said. "That's been on my mind, too."

"I just can't figure how he can act both guilty and innocent at the same time. There's something we're missing. Don't you feel it?"

"It won't matter. Not if Mark's here for the reason I think he is."

Birdie looked at the door in front of them. Jake could sense what she was feeling because he felt it, too. He almost didn't want to head in there. He didn't think he could take more bad news if they'd been wrong about Corvell, too.

Birdie ripped the bandage off first. She steeled herself and pushed through the doors. Darcy met them at the end of the hall. She, of course, understood the looks on Jake and Birdie's faces.

"I set him up in your office," she said. "He got here just a few minutes ago. Seemed agitated that you weren't in yet. I reminded him it's not even seven o'clock yet."

Jake understood the look on Darcy's face too, along with her tone. Whatever Ramirez said to her, she'd found it rude. Darcy Noble put up with zero bullshit.

"Thanks," Jake said. He'd downed two cups of coffee at home. He figured he'd need about three more on a day like today.

Ramirez was sitting at the table in Jake's office, where Darcy had deposited him. He rose as soon as Jake and Birdie entered.

"I had to come straight down," he said. "I knew you'd want to see what we have. I promised ..."

"Just let me have it," Jake said. He slid his coat off, took Birdie's, and hung them both on the hook by the door.

"Sit," Ramirez commanded them.

"Am I going to like this?" Jake asked.

Ramirez didn't immediately answer. Instead, he opened the file folder in front of him. Mark Ramirez often liked to speak through graphs and charts. Today would be no exception.

"DNA and blood evidence is back on your suspect, Alexander Corvell. We got some interesting results."

"Just tell me they're conclusive," Birdie said.

"They are," Ramirez answered. "Sort of."

Jake was about to blow his stack. For once, he just wanted a straight answer.

"He's not a match," Ramirez said. Jake felt like a ten ton boulder had just landed on his solar plexus. This couldn't be happening.

Not again. He could not ... would not ... believe he was back to square one.

"On every marker, the skin under Adah's nails, the semen, blood ... I told you. Our analysis was definitive. All foreign samples came from the same individual. That's been clear from the beginning. Based on the DNA collected from Corvell, he can be excluded. It wasn't his DNA. At least ..."

"Dammit," Jake said. He felt his anger rising. It was a struggle not to give into it.

"Who in the hell killed this girl?" Birdie shouted, her own rage starting to show. "After all this, are we left with it just being some random psychopath? We'll never find him. We're out of leads."

"Hold on," Ramirez said. "Let me finish. I said Alexander Corvell himself can be excluded. But the sample he gave proved something else."

Jake felt buzzing in his ears. His stomach rolled.

"Here," Ramirez said. He pointed to the data on one of the charts. Jake couldn't make his eyes focus on it. "See these markers? The areas in red and blue? These are Corvell's. These others are from the specimens taken off Adah's body. Do you see what I'm seeing?"

He had the graphs from Adah's killer printed on a transparency. He laid it over the sheet containing Alex Corvell's results.

"It's a DNA match," he said.

"You just said it wasn't a match," Birdie said, frustrated.

"It's a close familial match," Ramirez said, his tone gleeful.

"What are you saying, Mark? Speak English," Jake said.

"The samples taken from Adah belong to a close relative of Alexander Corvell's. You don't see these kinds of similarities outside of a parent/child relationship."

"His son?" Jake said. "You're telling me Adah Lee's killer had to be Alex Corvell's son?"

Ramirez sat back, smiling. "DNA doesn't lie. That's exactly what I'm telling you."

THIRTY-THREE

"As soon as we have a name to go with it, I'll have the warrant signed," Birdie said. Jake had her on speaker as he drove at NASCAR speed toward Frank's place.

"Good," Jake said. "Keep on that. Check through public records. BMV, social security, all of it."

"I know," she said. "I'm into it now. Just stay in touch. Bundy and Stuckey just called from Corvell's office. He's not there. It's closed up. I'm going to keep Bundy sitting there just in case. Denning and Holtz are on their way to Corvell's residence. Nobody is going to come in or out without us knowing about it. I'll meet you there in an hour."

"Got it," Jake said. He made a hairpin turn onto Baker Road, kicking up gravel and pissing off a flock of geese as they finished crossing. He clicked off the call and tossed his phone on the passenger seat.

His pulse racing, he finally turned down Frank's quarter-mile driveway. He saw no new tire tracks in the dirt road now turned to mud. As he screeched to a halt in front of the garage, he saw lights on inside.

He didn't knock. He didn't do anything to give her advanced warning he was coming in. He typed the security code into the panel on the garage door and waited impatiently for the thing to rise.

Barging through the service door, he shouted, "Kyra? Kyra?"

There was dead silence for a moment. But then Kyra emerged wearing one of Frank's robes and toweling off wet hair.

"What a pleasant surprise," she said, her voice dripping with sarcasm.

"Sit down," he said. "I need to know everything you told Alex Corvell about where Adah would be that night."

"I already told you that," she said. "He knew I was going to get her when she called to tell me she'd cleared Red Sky Hill."

"It was you? It was only supposed to be you picking her up?"

"Yes. Why are you asking me this again?"

Jake paced in front of the kitchen counter, then stopped short, rubbing his chin hard with his right hand. "Where were you?"

"What?"

"When you took that call from Adah. Where were you? Physically. At home? Your office? Your car? Where were you?"

She looked puzzled. Her mouth formed an "o" as she considered his question.

"I was at Corvell's," she said. "His office. I think I already told you that."

Jake slammed a fist against one of the cabinets. "No. You didn't. I don't think I asked."

"Okay, well, there it is. I had some other business to discuss with him. Mundane stuff. I was about to leave and my other phone rang."

"You were sitting in Corvell's office?"

"I think I was heading out to my car. I don't exactly remember."

"Corvell's son. What's his name?"

"Jake, what the hell are you talking about?"

"His son!" Jake shouted, taking a step toward her. Kyra sank into a chair at the kitchen table and set her towel down.

"I don't know his son," she said.

"You know he has one," Jake said. "You've met him?"

She turned her palms upward, shrugging her shoulders. "We didn't really talk about his personal life. I know he's got a trophy wife of some kind. Yeah. Maybe a handful of times I've seen his son. There might be an older daughter, too."

"In the office," Jake said. "Did you ever see him hanging around Corvell's office?"

She shook her head. "I don't know. Maybe. I certainly don't know the kid to talk to him. I told you. I've just seen him around a few times. Doesn't look a thing like his dad. Tall. Blond. Kinda skinny, I guess."

"His name," Jake said.

"Devin? Dylan? Something like that. No, wait. Dylan. A couple of months ago when I was in the office, the wife and the kid showed up. They were waiting for Alex to take them to dinner. She called him Dylan."

Jake took his phone out and called Birdie. She answered right away and said the name at the same time he did. "Dylan Corvell."

"What do you have?" Jake asked.

"Driver's license. Last known address is his parents' house. I've got the warrant, heading over there now. How fast can you get there?"

"Fifteen," Jake said. "I'm on my way." He clicked off the call.

"Stay put," he ordered Kyra. "Don't talk to anyone. Don't go anywhere. Don't do a damn thing until you hear from me again."

"Jake, what is going on?"

He was angry. If Kyra had just been straight with him from the beginning, this whole thing would have gone so differently. "Don't worry about it," he said gruffly. "I've just got to go clean up your mess."

He left her standing there, mouth gaping, water from her wet hair dripping on the floor.

H e and Birdie pulled up in front of Corvell's house at the same time. Jake flew out of the driver's seat, leaving his door open.

"What do you know?" Birdie asked, sprinting to catch up with him as he charged toward the front door.

"I think he was in the office when Kyra took that last phone call from Adah. Corvell either told his kid what was going on or he overheard. I have no idea whether Corvell himself was in on what Dylan did. Right now, I don't care. We're taking them both in."

"If he's here," Birdie said. She gestured to Deputies Amanda Chaplin and Jordy Holtz. "They can search the house and grounds." She handed Jake a copy of the arrest warrant. Another cruiser pulled up, more backup Birdie had called in. Deputies Morse and Corbin stepped out. Birdie gestured for them to join her and Jake on the front porch.

"Corvell!" Jake shouted as he pounded on the front door. Deputy Chaplin jogged across the yard to take a position at the back of the house. Holtz headed out to the stable. As far as Jake knew, there were no other outbuildings on the property.

"Open the door!" Jake yelled, ready to bust the thing down if he had to. There'd be no waiting around this time.

A moment later, Corvell opened it. He was in drawstring pants and a tee shirt, a ring of sweat around his neck as if he'd been working out.

"Step aside," Jake said. "We're coming in. Where's Dylan?"

Jake slapped his copy of the arrest warrant against Corvell's chest. "Dylan," Jake said. "Where is he?"

Corvell took a moment to read the warrant. His face registered no shock—held no expression at all.

"He isn't here," Corvell said.

"Sorry if we're not inclined to take your word for it." He waved the other deputies in. "We're going to turn this place upside down. You can make it easier on yourself if you just tell me where to find your son."

Deirdre Corvell appeared at the top of the stairs. Alex looked over his shoulder and shouted to her. "Just go back to your room, Dee. This doesn't concern you."

"Mrs. Corvell," Jake said. "I'm here for your son, Dylan. Is he home? Do you know where he is?"

"Go to your room!" Corvell shouted, as if she were a child. Deirdre looked startled, but she didn't move from her position on the upstairs landing.

"Go," Jake commanded the deputies. They knew from their previous warrant search that all the bedrooms were on the second floor. Jake had them march upstairs, brushing past a stunned Deirdre Corvell. She slowly descended the stairs and went to her husband's side.

"What do you think you're doing?" Corvell said. "This is a violation of my civil rights. My wife's civil rights."

"Spare me the lecture," Jake said. "You know damn well it isn't. And I'm done playing your games."

"Dylan isn't here!" Corvell shouted.

"Then he should have changed his address," Jake muttered.

"It took us a week to undo the damage you did to my home and property the first time. You so much as leave a smudge on the banister and I'll ..."

"You'll what?" Jake said. He turned to Deidre. "Mrs. Corvell? Since your husband doesn't seem willing to tell you, let me fill you in. I have an arrest warrant for your son, for the murder of Adah Lee Sommers. I'm asking for your cooperation in finding him. Or ... if I find out either one of you is hiding him, I'll arrest you for obstruction of justice, aiding and abetting, you name it. You can sit in a jail cell right along with him."

"Alex," she said, breathless.

"Not another word," he barked at his wife.

"Clear!" Jake heard the shout from upstairs. A moment later, Holtz and Chaplin came in.

"Nobody in the outbuilding," Chaplin said. "Only one other car in the garage. A silver Miata."

"That's my car," Deirdre said.

"I said not another word," Corvell said, turning and grabbing his wife by the shoulders. He gave her a quick, solid shake.

"Where does Dylan work?" Jake said. "Where does he hang out? The sooner you cooperate, the better."

"We have nothing to say to you," Corvell said. "We told you. Dylan isn't here. Your deputies have just told you the same thing. You are now trespassing. So either you arrest me, or get out."

"Alex, please," Deirdre said. "This is enough."

Alex Corvell's face turned two shades of purple. His eyes bulged and he advanced on his wife. Jake stepped in between them and put his hands on Corvell's chest, shoving him back.

"You touch her and I'll add domestic battery to the list."

"This is ridiculous," Corvell said. "Outrageous. My son isn't here. He's done nothing to warrant any of this. You need to leave."

"Your son's DNA was found all over the victim," Jake said. "He raped her, beat her, killed her, then dumped her body in Blackhand Hills State Park where a little girl found her. So we're not leaving here until we have an answer. Where's Dylan?"

"Not. Here," Corvell said. "I have no idea where he is. He's a grown man. And you're lying about everything else."

"No."

It was a quiet sound, almost inaudible. But it came from Deidre Corvell. She stepped back, sinking into a seated position on the bottom step of the massive double staircase.

Before Corvell could scold her again, before he could so much as breathe, Jake walked over to her.

"Mrs. Corvell? Tell me what you know."

"Deirdre!" Corvell shouted.

"Take him outside," Jake said to Holtz, who stood closest to Corvell. "Put him in cuffs and park him in the backseat of your cruiser until I say otherwise."

"You cannot talk to her outside of my presence. I am her attorney as well as her husband."

"You want him here?" Jake asked Deirdre.

She looked up at Jake, her eyes filling with tears. "No," she said. "Alex, it's time to tell the truth."

"Goddammit, Deirdre! She's out of her mind. She's been on medication. She does not speak for me. She does not speak for Dylan. She is not mentally competent. Anything she says will be inadmissible."

Holtz did as Jake asked. He and Morse muscled Alex Corvell out the front door. He resisted and the deputies held him in the doorway.

"What do you need to tell us, Mrs. Corvell?" Birdie asked. "Do you know where your son is? Can you tell us where he's staying?"

"I don't have to," she said. She pulled her cell phone out of the back pocket of her jeans. She tapped the screen and turned it toward Jake. It was a GPS map.

Jake took the phone. Birdie peered over around his shoulder.

"You're tracking him?" Birdie asked. "That's a tracker app, Jake."

"Deirdre, you little bitch!" Corvell shouted. "He kept his phone?!"

"Out," Jake said. Holtz and Morse dragged Alex Corvell kicking and screaming, stuffed him into their cruiser, and slammed the door in his face.

"I put it on there when he got his driver's license," she said. "I think he forgot it was there."

Jake looked closer. On screen, there was a blue circle outlining a photo of a blond teenage boy, grinning. It placed him about fifteen miles away in Maudeville. Jake knew the area. It was a trailer park.

"He has a couple of friends who live out there," Deirdre said. "Losers. Drug addicts. Dylan's been mixed up in it for a few years. We've kicked him out a few times. It never sticks. Alex always lets him back."

"He's been violent?" Jake asked.

She wiped away a tear. "Sometimes. If he's been drinking or using drugs. I always know. I just need to see him take one step and I know. Or the tone of his voice. He promises and promises, but nothing ever happens."

"Has he hit you?" Jake asked.

"He hit Alex. Multiple times. And yes, once he hit me. A few months ago. I tried to take his keys from him so he wouldn't try to drive drunk. He shoved me down the stairs, going into the garage. I broke my wrist. Alex had a client of his, a doctor, come over and take care of me. He wouldn't let me see my own doctor or go to the ER."

"Does he have a gun?" Jake asked.

"Not that I know of. We've tried everything. Alex has lined up job after job for him but it never lasts. He stops going. He checks himself out of rehab. I told Alex maybe we should stop bailing him out. Maybe jail would do him some good. He had a girlfriend. The sweetest kid you'll ever meet. Taylor. From a good family. She's studying to be a nurse. He hurt her. He'd never admit it, but I knew. I saw her at the grocery store and she had a black eye. I tried to ask her about it but she just took off. Scared to death. And when I told Alex, he blew me off. Told me he'd taken care of it and I shouldn't worry. And Dylan's been kicked out of school. Neither of them would tell me why. But I'm in a parent group on social media. There were rumors. A girl accused him of date rape. And Alex ... I think he handled that, too. Got the girl to sign something. I think it was an NDA. I was in denial. I can see that now. Alex kept telling me everything would be okay. Not to worry. I'm so sorry. I didn't know what to do."

"Thank you," Jake said. "You're doing the right thing. Will you send me this?" He handed her phone back to her and gave her his own cell number. A moment later, Deidre shared the link to her tracker app data with Dylan's exact location.

"He needs help," she said. "Do you ... do you really think he killed that girl?"

Birdie put a hand on her shoulder, trying to comfort her. "We think so, Mrs. Corvell."

"What should I do? Alex is going to be so angry with me. But we've done everything his way for too long."

"We'll bring your husband to the sheriff's office," Jake assured her. "We'll have a lot more questions for him. I'm going to leave one of my deputies here with you. Your husband won't be back for quite a while. Do you want him back in the house?"

She shook her head. "Better not. Not until he cools down. I don't … I don't feel safe."

It was all Jake needed to hear. He instructed Chaplin and Corbin to stay back and help Deidre Corvell with anything she needed. Then he and Birdie walked outside.

Corvell was yelling from the back of the cruiser, his voice muffled behind the closed window. Jake turned his back on him. When he reached his own car, he took out his phone and called Darcy at the office.

"I need the closest available units to meet me at 532 Trail Way in Maudeville Township. Sunset Acres Park. Tell them not to make a move until I get there. I'm fifteen minutes out."

Thirty-Four

Sunset Acres was one of the oldest, most rundown mobile home parks in the county. Inhabitants of the two nearby subdivisions had been petitioning the township to close it down or enforce their blight ordinances for years. As gallows humor, most of the field ops deputies referred to the place as Sundown Acres, owing to the park's large percentage of elderly residents and the fact that a not small number of calls out there involved well-checks or missing persons reports when someone's grandparent wandered off.

Jake pulled up to the row bearing all the modular homes with the 500 address. It looked like a ghost town. Each unit was more dilapidated than the next. Some of them had to be at least forty years old.

"Unit belongs to a Fred MacIntosh," Birdie said. She'd pulled up the address on the dashboard computer. "But he's listed as deceased as of 2020. Doesn't look like the trailer ownership was ever changed over to whoever is living there now."

"Fred was probably somebody's dad or grandpa," Jake said. He cut the engine and grabbed his vest from the back seat. He tossed Birdie hers. They strapped them on as three more units pulled up, having responded to Darcy's dispatch.

"Tenth one down on the right," Birdie said, showing her phone screen to Jake. She'd pulled up the satellite map of the area. A yellow dot marked unit 532.

Jake directed a unit to head down the row behind the MacIntosh residence. If anyone tried to run out the back, they'd be ready. He'd have the other two units on either side of the trailer, ready for anything.

It was time to go. Jake kept his hand on the heel of his weapon. A few neighbors peered out through windows, but quickly closed their blinds, probably used to minding their own business when something like this happened.

532 was practically caving in on itself. The screen door hung by one nail and flapped in the breeze. A wild-haired tabby cat sat on the porch and darted off as soon as it saw Jake and Birdie approach. The front yard was littered with beer cans and cigarette butts. Two windows on the side of the unit had cracks through them, repaired with duct tape; worn blue tarps covered part of the roof.

Jake and Birdie took opposite positions on the side of the front door. Jake gestured to the other deputies to fan out. One of them gave Jake a thumbs up, indicating the third unit had positioned themselves at the back of the trailer.

Jake knocked. "Sheriff's Department! Come to the door. I have a warrant. I need you to come out and talk to me."

He heard voices inside. Laughter. But also music playing at a high decibel. There was little chance anyone inside could hear him shout or knock. He banged louder.

"Open up or I'm coming in! I just want to talk to you, Dylan. Come outside."

The music got quieter, but no one came to the door. Jake shook his head in frustration. He pounded one more time.

"Dylan Corvell. This is Detective Jake Cashen. I just need to talk to you."

No answer. Just more laughter. Jake drew his weapon. Birdie did the same.

Birdie was on the side with the door handle. She carefully reached over and turned it. With a slight push of her fingers, the door slowly swung open. It wasn't locked.

Jake looked at Birdie, then down to Stuckey who was holding a small ram. Stuckey shrugged and held out the ram. Jake waved a hand across his neck, gesturing, "no." From the look of the door and handle, Jake guessed it had already been knocked down a few times.

With a swift kick, the door slammed inward. Guns drawn, Jake peeled left to the living room. Birdie went right, clearing the kitchen. A smokey chemical smell filled the trailer. Jake immediately recognized the scent as meth with a hint of body odor, sour food, and cat piss.

Two men sat on a battered couch staring at a large flat screen TV. They each had game controllers in their hands and were busy killing monsters on screen. One of the young men looked over his shoulder at Jake, then spotted Birdie and the other deputies. He didn't seem fazed. The kid was clearly baked. He stuffed his hand into a potato chip bag and nudged his companion. The other one, a kid with stringy red hair, turned.

Jake yanked a plug out of the wall, silencing the music and killing the video game. "Hey!" Jake shouted. "Stand up and show me your hands, put them on the top of your head, and walk toward me."

Still seemingly unfazed by the intrusion, the two stood up and followed Jake's direction.

"The hell do you want?" the redhead asked.

"Are either one of you Dylan Corvell?" Jake asked.

The two kids looked at each other, their eyes glazed over, hands still on their heads.

"No, man," the redheaded spokesman answered.

"Where is he?" Jake said.

"Sleeping, I think," Redhead answered. He pointed with his elbow down the hall.

"Dylan!" the other kid shouted. "Somebody wants to talk to you. Get your ass out of bed." He went back to his game, turning it back on.

Jake rolled his eyes. He kept two deputies on the gamer kids and started with Birdie down the hall. One room was the bathroom. There were two closed doors further down.

Then, something smashed to the floor. Jake and Birdie hugged the wall and crouched, guns drawn.

"Dylan Corvell!" Jake shouted. "I need you to come out, son. We just want to talk."

Breaking glass. A large thud. One of Jake's deputies barked through the radio. "We've got a runner! Slipped out a side window. Landed over the chain-link fence into the neighbor's on the east side."

Jake banged the back of his head against the wall. "You gotta be kidding me."

He and Birdie raced back to the front door. He shouted an order to the other deputies. "Don't let those two leave!"

By the time Birdie and Jake rounded the east side of the trailer, one unit had started to pursue Dylan from the row behind the trailer.

From the corner of his eye, Jake saw a rusted garbage can thrown from one of the other trailers across the street. Birdie took off like a shot. Jake was right behind her.

Dogs started barking. Jake saw a skinny kid with blond hair trailing behind him as he darted in a zigzag pattern through the yards.

Birdie shouted into her shoulder radio, telling the other units which direction Dylan was headed. Birdie was fast, but Jake was faster. He overtook her and started to close the distance between Dylan and himself.

The kid was surprisingly agile. He vaulted over a wooden fence and kept on going.

"Christ," Jake muttered. It was hard to be nimble wearing his protective gear and a ten-pound belt. But he cleared the fence no more than five seconds after Dylan.

"Dylan! There's nowhere to go! You're going to get hurt!"

Dylan took a sharp turn. As Jake gained ground, the kid picked up a Big Wheel from one of the yards and hurled it in Jake's path. Jake quickly dodged it. Dylan ducked under a clothesline. A pair of ratty boxer shorts flew off and landed on Jake's face. He tossed them aside. Birdie was right behind him.

Jake kept going, nearly tripping over a garden hose as he rounded the corner. Up ahead, the alley dead-ended into a ten-foot-tall chain-link fence.

"Stop!" Jake yelled. "There's no place else to go!"

Dylan looked over his shoulder. But he kept on running. He took a sharp turn down another row of trailers. Birdie caught up to Jake.

An instant later, they heard a loud metal crash and a scream. "Get it off me! Get it off me!"

Guns drawn, Jake and Birdie rounded the corner together, then stopped short.

Dylan Corvell was on his back, lying in a pile of garbage, a metal can overturned near his feet. He kicked his legs and writhed on the ground as a large, angry German Shepherd sunk its teeth into Dylan's arm. The dog foamed at the mouth and emitted a low, lethal growl.

"Shoot it!" Dylan yelled. "Shoot it!"

Jake raised his weapon. Birdie, to Jake's right, took one step forward. She shouted in a loud, clear, crisp voice, "Break!" Then she thrust her left arm out and bent her hand sharply downward at the wrist.

The dog reared its head, released Dylan's arm, let out a keening wail, then immediately dropped to its belly, head flat on the ground.

Dylan curled into a fetal position, whimpering. The dog stayed frozen on the ground. Jake looked at Birdie. "How the hell did you know that would work?"

She shrugged. "I ... well ... I didn't. He just looks like one of the K9 units that served with my battalion."

Another shout came from Jake's left. "Boris! Boris!"

A woman with long, kinky gray hair wearing a bathrobe and little else came running toward them, waving her hands.

"Don't shoot him! Don't shoot him! He's a good boy. He's a good boy!"

Jake and Birdie pointed their weapons downward. The woman grabbed a long leash trailing from Boris's neck. She pulled the dog back. He slobbered his owner's face with kisses.

Jake quickly advanced, though Dylan wasn't moving. He just lay there sobbing, covered in mud and dog shit, holding his bleeding arm to his chest.

Birdie started shouting his Miranda rights at him while Jake worked loose his handcuffs and pulled Dylan's arms behind him.

THIRTY-FIVE

An hour later, Jake had Dylan Corvell deposited into one interview room, his father, Alex, in another. He sent Lieutenant Beverly to supervise the searches of 532 Trail Way, Dylan's car, and the room he kept at his parents' house.

While Birdie dealt with Alex, Jake walked into the room with Dylan and slapped a file folder on the table. Since the second Jake put the cuffs on him, Dylan had morphed into a cocky little jerk. He sat with his arms crossed, sunk down into the chair, his legs splayed wide. He wore a bandage on his wounded arm, but the EMTs said it was superficial and didn't even need stitches. They cleaned it, dressed it, and handed him back over to Jake.

"I got nothing to say to you," Dylan said, smiling.

"Don't care," Jake said. "I'll do the talking, then. I'm going to explain what's going on. So we're clear. So there's no misunderstanding."

Jake opened the file folder and pulled out a zoomed-in photograph of Adah Lee's body the way it was found. In this image, you couldn't see her face. Just her hands and torso.

"Look closely," Jake said. Dylan flicked his eyes toward the picture but acted unimpressed.

"I notice you've got fresh scars on your neck, Dylan. Like somebody might have scratched you."

The kid curled his lips in a smirk. "I've got a girl who likes things a little rough. She got carried away."

"Obviously. See, I'm thinking you're dumb, but you're not stupid. This girl here had long nails. She fought pretty hard. She took a chunk out of you. There was skin and blood under her nails. Your skin and blood."

Dylan leaned forward, still smiling. "I told you. Some girls like things rough. I've got a few battle scars. But sometimes they turn into hellcats. You know? Or ... maybe not. You look like the vanilla type to me. Or maybe your hand is all you can score."

Rage boiled through Jake, but he took a breath and did a mental five count.

"This girl was raped, Dylan. Beaten. Strangled. By you. It's over. You're caught. DNA doesn't lie."

Dylan shrugged. "I like kinky girls. More to the point, they like me. Trust me. They get rewarded."

"Rewarded," Jake repeated. "Adah Lee got dead. She got thrown away like garbage. That's what you thought she was, isn't it? You thought she was nobody. Who was going to care if a girl like that disappeared? Nobody really knew she existed outside of her own family."

"That's not my problem. Yeah. She was some hillbilly. Who cares?"

"I do. Her family does. Do you know who her family is?"

"I told you. A bunch of inbred hicks. Trying to marry her off to her own brother or something. Why should I give a shit? Why should you?"

There was no point talking to him. No point arguing. "You know," Jake said. "You're right. I don't care what you have to say or don't say. I know what you did. It's all here. Running through your veins, Dylan. You don't have to talk. You don't have to explain or bother lying to me. Because you don't matter. Everything that matters is in this file. This file puts a needle in your arm."

Jake stood. Dylan lifted his eyes, watching him. But the smirk didn't leave.

"Get comfortable," Jake said. "It's going to be a long day for you."

Birdie opened the door and poked her head in. "Sorry to interrupt. I just wanted to let you know. The prosecutor's almost done with Mr. Corvell. He's having the paperwork sent over from his office. Full immunity."

She flicked her eyes over to Dylan, pretending she was just noticing him sitting there. "Oh, sorry. I really didn't mean to interrupt you."

Dylan sat up a little straighter. His color got a little more ashen. But he kept his mouth shut.

"Thanks," Jake said. "I was just about to head over there."

"You want me to sit with this one, sir?" she asked, her tone as meek as she could make it. An act Dylan Corvell seemed to buy. He started to chew on his thumbnail.

"He'll be okay for now," Jake said. He didn't even turn to look at Dylan as he walked out of the room and locked Dylan in behind him.

"Is he scared enough?" Birdie asked, straightening her posture as they walked down the hall.

"That'll help," Jake said. "Is Ansel really here?"

"Yes, actually. I don't think he's considering full immunity though. Corvell said he wants to talk to you. He sent Ansel out of the room."

As they rounded the corner, Boyd Ansel, Worthington County's prosecutor, stood in the hallway outside the other interview room. He carried a briefcase in his left hand and hailed Jake as he approached.

"Get anything from the son?" Ansel asked.

"Just attitude. What are you offering his father?"

"Depends on how much he cooperates. I think he's finally figured out sticking with his son is like strapping himself to dynamite. Let's just say his self-preservation instinct has kicked in. I told him he's gotta plead. I can work out a lesser charge, recommend a long house arrest and probation, but he's not walking away from this."

"He went for that?" Jake asked.

"It was his idea," Ansel answered. "I'll let him explain for himself why."

"It's aggravated murder for the kid," Jake said. "Plus, about six other felonies."

"The only thing I'll bargain with is his life," Ansel said. "Whether he spends it waiting to be executed or waiting to die of natural causes in a prison cell."

"Thanks," Jake said as he opened the door. Alex Corvell looked tired, but clean-shaven, freshly barbered, and in a crisp black suit and yellow tie.

"Is he okay?" he asked. "Will you at least tell me that?" For as arrogant as Corvell had been through all of this, that seemed to melt away.

"You told Boyd Ansel you'll cooperate?"

"In exchange for some assurances, yes. I can't go to prison."

"That's not up to you."

"I know. It's up to the two of you. But Jake, if you send me to prison, I'm a dead man. I know better than to cross Rex Bardo."

"Except you did," Jake said. "The second you started covering up for Dylan. And when you started working with Kyra before that."

Corvell dropped his head. "You're not a father. You can't know the hell this has put us through."

"Your hell? Christ, Corvell. A girl is dead. Tortured, raped, mutilated, strangled, then dead. You don't know what hell is. Only the one you've created for yourself."

"He's my son!"

"His mother seems to understand what a monster he is. She wasn't willing to throw herself on a fire to save him. But you were. As far as I'm concerned, there should be no mercy for you."

"I'm his father. I'm sorry. But I still love my son."

"You've been playing games. Stalling for time. Your alibi. That's what that was, wasn't it? You knew it would only take me about ten minutes once I got your financials and cell data to find out you lied. But you knew your DNA wouldn't be on that girl. You knew every piece of physical evidence would clear you. So you threw up roadblocks to stall for time. For what? You were going to help Dylan disappear."

"They will kill him," Corvell whispered. "I couldn't trust you. I couldn't trust the Bardos. I was the only shot he had. If you had a son of your own, you'd understand. I just wanted to give him a chance. But he would have been far away. I would make sure he couldn't hurt anyone else."

"What was the plan? Venezuela? Argentina? Had to be somewhere he couldn't be extradited."

"Please, I'll tell you everything. I just need to know you won't put me in prison. I know Ansel can ensure that. Ask him."

A second later, Ansel walked through the door. Of course, he'd been listening from the other side of the one-way mirror.

"It's your call, Jake," he said. "I'll sign off on whatever you want."

Jake wanted to see Alex Corvell rot in prison right next to his son. But he knew Corvell was right. He wouldn't survive it. He knew too much about the Bardos. And he tried to help his son get away with killing Adah.

"Everything," Jake said. "Every detail. What you did. When you did it. Then Boyd tries to get you probation and house arrest. Not some ninety-day bullshit. Years, Corvell. You're eating a felony, you get to wear that for the rest of your life. You'll give up your law license."

Corvell didn't look the least bit shocked by any of Jake's conditions. He turned to Ansel.

"I didn't know," he said. "I had no idea Dylan was listening in when Kyra got the call from Adah. He was in the office. I was trying to put him to work, doing some grunt work for me. My son has been rudderless. I've been trying to help him find some direction. But nothing worked."

"You knew he'd hurt women before," Jake said.

"I never saw that. Maybe that was on purpose. I didn't want to believe it. I suppose none of that matters now. I won't waste your time. But that night, when Kyra got that call, I had no idea Dylan would do what he did. I didn't even know he went to her. Not beforehand. But later, it was maybe midnight that night. He came home. He was all scratched up and covered in blood. I thought he'd been in a car accident."

Jake felt his whole body go rigid. No one was there for Adah. She'd been literally thrown to the wolves.

"What did you do?" Jake said, his own voice sounding foreign to his ears. Cold. Flat. Dark.

"He told me. He said it was an accident. That he was just trying to help that girl get where she wanted to go. He said he thought that's what I would want. He said one thing led to another and she threw herself at him. That it got rough. I was confused. I didn't know who he was talking about. Then he said her name. I felt the floor just disappear beneath me. I couldn't breathe. I didn't want to believe it."

"Did you see her?" Jake asked. "Was she still in his trunk, Alex?"

"No. God. No. No. It was all over. Dylan had already ... disposed of her. He didn't tell me where. I never knew that. He just told me he'd taken care of it. That nobody was ever going to find her. He begged me. He kept saying Daddy, please, I'm sorry. He just fell apart. Clinging to me. I love him. I'm sorry for what he did and what he is. But I still love him. That night, he seemed like just a scared little boy. I'm sorry. It broke me. I panicked."

"Panicked," Jake said. "You made plans. Schemed. Didn't you?"

Corvell scratched his chin. "I swear, I just wanted to get him somewhere safe where Rex couldn't find him. Then ... days went by. Nobody came to the front door. Everyone assumed Warren Sommers hurt her. He's a vile human being. He deserves to rot in jail. I'm sorry, but I didn't have any sympathy for him."

"He's the monster," Jake said. "You didn't think your precious Dylan was the same thing."

"He's not! He needs help. That's all."

Jake wanted to throw up. "Keep going."

"I just needed time. You're right. I stalled for it. I did a few things. First, things I was hoping would keep things focused ... elsewhere."

"You leaked Adah's possible paternity to the press," Jake said. "You were hoping to make a bigger circus out of this. Make my job harder."

"Yes," Corvell whispered. "Then, I did things I thought would draw attention to me if the investigation ever turned that way. Just time."

"Your bank account?" Jake asked.

"Yes. I put a large deposit into my personal account. I knew if it came to it, you'd look there. It was just cash I kept in a safe for emergencies. I knew the timing of the deposit might cause questions. Raise suspicions. I swear, I just needed some time."

"This was the day after Adah went missing," Jake said. "Within twelve hours. The girl is dead. Brutally murdered, and you have the presence of mind to make banking transactions in an attempt to throw me off?" Jake knew it was just a more sophisticated version of throwing garbage cans and a Big Wheel in his path the way Dylan had when he ran.

He didn't answer. Jake believed this guy thought everything he did was justified if it was to protect his miserable son.

"Your ridiculous alibi," Jake said. "That was just to throw me off and make me spend time chasing my tail."

Corvell squirmed in his chair. "He was supposed to go. I gave Dylan money. A bus ticket. He was supposed to get on it and cross the southern border. From there, I arranged for passage to Central America. Yes."

"But he was too stupid or too stubborn to do what you told him. Even down to keeping his cell phone on him."

Corvell's eyes filled with tears. He stared up at the ceiling.

"He put the money into his arm or up his nose? Is that it?"

"Probably."

"He figured Daddy would just bail him out again. That he had nothing to worry about. That he'd really done nothing wrong," Jake said.

"Yes."

Corvell buried his face in his hands and sobbed. In a strange way, Jake could almost feel sorry for him. Not only was his son a psychopathic murderer, he was a damn idiot.

"Come with me," Jake said.

"What?"

"Get up and come with me. There's one last thing I want to watch you do."

Corvell looked desperately at Boyd Ansel. Ansel merely shrugged and held the door open for him and followed them both down the hall.

Two minutes later, Jake opened the door to the other interview room. Dylan Corvell sat up straighter when he saw his father. That smirk crept back into his face. He rose and held his hands out, displaying his cuffs.

"Time to take these off," he said. "You have no idea who my father is."

"Tell him," Jake said to Alex Corvell.

"Dylan, son. It's over. I can't help you anymore."

For a moment, Dylan's smarmy expression stayed locked in place.

"It went too far," Alex said. "And it was wrong. I can't fix this. I can't get you out of this. They know what you did to Adah Sommers. They can prove it. Please. Just tell them what they want to know. At least then maybe you won't face the death penalty. Please. Don't put your mother through that. Don't make her have to watch them strap you down and kill you by lethal injection. I'm begging you. Cooperate with them now."

Dylan's face went sheet white. "You son of a bitch. He's lying. He's lying! He killed her. I didn't have anything to do with this. Dad. Daddy! Please!"

"No, Dylan. I'm sorry. Not this time. It has to stop."

Dylan shook his head. He went from scared to furious in one breath.

"I'll kill you. I'll kill you! You son of a bitch. What did you tell them about me? What did you say?"

Dylan Corvell lunged at his father. Jake got in between them just in time but not before Dylan shoved his father back against the wall. Alex staggered and nearly fell. Ansel caught him.

Jake threw Dylan back. He thrashed, threw punches. But Jake quickly immobilized him and wrestled him to the ground.

Dylan's screams echoed off the concrete walls. Four deputies poured in. Jake let them have Dylan. They hauled him to his feet and carried him out the door and back to his holding cell.

THIRTY-SIX

King Rex Bardo had a swagger to his walk today. His bruises had faded, but he had new hardness to his face. He swung one leg over the bench and sat down across from Jake.

"People are gonna start thinking we're friends," Rex said, with no humor in his voice.

Jake had a flat manila envelope under his hands as he rested them on the table.

"I made you a promise," Jake said. "I know you probably already know the highlights, but I figured you'd want to hear it directly from me, too."

Rex didn't blink. He kept silent.

"Dylan Corvell will plead guilty in exchange for Boyd Ansel not seeking the death penalty. It's over."

Rex arched a brow, but still didn't utter a word.

"Even without Dylan's confession, the evidence was solid. No one else was involved. Not just the DNA. Reports just came back. The carpet fibers found on Adah matched the ones in Dylan's trunk. Her blood was found there too. Dirt from Blackhand Hills was in the treads of Dylan's tires. It was all him and only him."

Still, Rex remained stoic.

"I'm sorry," Jake said. "I wanted it to be something, I don't know. I don't know what I mean. But it was a psychopath who liked to hurt women. Adah was just in the wrong place at the wrong time. Everybody who tried to help her just couldn't. Warren's to blame for making her life so hard and pushing her to escape from it. Alex Corvell's to blame because he raised a monster for a son and made one too many excuses for him."

"Is that all?" Rex asked.

"What?"

"Alex. Warren Sommers. This kid. You think you've wrapped everything up?"

"Sommers is done," Jake said. "He's not going to be in a position to hurt anyone else, either. His entire compound out there has been cleared out. Those who want to start over are getting that chance. Scarlett is getting that chance. Her son Isaac just started a new job. He's making good money as a carpenter. I've got a social worker who set him up with a place to live. Big enough for Scarlett and Zenni to stay there, too. And they want to. She's ready to start over. Zenni enrolled at Stanley High School, starting in the fall. A bunch of the rest of those kids did too. We're finding good foster families for the ones who wanted to leave Red Sky Hill without their parents. That's most of them. There are no more whisper kids, Rex. They're being taken care of. Given a chance."

"Sounds like a happy ending, then," Rex said.

"If something good could come out of this, it's that. Adah died for that. In her death, she was able to shine a light on everything that was going on out there. And put an end to it."

"So I should be grateful?"

Jake clenched his jaw. "That's not what I'm saying."

"If it helps you sleep at night. Who am I to tell you what to think?"

"I delivered on my promise," Jake said. "I want to know if you'll deliver on yours?"

"And what promise would that be?" Rex asked, leaning forward, getting into Jake's face.

"This ends here. Adah got her justice. There's nothing else for you or anybody to do. This has to be over. I don't want my town ripped apart by some civil war you want to start."

Rex sat back. He paused for an uncomfortable moment, looking up at the one window in the visitor's room. Then he turned back to Jake.

"How's my niece?" An ominous request.

"Fine," Jake said. "At least I hear she's fine. We don't exactly keep in touch."

"Good," Rex said. Jake didn't want to push things any further. He knew Rex understood what he was saying. There was no need to retaliate against Kyra. Jake wouldn't go so far as admitting he knew where she was. Though he guessed Rex already knew.

"Will you say it?" Jake asked. "Will you keep up your end of this? I told you I'd find Adah's killer and I did. He's never getting out."

Rex said nothing. Ultimately, Jake knew it was as close to an agreement as he'd get.

"There's something else," Jake said. He took his hands off the envelope on the table. Rex kept a stony expression.

"You had your mother make a request on your behalf. About Adah. Her DNA. If you want to know the truth. Whether she was really your daughter."

Rex looked at the envelope, but didn't move to take it.

"Do you want to know?" Jake asked. He hadn't looked inside it himself. The results had come in a sealed envelope, which was now inside the larger one.

"Does it matter?" Rex asked.

"Only you can answer that. But this wasn't your fault. Or it wasn't because of you. Adah didn't die because of what's in this envelope."

Rex grabbed the envelope. He stared at it for a moment. Jake half expected him to walk it over to the nearest trash can and throw it in. But he didn't. He tore open the top and pulled out the smaller envelope inside. He crumpled it in his hands. For the first time, his face changed. He furrowed his brow in obvious distress. Then he took a breath and carefully tore off one end of the envelope.

Jake watched as Rex opened the single folded piece of paper inside. His eyes darted across the page. Then he looked up at Jake, that hard, unreadable expression back in place. He flicked the paper back to Jake.

Jake almost didn't want to look. Rex was right. It didn't matter anymore. Adah was dead. She'd never know the truth about her own paternity. Maybe she wouldn't have wanted to. Or maybe knowing might have changed everything. Would she have made a different choice that night? Stayed behind? Or would she have simply run to Melva and stayed with her?

Jake picked up the sheet of paper and read it. The results were conclusive. Of course they would be. Their DNA matched. Adah was Rex's daughter. Perhaps the only child he would ever have.

"I'm sorry," Jake said.

"I know," Rex answered. "Take that. Burn it. Melva already knows. She has from the beginning."

Rex rose from the bench. Without saying another word, he walked up to the door and pounded on it. A moment later, one of the guards opened it and led King Rex back to his cell.

THIRTY-SEVEN

Three days later, Jake stood in Sheriff Landry's office. Just a few people had gathered. Only the ones Birdie wanted. Lieutenant Beverly. Deputies Denning and Chaplin. Darcy. Jake himself.

Then, off of the side, out of the photographer's range, stood Gemma and Travis. Travis looked good. For the last few weeks, he'd trained hard in the workout room, getting leaner, more cut. Ready to surpass any physical challenges West Point had to throw at him. He'd be leaving in just two months.

"It is my great honor and pleasure to present this to you. You've worked hard for it. You've earned it. Probably more than any other individual wearing this badge." Landry gave Jake a look. There was laughter in the room.

"Don't look at me," Jake said. "She's right."

Erica stepped up. She looked radiant today in a fitted black suit. He didn't think he'd ever seen her wear heels. Or much makeup, for that matter. But today, Jake realized what a knockout Birdie really was. No. It wasn't even that. For the first time, if only briefly, he didn't immediately think of her as Ben Wayne's kid sister. She was fierce, smart, talented, experienced, and ready.

"Congratulations, Detective Wayne," Landry said to an eruption of applause. Gemma dabbed her eyes with a tissue.

Landry shook Birdie's hand. Birdie smiled. "Oh, come on!" she said, then pulled Landry into a proper hug. Then they both turned, standing side by side as the photographer took their picture for the union newsletter. Another copy would appear in the *Daily Beacon*.

There were men out there who wouldn't be happy about today. Jeff Hammer. Some of the desk sergeants. Wannabes who didn't have half the talent Birdie did, but thought her promotion would take something away from them. But Jake knew Birdie was capable of taking care of herself. At least in his head. In his heart, he didn't think he could ever stop looking out for her. But that was part of a different oath he'd taken as he stood over her brother's grave.

"Come up here, Jake," Landry said. "You're not getting off that easy today."

Grumbling, he walked up and stood beside her with Erica on the other side. He did his best to smile, but knew he'd look awkward and grumpy in the photo. It couldn't be helped. And Gemma would rip into him for it.

"Drinks at Sips are on me!" Gemma called out. "But only for the people in this room!"

"Good luck with that," Lieutenant Beverly said. He was right. Though many of them would be the sore losers from the department, they'd all show up to mooch off Gemma's hospitality at Cashen's Irish Pub, or what everyone now called Sips. Though it irked Jake to no end because Cashen started with a C, dammit.

There were well wishes. The group broke off into smaller groups of conversations. Birdie was gracious. Happy. Jake was hoping he could sneak out and head back to the office. He still had a few bits of paperwork to close out Adah's murder file and hand it off to Boyd Ansel.

"Where do you think you're going, baby brother?" Gemma said. She never missed a thing where Jake was concerned.

"I'll head over to the bar in a bit," he said. "Just a few things I still need to take care of."

"Nonsense," she said. "If Meg Landry can leave now, so can you. Whatever you've got on your desk can wait until tomorrow. This is your celebration, too. I know how hard you've fought for her. So does she."

"Gemma, I ..."

"Shush. You know I'm right. Let's get out of here. I'll drive you home later so you don't need to worry. Just relax and enjoy the night with these people. You've done some good things lately. Soak it in."

"Whatever she's telling you, listen to her," Landry said, looping her arm through Gemma's. "I'll buy the second round."

He was outnumbered and outmaneuvered, it seemed. Birdie winked at him from across the room. "Do you mind if I ride over with you?" she shouted. "My car's on the fritz."

Jake sighed. "It's that damn alternator. I keep telling you to get it looked at."

She laughed at him. Jake turned. Gemma tried to grab his arm. "Gemma, I need to grab my stuff out of the office. I'll get Birdie's purse and coat, too. Do you mind?"

"Five minutes," she said. "That's all you get. Then I'm sending out a search party."

He was about to give it back to her when his cell phone rang. At about the same time, Meg's rang too. Frowning, Meg brought her phone to her ear. Jake did the same.

"Jake?" Jake's caller ID told him it was Deputy Corbin. "I'm really sorry to call so close to the end of your shift. But I got a call I think you should know about. We got sent out for a well-check. 1893 Springer Lane."

It took a beat for the address to click in Jake's mind. When it did, he felt his stomach drop to the floor. "Alex Corvell," he said. "Did you find him?"

"Yeah," Corbin said. "It's just … Jake. He's dead. Stone's already on his way too."

Jake clicked off. Meg was slowly bringing her phone down away from her ear.

"Sorry," he said to her. "I'm going to have to try to catch everyone at the bar later. I assume your call was about the same thing?"

"I don't know how this could happen," she said. "They were supposed to be watching him 24/7."

Jake frowned. "What are you talking about? That was Corbin. He caught a well-check out at Corvell's. He's dead. I've got to meet Stone out there and see what's what."

Meg's jaw dropped. "Corvell?"

"Yeah. They just called you too?"

Birdie must have sensed something between the two of them. Hugging Travis but with her eyes on Jake, she broke away and walked over to them.

"I just got a call that Alex Corvell turned up dead. I hate to cut this all short, but I've got to get out there."

"I'll go with you," she said.

"You don't have ..." Jake started.

"Jake," Landry snapped. "I didn't hear anything about Alex Corvell. That's not what my call was about. That was the shift sergeant at the jail. Twenty minutes ago, Dylan Corvell was found hanging from his bed sheets. He's dead."

THIRTY-EIGHT

E than Stone stood just inside Alex Corvell's garage door. He typed into his tablet, his brow knit. Jake and Birdie had just finished supervising a sweep of the entire house. No one else was inside.

Alex Corvell sat slumped over the steering wheel of his BMW. The beds of his fingernails were already starting to turn blue.

"How long do you think he's been like this?" Jake asked Stone.

"I've got to do my thing back at the lab," Stone answered. "But if I'm eyeballing it, I'd say close to twelve hours. He made good work out of it."

Stone pointed his stylus toward the windows on the far wall of the garage. They'd been taped over with black garbage bags.

"He wanted to make sure things were as airtight here as they could be," Birdie said. She'd chucked her heels for a pair of black converse sneakers.

"Corbin," Jake shouted. Deputy Corbin stood just outside in the driveway. He'd been canvassing Corvell's neighbors. "Any word on where the wife is?"

Corbin walked inside. "Sybil Lockhart. Next-door neighbor on the south side. That's who called for the well-check. She walks the Corvells' dogs when they're out of town. She said Corvell was supposed to pick up his wife's two dogs around noon. He didn't show. Wouldn't answer her calls. She knew that wasn't like him. Mrs. Corvell is in Fiji. She left a few days ago. Told the neighbor she didn't know when she'd be coming back. Neighbor heard she'd filed for divorce."

"Good for her," Birdie muttered.

"Jake?" Deputy Holtz appeared in the doorway leading into the house. "You might want to come take a look at this."

Birdie followed him as he stepped inside. Holtz led them to Alex Corvell's home office on the main floor off the living room.

Another deputy was busy photographing the room. He snapped a few shots of something on Corvell's desk.

"He left a note," Holtz said. "It was sitting just on top of his desk."

Jake stepped forward. Sure enough, a half a sheet of notebook paper was torn off and sitting on top of Corvell's ink blotter. It was simple. To the point. But unmistakable.

> Dee, I'm sorry. I know you think I'm a coward. That I was too permissive. Made excuses. You're probably right. This is my fault and only mine. You deserve to be happy and free of this. The important papers are in the safe. You know the combination. I love you. Goodbye.

Jake walked away. Ethan Stone met him in the foyer. "We're about to load him up and get him over to the lab," Stone said. "I'll have some preliminary findings for you by tomorrow. But I'm not expecting anything earth-shattering. The car was running. Garage was sealed off. Carbon monoxide. Probably didn't take long. He'd have just fallen asleep. Not a bad way to go if you're gonna do something like this. Neater than a bullet. Cleaner than pills. Just roll the car off and everything's back to normal. No clean-up."

It was a grisly assessment, but accurate.

"I'll talk to the neighbor again," Birdie said. "Figure out how to get a hold of Deirdre Corvell."

There was nothing left to do here. Stone and the deputies had everything in hand.

"Jake?" Birdie said. "What is it?"

Before he could answer, his phone rang. It was Meg. "Cashen," he answered.

"Hey, Jake. Just finishing up at the jail. We'll launch an internal investigation, of course. But there's not much else to do. They did a bed check about twenty minutes before Dylan was found. He wasn't on a suicide watch. He'd been talkative. A bit of a jerk, but didn't seem depressed. You just never know though. He was facing a pretty bleak future. On the surface, it just doesn't seem like anyone did anything wrong. I'll have to put out a statement, of course. What a way to end the day, huh?"

"Yeah," Jake said. "We're finishing up here. Same story. How about we circle back in the morning and figure out what we want to say?"

"Sounds good. Try to shut your brain off. Do what you promised. Head over to Gemma's. I probably won't make it. I've got to stay here for a bit longer."

"Yeah," Jake said, then he clicked off. He slid behind the wheel. Birdie got in beside him.

"You don't like it, do you?" she asked.

"No. It's just ... I don't know."

"Too much of a coincidence? It looks like father and son checked out about the same time."

"Yeah," Jake said, putting the car in reverse. He put his arm over the seat and looked behind him as he backed up.

"You think this was Rex?" Birdie asked.

"I don't know," he said. "I felt like we understood each other when I saw him the other day. But I'm not naïve enough to think he couldn't have just been saying what he knew I wanted to hear. The Bardos had a problem."

"Revenge? Retribution for killing Adah?"

"Sure," Jake said. "But Alex Corvell. He was the problem. They know Corvell cooperated with us. Turned on his own son. And he was facing his own uncertain future."

"He was a liability," Birdie said. "It has to have occurred to Rex that Corvell might have had an incentive to cooperate with the feds at any time. He knows too much about Rex and the Hilltop Boys."

"Yeah."

"You'll never prove it. You heard Stone. He's going to have to rule this a suicide. There's nowhere for this to go."

Jake didn't answer. He kept driving, a nagging feeling eating at him.

"I would only say this to you," Birdie said. "But I don't see why we should care. Dylan was irredeemable. He was going to end up dead in the showers or the exercise yard someday. You know that. And Corvell? He wasn't innocent either. Just ... call it even. Move on. I'm sure Rex will."

"Move on," Jake repeated. "But to what?"

He slammed on the brakes. Birdie rocked forward. He turned to her. "You're right. I don't care about the Corvells. But if Rex is settling scores, there's somebody else he might want to square up with."

"What?" Birdie said.

Jake revved the engine and turned the car around with a violent swerve. He stepped on the gas and headed west as fast as he could.

"Jake, what?"

Jake turned to Birdie and uttered a single word. "Kyra."

THIRTY-NINE

"She wanted to lie low," Jake shouted as he sped toward Frank's. "I told her the day we arrested Dylan Corvell that it was over. She still didn't feel safe. She didn't kill Adah. But she knows if she hadn't gotten involved none of this would have happened. Rex will find out, if he hasn't already, that Kyra led Dylan to Adah."

"You've still been hiding her? This whole time? I mean, I knew you said you'd gotten her somewhere safe. I didn't think she was still relying on you."

"Don't judge me. Not now," he said.

"I'm not." Birdie grabbed the ceiling of the car to steady herself as Jake took a sharp turn. "Jake, I'm not."

"She asked me if she could take a few more days to figure out her next move. It was over. She's not a witness to anything anymore. Dylan confessed. Alex confessed. She's off the hook."

"But not to Rex," Birdie said.

Jake slammed a hand against the steering wheel. "Dammit. I should have just let her go."

"No, you shouldn't. She's not innocent in this. She never was. She lied to you from day one. Told you half-truths. If she'd been straightforward, we could have solved this thing in half the time. Maybe it would have saved Scarlett Sommers from that last beating."

She wasn't wrong. But it was too late for all of that now. Jake sped down Frank's driveway. From the corner of his eye, he saw Birdie's face fall. He'd never told her where he'd stashed Kyra. He'd only told Landry. Rex couldn't know. No one else did. She had to be here. She had to be okay.

He stopped the car and practically flew out of it, racing toward the garage. He punched in the code. Birdie was just behind him.

"Kyra!" he yelled. The house was silent and dark. Jake ran to the bedrooms. All empty. Each bed was neatly made. He went into the main bathroom. Beads of water clung to the shower glass, but everything else was neat and clean. No toothbrush in the holder. Nothing out of place.

"Anything?" Birdie called out. She'd gone down to the basement. Jake stormed down the hall back to the kitchen as Birdie came up.

"Nothing down there," she said. "Doors are all locked."

Jake went to the refrigerator and opened it. The food had been cleared. There were no dishes in the sink. He opened the dishwasher. That was empty, too. All bowls, plates, and silverware were accounted for in the cupboards.

"She's gone, Jake," Birdie said.

He leaned against the counter. "She didn't have a cell phone.

There's no working landline. No computer. No Wi-Fi. She didn't have a car."

Jake went to the front door and looked down the driveway. There were no tire tracks except for his own. Birdie went to the slider at the back of the house. Jake went to join her. He looked down to the yard and small trail leading out to the woods. It was muddy now, having rained for the last two days.

"No footprints," Birdie said.

Gone. She was just gone. Vanished.

"There's no sign of a struggle, Jake. Nothing's out of place. I don't get the sense anything bad happened here. She could have just decided to leave. She knew the Corvells had been arrested, right?"

"Yes," he said.

"Then it seems to me that's the perfect time to get gone. If I were her, I wouldn't have told you either. She knows you talk to her uncle. She knows you know her part in all of this. She's smart not to trust anyone and just make her own plans."

"How?" Jake said. "She had no way to get in touch with anyone."

"That you know of. Jake, that woman's like a cockroach. She'll survive anything."

"Yeah," Jake said. "I hope so."

"When she wants to reach out to you, she will. That's what she's done every other time. You know? There's a part of me that still respects her. I think I believe what she told you. It pissed me off too that Melva Bardo didn't do more to protect those kids. So Kyra's intentions were good. But not the way she went about it. But that's her burden to live with. Not yours. You did what you could for her. More than enough. Let's go. Leave this behind."

Jake looked around one last time. It was as if Kyra had never been here at all. Yet he still felt her presence somehow. The house itself felt like her message to him. Everything where it was supposed to be. Nothing of her left behind. Jake had no way of knowing it for sure, but it felt like a goodbye.

He just hoped he was right. He hoped Rex hadn't found her after all. But something she told him rang in his ears now. If something happened to her. If she was gone. The Bardo family would collapse. Their enterprises would fall apart. She said she was the one holding everything together, not Rex. It could have been a lie. Another of Kyra's manipulations. But if she was telling the truth and she was gone for good, something bad was coming. Jake could feel it.

Jake walked with Birdie back to the car.

"It's gorgeous out here. I'd forgotten. Ben brought me out here a few times when we were kids. Is it yours now?"

"Kind of," Jake said. "It just feels haunted now somehow." That was exactly it. Frank's ghost, now Kyra's. Though as far as he knew, neither of them were dead.

"I get that," Birdie said.

"I'm sorry," he said. "I know you didn't approve of me helping her the way I did."

Birdie smiled and came to him. She took his hands in hers and went up on her tiptoes. She placed a gentle kiss on his cheek. Like a sister. But it sent something else through him. His urge to keep her safe. To shield her from the bad things that would always come.

"Come on," she said. "There's still time for at least one round at Gemma's. Don't make me miss my own party ... partner."

Partner. She was like him. Or at least, she was more like the person he wanted to be. Noble. Brave. Loyal. Things would be different now between them. He was proud of her. He trusted her. He knew she trusted him. With her life. But it was part of her job to protect him now, too. As she walked around to the passenger side of his car, Jake knew he could trust her with his life as well.

Turn the page and keep reading for a special preview of Their Deadly Truth, the next book in the Jake Cashen Series.

PREVIEW OF HER DEADLY TRUTH

"Are you sure you can't get someone else to stay with him?" Crystal Adamski leaned against the bus window, chewing gum. "Everybody's going to be there. Bryan Jarvis is going to be there. I heard he broke up with Kimmy Pawlak. He was looking at you at lunch. I mean ... really looking at you."

Gemma felt a warm rush at the mention of Bryan. He was a year older. An eighth grader. He played quarterback for the junior high football team. Crystal had to be making it up.

"He was not," Gemma said.

"He was too! I swear. You walked by to throw out your tray and he was staring you up and down, Gemma. Shannon lives right down the street from him. She said she'd ask him if he liked you."

Gemma couldn't breathe. She'd had a crush on Bryan since the end of last school year.

"Please promise me you won't say anything to him," Gemma pleaded. "Don't you dare tell him I like him. Tell Shannon not to butt in either. And no. I'm stuck. I begged my mom last night. She can't get anyone to cover for her at work. My grandparents want to go out to dinner for their anniversary. It's just me."

Me and Jake, she thought. It really wasn't fair. She shouldn't have to be the built-in babysitter for her seven-year-old brother all the time. And it was never just him. Mom would always let him bring his grubby little friend Ben Wayne over and she'd be stuck watching the two of them.

"You're missing everything, Gemma," Crystal said. This time, she'd be missing an after-school party at the bowling alley.

The bus was getting close to her stop. Gemma's would be the last on the line. She didn't mind. She'd move up to the front of the bus and keep Mr. Kirby, their bus driver, company. Kirby retired from the DNR and used to work as a park ranger. He always had funny stories to share and kept candy in a bucket behind his seat. A couple of times a year, Gemma's mother would send her with a fresh bag of Jolly Ranchers to refill it.

The bus jerked to a stop and Kirby opened the front door. Crystal rose and scooted past Gemma. "See what you can do," she said. "It won't be the same without you."

Gemma watched her friend get off. She sat quietly for the next four stops, staring out the window. She watched the leaves starting to fall from the trees as the bus picked up speed. Peak color was at least a week away. Pretty soon, her mother would make the same joke she made every year. She was about to become a whitetail widow when her dad and Grandpa Max went off to hunt almost every single day. Now they were starting to take Jake with them, though her brother could never sit still. Her dad threatened to glue his little butt to the tree stand.

As the bus lurched forward and more kids got off, Gemma made her way up to the seat right behind Mr. Kirby. He smiled at her from the rear-view mirror.

"You okay?" he asked her. "You seem kinda mopey."

"I'm fine," she answered. "Just tired. I've got a pile of homework to do before my brother gets home and all hell breaks loose."

Laughter came into Kirby's eyes. "That boy runs like he's got a motor inside of him. I heard your dad say he was going to make him start wrestling this year. Burn off some of that energy. That'll be good for him. I've been helping out in the room. I'll keep an eye on Jakey Jake."

"Somebody ought to," Gemma muttered. Kirby was right. Jake refused to sit still. He was always climbing something, jumping off something, making messes he never cleaned up.

Kirby came to Gemma's stop. She looped her arms through her backpack and grabbed a butterscotch from Kirby's candy bucket.

"Have a good one," Kirby hollered as Gemma went down the bus steps. He put the stop sign out. Then he waved Gemma across the street.

Her backpack was heavy, laden with her math and science books today. She had two tests tomorrow. Two worksheets to finish. Jake would be home in an hour and a half. She might as well get everything done before he barreled in and disrupted her peace and quiet.

She walked up the long sidewalk to the small, three-bedroom house she'd lived in since she was a baby. Grandma Ava called it a "fixer-upper." Grandpa Max called it a money pit. He and her dad had been working on remodeling the basement bathroom. Last summer, they'd put on a new roof.

Jake had left his bike laying in the grass. Sighing, Gemma leaned down and picked it up. She walked it up driveway and leaned it against the side of the house. She grabbed the side door leading into the garage. Mom liked her and Jake to come in from that way so they could drop their backpacks and take off their shoes in the mud room. The knob wouldn't turn. Gemma pushed, but the door didn't budge. It was still locked from the inside.

"Great," she muttered. She hoped she remembered her key to the front door. Her mom wasn't supposed to be home until almost five. Her father, not until ten or so. Gemma would have a blissful ninety minutes home alone. She walked around the house and back up the front sidewalk. The wind kicked up, blowing her hair straight up. Ahead of her, Mom had painted the front door a cheery yellow. She kept pink geraniums in flower boxes under the two window sills on either side of it.

As Gemma stepped up to the porch, she noticed something off. The front door stood slightly ajar. She could see the kitchen light on in the middle of the day. Dad didn't like that. He'd lecture Gemma and Jake about turning off light switches. He sounded just like Grandpa Max when he did it. "You don't pay for the electricity around here!"

"Mom?" Gemma called out. It was still warm enough to keep the windows open, but leaving the door open like that would let every fly in Blackhand Hills inside.

"Mom?" she yelled again. Her mother worked part time at the bank in downtown Stanley as a teller. A recent development, but since Jake was in school full time, her mother wanted something to do. Had she come home early today?

"Mom?" Gemma called out one last time. The house was too quiet. The smell wasn't right. Mom usually put something in the crock-pot for dinner every morning before work.

Gemma put her backpack down on the living room couch and made her way to the kitchen. She took two steps past the counter and stopped.

There was a moment. A heartbeat, maybe two, as Gemma's brain slowly processed the scene in front of her. Her mother was there, but lying on the kitchen floor on her stomach. She looked like she was sleeping, her legs partially curled under her.

"Mom?"

Gemma took a step forward. A fly buzzed by her ear. Then another. Something had spilled on the floor right next to her mother. Something dark. Had she slipped in it?

"Mom!"

Gemma dove forward. Her mother wasn't sleeping. She hadn't slipped. She hadn't spilled anything. Blood seeped through the grooves in the patterned-linoleum floor. It was everywhere, spread out in front of her mother's head. It matted in her hair, making it look dark where she was normally blonde.

Slowly, Gemma reached for her mother's shoulder. She turned her to her side. Her mother stared at her with sightless eyes, all color drained from her face.

Gemma stumbled backward, landing on her butt. Her mother clutched the wall phone receiver in her right hand. Gemma could hear the harsh pulse of the busy signal.

Gemma didn't scream. She didn't panic. She went cold. Detached. As if everything were happening to someone else.

There were things to do. What were they? Gemma reached out and placed a finger in the crook of her mother's neck, feeling for a pulse. There was none. Her mother was cold to the touch.

Dead. Gemma cocked her head to the side. Was this real? She should scream. She knew she should scream, but couldn't. Why couldn't she move? Why couldn't she get to her feet? She was frozen. Staring at her mother. Knowing what she was seeing.

Mom is dead. My mom is dead. I have to move. Why can't I move?

Gemma took the phone from her mother's hand. It took force to release it from Sonya Cashen's lifeless grip. Gemma found her way to her feet. She put the phone on the cradle, then picked it back up. She dialed 9-1-1.

"Please state the nature of your emergency," a voice said.

Gemma had dreams before. Ones where she tried to talk or tried to scream and no sound would come out. This was like that. Except she could hear herself talking. She just didn't know what she was saying. How could she be saying these things? "My mom is hurt. She's dead. I think she's dead. There's a lot of blood."

Little bits of the dispatcher's words cut through.

"Ambulance ... are you alone ... who else ..."

"Please come," Gemma heard herself say. "Please hurry."

The dispatcher asked her again. "Honey, are you by yourself?"

By myself, Gemma thought. Her father had been working afternoons but was supposed to switch to midnights. Gemma thought that was supposed to start tomorrow. Was it today? Did she have her days mixed up? Maybe her dad was still asleep. Then he'd wake up right after Jake got home.

Jake. Jake.

Gemma tried to clear the mud in her mind. It felt like something slammed into her chest.

"Please hurry," she said into the phone. "I have to go find my dad."

Urgency came back into Gemma's body. Her heart raced. She set the phone down. She could hear the dispatcher's voice yelling to her, but Gemma couldn't stand still now. Adrenaline raged through her. She ran to the upstairs bedrooms, taking the steps two at a time.

"Daddy!" she cried out, though she hadn't called him that since she was five. She burst through the door into her parents' bedroom. The sheets were crumpled, but her father wasn't there. Grief choked her. She needed him. "Dad, please!"

Gemma ran to the attached bathroom, but her father wasn't there either. She ran to Jake's room. Then she flew back downstairs.

She half expected it to be a dream. But it was a nightmare. Her mother was still lying on that kitchen floor, motionless.

Gemma would never know what made her do it. It was just a feeling, a sense. But she ran out the back door and into the yard.

That's when she saw him. Her father was out there. There was a willow tree. Her father hated it. He'd been meaning to chop it down. But it was easy to climb and he'd built Jake and Gemma a small tree fort in it.

She found her father on the ground, leaning against that willow tree. She could see the great wound to his head from here. She didn't have to get any closer to know he was dead, too. And she saw the gun in his lap. Still clutched in his right hand.

Gemma took a few halting steps backward into the house. She could hear the faint wail of a siren in the distance. Though it was getting closer.

"Too late," Gemma whispered. They were too late. She was too late. Nothing made sense. This couldn't be real.

All urgency left her. The cold came back in its place. Gemma walked calmly back into the kitchen. She could still hear the dispatcher yelling for her to pick up the phone. She did.

"I hear them," Gemma said. "They're on their way. I have to go now."

"Honey, it's okay. I can stay on the line with you until they get there."

This puzzled Gemma. Nothing was okay. There was nothing left to say to this woman. Nothing she could possibly say to Gemma that would hold any meaning.

"I have to go now," Gemma repeated. A single thought went through her mind. The urgency came back.

Jake. I have to take care of Jake. He can't come home to this. I can't let him see it.

She hung up the phone. She closed her eyes for a moment as she sought clarity. As she tried to figure out what to do. There was a voice in her head. As if her mother's ghost were already trying to speak. You have to keep Jake safe from this.

Then she picked up the phone again and dialed the Waynes' house. Judith Wayne, the mother of Jake's best friend, answered in a cheery voice that tore at Gemma's heart. She was someone's mom. Ben Wayne still had a mom. She didn't.

"Mrs. Wayne," she said calmly. "This is Gemma Cashen. There's been an emergency. Can you do us a favor? Can you pick up Jake from school and take him to your house? Can you keep him there?"

"Of course, honey. What's wrong? Are you okay? You don't sound okay. Is your mom there?"

"Just, please go get my brother."

Gemma hung up the phone. She felt tears coming, but choked them back, going cold again. She couldn't cry. She had to think. She had to be strong. She walked out of the kitchen, through the front door, and sat on the porch steps as the ambulance roared into her driveway.

A young couple dead. A haunting echo of one boy's darkest day. A detective who can't walk away — even if it costs him everything.

One-Click So You Don't Miss Out!

Interested in getting a free exclusive extended prologue to the Jake Cashen Series?

Join Declan James's Roll Call Newsletter for a free download.

About the Author

Before putting pen to paper, Declan James's career in law enforcement spanned twenty-six years. Declan's work as a digital forensics detective has earned him the highest honors from the U.S. Secret Service and F.B.I. For the last sixteen years of his career, Declan served on a nationally recognized task force aimed at protecting children from online predators. Prior to that, Declan spent six years undercover working Vice-Narcotics.

An avid outdoorsman and conservationist, Declan enjoys hunting, fishing, grilling, smoking meats, and his quest for the perfect bottle of bourbon. He lives on a lake in Southern Michigan along with his wife and kids. Declan James is a pseudonym.

For more information follow Declan at one of the links below. If you'd like to receive new release alerts, author news, and a FREE digital bonus prologue to Murder in the Hollows, sign up for Declan's Roll Call Newsletter here: https://declanjamesbooks.com/rollcall/

Also by Declan James

Murder in the Hollows

Kill Season

Bones of Echo Lake

Red Sky Hill

Her Last Moment

Secrets of Blackhand Creek

Lethal Harvest

The Whisper Girl

Their Deadly Truth

With more to come...

STAY IN TOUCH WITH DECLAN JAMES

For more information, visit

https://declanjamesbooks.com

If you'd like to receive a free digital copy of the extended prologue to the Jake Cashen series plus access to the exclusive character image gallery where you can see what Jake Cashen and others look like in the author's mind, sign up for Declan James's Roll Call Newsletter here: https://declanjamesbooks.com/rollcall/

Made in United States
Cleveland, OH
28 July 2025

18887658R20218